WITCHES OF ETLANTIUM BOOK 3

Copyright 2013 Thea Atkinson

Published by Thea Atkinson

No part of this publication may be reproduced in whole or in part, or stored in a retrieval system, or transmitted in any form electronic or otherwise without permission from the author.

Chapter 1

They were all starving and Alaysha knew it. Worse, she knew the thirst would kill them before the starvation had a chance.

She wouldn't mind dying so much; the hunger or thirst could take her if they wanted. She didn't even mind the hunger pains that had taken residence in her belly. She deserved all of it, truth be told. The lives she'd taken over the years as her father's personal weapon of war laid heavily on her conscience. The sister who'd died because of her at the fiery hands of a witch who could control her element so perfectly that she could send flame leaping from person to person, that sister deserved her vengeance.

The memory alone of her homeland's collective screams of agony, of her sister's eyes as she met Alaysha's, the knowledge that Saxa, her only friend, was still left in Sarum at the mercy of Aislin's temper; all those things made Alaysha welcome the ache of hunger and thirst. She didn't even want to think about Yenic.

She deserved to die, yes; so too, did Edulph, who trudged along in front of the queue; his hands bound. But these companions who'd opted to follow her: Aedus, Gael, Theron did not.

She stole a glance at the shuffling feet of those companions, dragging across the cracked earth of the burnt lands. She'd marched behind them saying it was because, as a soldier she could protect their rear, when in truth, she couldn't stop thinking that their faces, when they looked at her, were filled with blame; their eyes begging for her to bring the rain and quench their thirst.

She looked past them to the vast, dry desert they'd been walking through for the last seven days. She looked sideways. Behind. The cracked earth extended past all horizons, and it had been five days since they'd found anything edible. The stores they'd rammed into sacks upon their escape from Sarum had long since gone. The last of the water skins had been on ration since early yesterday and had been guzzled by their thirsty tissues so quickly that no one needed to relieve their bladders.

Barruch could barely lift his hooves over the earth enough to move forward. It was with a sad sting of pain that she knew he'd seen his last sunset. Alaysha kept her palm on his neck and shuffled along with him, afraid to leave his side.

"Stop," she said and realized nothing had left her mouth in the way of sound. Even so, the pause of her own bare and cracked feet sent some subliminal message to the others. They paused and turned dumbly toward her, expressions a dead wash. No energy to even look curious, she realized.

Alaysha licked her lips and felt her tongue stick to the corner. It took three dry swallows before she was able to gather enough suppleness in her throat to try again.

"I can't." She let the muscles of her legs falter and felt her backside strike clay earth. A shadow passed in front of her vision. She didn't need to hear him speak to know it was Gael.

She peered up at him, taking in the massively broad shoulders and by now ragged and filthy hair two shades darker than his sister, Saxa's, and she found enough strength to shrug. How could she find the words to tell him she couldn't force her beloved mount to take one more step?

"He has been brave, this one," Gael said, and patted Barruch's neck before he crouched next to Alaysha.

She could only nod.

"We'll rest," he said, and signalled to the others, all

three. Aedus, Theron, and Edulph fell to the ground as though he'd cut their legs from beneath them.

"This is ridiculous, Gael. We should never have come this way." She wrapped her arms around Barruch's leg.

Gael's silver gaze ran over her face, landing like a moth on her lips. Self-conscious, she tried to lick them. They felt split and puffy. She gave up when she tasted blood.

His palm found the hollow beneath her ear and his fingers kneaded her neck. "Theron says it's passable."

"If it was passable, Aislin's men would have followed us." She eased her eyes closed, thinking how good it felt to let them rest, then forced them open, afraid she'd fall asleep right there. She was exhausted; the few hours' rest she'd managed at the height of the sun had long been used up.

"If he says it's passable, we must believe him. He's been through this before."

She squeezed Barruch's leg and felt it tremble. Her eyes stung but no tears came to relieve the burning. She felt Gael's palm move to her back and reach beneath her arm. "Come. You're stronger than this."

She panicked; he would lift and carry her, all because he wouldn't leave her to die with her mount. A quick shot of energy helped her push away from him. "No, Gael. Save your strength."

"For what? A hectare? A leagua? Just to leave you here alone?"

She'd been right; he had planned to carry her. "I won't be alone."

Barruch nuzzled her hair. His hot breath cascaded over her, making her wish she had enough energy to stand and hug his neck. It was smothering hot but no perspiration eked through her skin. She knew her body was breaking down. It was just a matter of time before self-preservation kicked in and the power took over. She'd drink them all dry for the small chance the power would give her enough fluid to see her to the ends of the burnt lands.

She tried to swallow again and found the wherewithal to speak. "You'll have to kill me soon."

He leaned closer and held her gaze with his own. She saw resolve in the green of his eyes. Yes. She'd forgotten how his eyes shifted colour like that from steely silver to mossy green.

"It won't come to that," he said. "We still have some water. You can have mine."

She shook her head; what they had left of water wasn't near enough to keep dehydration away for very long, but her power wouldn't care. It would thirst what it could.

"When Barruch goes, you'll likely take what meat from him that you can manage; I'll help with that. After that..." She didn't want to say it couldn't possibly buy them much time. That they'd likely vomit up the muscle anyway and then expire from exhaustion and further dehydration. But if any of them lived while she still did, they'd be gone long before they had even that chance. She'd simply, without wanting to, drain them of whatever fluid still flushed their tissues.

"If I mean anything to you, Gael, you'll kill me." It was a terrible thing to do, manipulate him, but it was her only hope. Neither of them had spoken of the night in the tunnels when he'd consoled her over her sister's death and Yenic's capture and seemingly ultimate demise, the night she'd repaid him with her body. It was a sweet memory but one best left to die its own death.

"You said you'd do anything for me." She gripped his arm fiercely.

He pressed his lips together and the top one cracked and bled when they met. His tongue dipped into the fissure greedily.

"Gael," she pressed.

He shook his head. "I'll give you my own moisture before I let you die." He stood and looked down at her. She could tell he was working hard not to sway off his feet.

"Please, Gael. This place has no water. Not for leaguas, maybe hundreds of leaguas. I'd know it; I'd smell it if it were here."

It was true. Almost. She'd sent her thirst out once, trying to scent fluid as their skins began to dry up, and she'd smelled fluid, wanted, needed, desirable fluid so sweet she felt the power begin to uncoil within her. It wanted to *gather* water, not find it. Not search when there was a quick and ready source right within speedy reach: the last of the skins, the water in the soft tissues of Aedus' body, in the beating heart of Theron. In their blood. She'd take it all if she let the power so much as sniff it.

A fortnight ago, she'd have revelled in the ability to discern the nuances of power, relished with giddiness the ability to pull it back. Now she was just terrified to let it peek out at all.

She could feel the weak pulse of Barruch's heart in his leg. She wished she could weep. The tears hoarded themselves, and rage came at the futility of it all, her inability to grieve for a beast that had been more family to her than any blood had ever been.

Her mind was invaded by visions of her past. Her nohma's smile, her tender touch, the feel of her heartbeat, the soft shushing sounds she made as she pressed a cloth sopping with goat's milk into a hungry mouth. Every tissue in Alaysha's body cried out with the memory, so real she could smell the honey in the milk, feel the wetness of tears against her cheeks at the relief of finally eating. The feel of her belly gurgling as the first drops of milk dropped in. The satiation. The drowsy sleepiness that took her limbs at being full for the first time. Such deliriously divine sleepiness.

"Alaysha."

She worked to open her eyes and was surprised to see Gael's face so close to hers that her cheek could touch his with a mere movement.

"I'm fine," she told him.

"Not fine."

His breath was hot on her skin, too hot.

"Neither are you," she said. In response, he twisted away so she couldn't see his eyes. She started to speak again, to implore him to kill her before he lost his strength, but a blue-veined foot stole her attention.

"Theron," she murmured and looked up to see a peaked face drawn with fatigue and hunger. "We won't make it," she told the shaman.

He pursed his lips.

"Look around," she said. "We're dying. There's not a drop of water."

His mouth worked even as his glance darted to Barruch who snuffed haughtily under his study. Leave it to that arrogant horse to show disdain at such a time. She was so taken by the humour that she missed the shaman's words.

"What did you say?" she asked him.

He had the grace to look ashamed. "We said not every drop is dried up; no, not at all." He put a tender hand on Barruch's neck.

"No," she said, realizing with shock what he meant.

"The beast is dying too, young temptress."

Strange, that she could entertain thoughts of Barruch dying, but not of taking his life. Somehow that was too barbaric. "He's family. My family. And I won't take him that way."

"He's a beast who can give us fluid."

The insult of it lent her the strength to stand and face the shaman.

"No, Theron. No."

She felt Gael's hand on her shoulder. "Tell him, Gael," she pleaded. "Tell him I won't bleed this beast so he can, we can, drink the blood." She thought her voice rose; she'd meant to let it shout at the indignity and couldn't understand why it came out so low, so gravelly.

Theron's voice swept over her so softly she had to work to hear it. "Not us, young temptress, oh deities no, no, no. Blood is food more than it is fluid to such as a lowly man. We'd gain nothing from it." He gave the beast a pat. "It is for you."

She took an involuntary step away from him, and he took one toward her.

"It's the only way," he said. "This witch must pull from it as much fluid as she can and then release."

She felt her head shaking in refusal but couldn't for the life of her find the words to accompany it. Fortunately, Gael spoke for her.

"She doesn't have that kind of power."

"Power," she heard herself saying at the ridiculousness of his statement. "Power? It has nothing to do with my power."

"I didn't mean--" Gael began.

"I know what you meant, Gael," she said, looking at

Theron. "I can't do that to him." Her voice was nothing but a dusty groan, and when the shaman placed his palm on her heart, she thought she'd find the liquid for tears after all. "No," she said again, and put all she had into the word.

The shaman's narrowed gaze spoke of suspicious comprehension. "Yet the witch would sacrifice herself? To what end? So we can carry on another handful of steps?"

"If you hadn't made us come this way we'd not be making these decisions."

"And Aislin's men would have us and you'd be dead at her hands, like your sister." Gael's voice, the traitor; that he would bring up her sister. It was cruel. Too cruel. She slapped his hand away.

"The truth is always painful when it strikes at the heart," he said. "But they won't follow us; they'd be fools to do so." Gael shuffled his feet. "As we are, I suppose," he mumbled.

Theron turned to face him. He looked small and frail against the massive height of the warrior. "Does the warrior think Bodicca a fool?"

"If Bodicca brought Yenic through these burnt lands, then yes, she is a fool. I expect we can tell her carcass so very soon."

Theron shook his head stubbornly. "The large woman would have made it. She knows the secrets of traveling the burnt lands."

"How, Theron?" Alaysha asked. It didn't matter the secrets that existed if the woman didn't have water enough to make it across. And no amount of water was enough. Their own situation proved it.

"Bodicca's homeland lies on the other end," the shaman said. "I've been this way before." He paused as he met and held her gaze with his own. "Twice."

"You've seen the other side?" She could barely believe her ears. This frail man, travelled the burnt lands.

"Yes." He took a deep breath. "We know it's possible to cross. We need the horse's blood."

All she had was the best argument. "I don't have the power."

"Leech the water from the blood. Let it go. We'll collect it."

"I can't. I'll drain you all."

A shout came. Edulph. Impatient still, even in his weakened state. He was one added burden, had been all along. They'd found Aedus's prodigal brother in a pit inside the mountains of Sarum, burned and afraid, tortured by Aislin in an attempt to wrest him of any information he had about the wind witch. All along they'd thought Edulph had abducted Gael's nephew and all along her bondman Yenic knew he hadn't, that it was his own mother who had been the culprit. Thoughts of Edulph now brought tortured thoughts of Yenic and his betrayal.

How she had crossed into territory where enemies could be trusted and loved ones feared she'd never fully fathom.

She ignored Edulph even as Aedus wrung her hands over him, but dared not get too close. Alaysha knew the girl still felt the missing finger her brother had severed as though it were still part of her hand, and even if she'd adapted, it was a constant reminder of her brother's treachery. Such a loyal girl, that one. If no one else proved trustworthy, that ragged, ferret-faced urchin would. Alaysha would do nothing to endanger her, certainly not on an uncertain try to psych the living fluid from her horse, not knowing if the power would overtake control and drain them all instead.

"No," she said. "I can't risk it."

Strangely, Theron shrugged. "If the witch doesn't try, we'll be dead anyway. A shaman even as wise as us is still merely an old man. I have no use. Edulph is nothing but a waste of good fleshing."

Gael stepped toward her, and she held her hand up to stop him from speaking. She knew what he was planning to pledge--the same as Theron was, and neither mattered.

"I can't risk her," she said. "Not Aedus."

The shrug again. "She's already at risk." Gael waited a moment, giving her a knowing glance. "We all are, anyway, aren't we?"

So he did know. She was on the sharp verge of thirsting them all dry, that it wasn't just a remote warning, and he understood the danger. She wanted to sink onto the ground and stay there. Instead she sighed. Swallowed, even though there was no liquid to move down her throat.

"Theron, can't you break the earth, seek water below?" She knew his witch had made the earth split when Alaysha had brought too much rain. She knew Yenic could channel his mother's fiery power; surely Theron could do the same as the clay witch's Arm.

He grinned, with an ironic twist to his mouth. "Not without blood," he said.

Not without blood. Barruch's blood once again. Blood she would have to shed or psych of its water if they were to survive. Just the thought made her chest burn. She had to inhale and exhale repeatedly just to keep from panicking at the futility of it.

She felt her legs tremble, heard Gael's voice as a whisper, coaxing her, telling her it was okay.

"I've killed before," she said, searching out his eye. "You know I have. But this is different." She heard the pleading in her voice, like a toddler begging her father not to spank her. Father, she thought morosely. It was all her father's fault she was in this spot in the first place, her father's fault she was a killer.

Gael's arms went round her, and she fell against his chest, choking back sobs.

"You don't have to kill the beast," he said next to her ear. "You only have to thirst his blood once it flows. I'll do the deed for you."

She discovered her fists were beating against his back; that she was squirming in his arms. "You'd kill him? You'd kill my Barruch?"

Gael's hands found hers and held them tightly against his sides. His body pressed into hers in command for her to be still and yet with a gentle intimacy that actually stilled her. "I would kill anyone--any beast, any witch, any woman--to save you."

She peered up at him. He'd not mentioned their night together, as he'd promised, not once since she'd lost Yenic and her sister and her father, Yuri, all in one day and needed the comfort he'd offered. He'd not once told her again that he loved her. That he would say anything now was proof of how bad off they were, how close to dying--and that he knew how close she was to unintentionally psyching them dry.

"Just do it," she croaked and staggered away from Barruch. If it must be done, then on with it, but she couldn't look into those lovingly haughty eyes and watch the life drain from them, see his realization of her betrayal.

"Do it," she sobbed and stuffed a fist into her mouth. She stared back over the dried earth they'd traveled. She forced herself to think back on the days that had set them on the path in the first place, fleeing her homeland with an old man, a young girl, a criminal, and a warrior, and leaving behind the only true friend she'd made.

The thought of Saxa and her willowy frame, the soft voice and silver light hair brought her to thoughts of Yenic, and thoughts of him brought her to her twin sister.

Then the meandering thoughts stopped. They had to.

Her sister, newly discovered, was no more. Aislin, the witch of flame, had killed her trying to goad Yuri into relinquishing Yenic.

It was all a tangled, nightmarish mess, all set in motion by Yuri's greed for power, his megalomaniac desire to control each of four witches that a season ago Alaysha hadn't known existed.

She squeezed her eyes shut, expecting to hear the familiar whinny as Gael's blade moved across the broad neck. Each limb felt taut with anxiety. She scraped a bare foot across the earth, remembering how it felt on Barruch's back, how he'd struggled to reach her when she'd caused the flood at the mud village. She hadn't thought he'd live through that. She smiled nostalgically. She remembered seeing him at the edge of the river when he'd brought Gael out from the city during Aislin's rampage.

She recalled how handsome that horseflesh looked to her each time, how it made her stomach flop over itself in relief.

Her friend. Her family. Her one connection to the humanity she thought she'd given up each time she had to kill for her father.

Dear deities, how could she let this happen? She couldn't, that's what. She wouldn't.

She spun around, intending to shout for Gael to wait, hoping it wasn't already too late.

She would have gotten the words out too, if Aedus hadn't yelled first, pointing to the horizon, jumping up and down when the girl shouldn't have the energy to stand, let alone hopscotch from one foot to the other.

Theron's posture revealed his surprise, and as confused as Alaysha was to see a hulking shape coming toward them, her first thought was to make sure Gael hadn't gone ahead and murdered her Barruch. She felt her heart squeeze in her chest, the fear that it was too late keeping it from pumping.

"Gael?" she croaked.

He met her eyes and she felt her whole body slump with relief when he spoke.

"He's safe yet, Alaysha," he said and she breathed easier at his words.

The horizon could finally take her attention then. "What sort of beast is that?"

Gael shrugged, but it was Theron who spoke, his voice such a strange tone Alaysha didn't realize at first that it was dread.

"That would be an Enyalian. And an Enyalian means this shaman and these good people are as good as dead."

Chapter 2

Alaysha watched as the strange hulking beast on the horizon grew bigger as it drew closer. With relief she saw that what Theron called an Enyalian was alone. What harm could come from a lone rider?

"Should we fear one Enyalian, Theron?" she asked him, and didn't feel so reassured when she saw his reaction.

"She'll have seen us," he said, casting panicked looks around him. Alaysha noticed he took to stepping side to side anxiously, his filthy cassock swaying over his blue-veined feet.

"She?" Alaysha asked and glanced at Gael for confirmation. "Did he say she?"

Gael nodded and Theron edged closer, staring thoughtfully at the warrior.

"All Enyalia are shes." He took measure of Gael, and seeming to decide something of importance, began pressing Gael to sit on the ground. At first, Gael resisted, but when Theron grew persistent, the warrior settled on his buttocks next to Barruch with a shrug. Despite his seemingly relaxed posture, Alaysha noted his fingers clenched the handle of his blade beneath his arm.

"What's going on Theron?" she asked as the shaman did the same to Edulph who had a harder time finding a dignified sitting position with his hands bound in front of him.

The shaman took Aedus's hand and led her closer to Alaysha.

"Any number of Enyalia is dangerous--life threatening even, yes, yes, yes--especially for a man." He moved them to stand in front of Barruch. "Let her see this witch first," he told Alaysha then looked back at Gael. "Spring when she's noticed you, but only if she notices you. Otherwise, look weakened or dead or near dead." He paused when he'd checked Edulph, seeming to decide the madman's fate. "If the foolish madman wants to live, he'll pretend he's dead."

"And then what?" Aedus piped up. "If she wants to kill us, she needn't waste her energy, Theron. She just needs to pass us by and let this cursed land do it for her."

Alaysha wished she didn't have to hear the note of sourness in the girl's tone. To have lived and thrived on your own as this girl had done, only to be put in harm's way repeatedly because of Alaysha and all the messiness her life had become, must be an insult to the girl's tenacity.

Theron glared at the girl. "The Enyalian won't take the chance, oh, no." he said, looking past Alaysha at the approaching beast. Alaysha followed his gaze. Indeed, it was a beast--unlike any horse she'd ever seen, but the figure atop didn't ride so much as slump over it.

"We can protect ourselves," she said aloud. "If we stick together."

Theron shook his head. "Maybe if we weren't so weak. Maybe if we had more men..."

"She is one woman and we have a witch," she said indignantly.

He grinned. "A witch without the control to be discreet in how her power works. Better the warrior out there than the witch right here, we say. Yes. Oh, yes."

Aedus threw her hands up. "Then what's the point, you fool?"

Theron looked at her. "Better than this small child has called us a fool. Indeed, a fierce Enyalian herself did so, didn't she? Yes. So long ago."

Alaysha could swear he looked nostalgic. "How do

you know these warriors? Who are they?"

He chewed his cheek, sent a furtive glance forward. The figure had come so close, Alaysha nearly staggered in surprise at the queerness of the beast. She could make out a long neck, and what had looked like two figures atop the one back she could now see was one woman slumped forward across a large hump. The legs of the beast, long as they were, seemed supple and strong despite the heat. The woman's legs hung down well past the belly of the beast but looked red and raw. Not bleeding--just raw.

That was the moment she realized it.

"We're not in danger," she said aloud. "She's hurt."

Theron squinted, shading his vision from the sun with his palm. "It's worse than that," he murmured. "Worse even than our deaths. Oh, no, no, no, no."

Alaysha saw it the same moment he did it seemed. Both of them stumbled forward to help the woman from her mount.

"Oh, dear deities," Alaysha heard herself say, through the heavy breath of her exertion. She heard Gael's voice behind her as he spoke.

"Bodicca," he blurted even as Alaysha's hand reached the woman's leg. It was indeed raw, covered in boils in a long strip of flesh that appeared to be from a trail of something wet and greasy.

"Sweet Liliah," she heard Theron say. "Melted down. Poured on her, poor thing."

Alaysha swept a look over his face. He looked stricken and it wasn't just from the wounds; it was as though he felt connected to the woman's pain.

"So brave," he murmured. "Poor brave thing." He tutted and did more to ease her down than either Alaysha or

Gael did. They were awkward trying to wrest her from the beast without causing her further pain. Theron was adept, gentle. He stripped away his cassock and laid it on the bare earth. He stood in his flaxen shift, with his scrawny arms hanging at his sides. Strangely enough, scrawny as they were, they looked to have some semblance of old sinew and muscle. The tattau on his ribs stretched and sagged with his skin.

"Check the other side," he commanded. "She'll have water skins. Yes, oh, yes, she will. Plenty."

Aedus made for the other flank and whooped in victory. Then Alaysha lost sound of her as the girl presumably guzzled from the skin.

"Careful," she shouted at the girl. "Not too much. Lots of little, Aedus, so you can keep it down." She turned to Gael, who was already striding round the beast.

"I'll see to it and get you some," he said, his expression shifting to barely hidden revulsion as he spied Bodicca's back.

"It's a mess, Theron," Alaysha said. "Thank the deities she's passed out."

He said nothing to that, merely began digging through the pack he'd been carrying since they'd fled the city and refused to relinquish to anyone even though it was no doubt a heavy parcel for him to manage. She doubted he'd have any medicines or herbs to heal the mass of bubbled flesh that trailed in splotches and streaks down the warrior's body.

"What did this," she mused aloud. "Boiling water?"

"Boar fat, we should imagine. Melted down, yes, oh, yes, but oh, so hot," he mumbled, then choked and gagged loudly as he inspected the warrior's back.

Alaysha could stand no more. She turned in relief to Gael who held out a water skin.

"It's hot, but very sweet." He flashed another, uncharacteristic grin. "Aedus is giving Edulph some."

She kept her lips tightly closed thinking about that horrible villain finding relief. "And Barruch?"

"She's already cut a hole big enough to let him at it." The large warrior looked back over his shoulder and Alaysha followed his gaze to see Edulph cupping his hands into the broad leather. Aedus was scolding him not to waste any.

Alaysha gulped at the mouth of the skin, watching them curiously. "Is this it?"

"There're two more. Looks like she hasn't been able to drink much."

"I imagine not." Alaysha hated to do it, the reluctance to even think what was invading her mind was strong, but not strong enough to overcome the worry of it. She couldn't stop herself from wondering aloud what they would all need to know eventually.

"If she's here, where do you think Yenic is?"

Bodicca had taken him when the struggle between Aislin and Yuri had looked to go bad. Gael had told her back then that where Bodicca had taken Yenic meant that he was undoubtedly dead. If she was here, alive but sorely injured, it must be true. She tried to force her lungs to expand.

"Do you think he's gone then?"

Gael sighed and nodded at Theron. "He'll do his best to find out for you."

She met Gael's eye and saw something shift within the depths. Hurt, maybe.

"Not just for me, Gael," she said, trying to placate his pain. "For Saxon, too. If Yenic lives we may yet get Aislin to release your nephew."

He nodded mutely, but Alaysha could see he still felt

miserable. Better she focus on something she could fix, something tangible. She made her way to the shaman and searched his face questioningly, hoping he would understand what she wanted without having to say it.

"She lives, "Theron said.

She breathed deeply, wanting to ask about Yenic. "That's good."

"Perhaps," he shrugged.

"What does that mean, Theron?"

He groaned as though he thought her simple and Gael stepped closer. "The Enyalia, Alaysha. They are a caste of fierce warrior women."

"I assumed as much."

"Did you miss the term 'women'?"

"What are you talking about?"

"The Enyalia allow no man to enter their lands. I should have known by her height, her demeanour toward men that Bodicca was one of them, but it was so strange to see one in your father's city."

"Gael, get to the point. It doesn't make sense that they did this to her. What does it mean?"

Theron scuffled his feet and made a furtive movement toward Bodicca, almost a feigned need to inspect her back again, and it made Alaysha even more suspicious. "Gael? Theron?"

The shaman rolled his eyes. "They allow no men," he said. "If Bodicca is here, then Yenic is dead."

Gael reached for her hand and held it next to his heart where she could feel the thudding within. "Alaysha," he murmured. "I think he's saying that no man who enters Enyalia lives to leave."

Chapter 3

Alaysha was pretty certain her hunger and thirst had made her delirious. Yes. Seven days across the burnt lands with barely any water--rationing what they did have, baking in the unyielding sun, worrying about accidentally killing those of her companions whom she loved. All of those things had sent her over the edge into full blown sun sickness.

It had to be so. Bodicca did not lie at her feet, covered in sores from some horrible burning. She wasn't there lying alone, without Yenic, whom she herself had taken captive from Sarum in retaliation for Aislin's kidnapping of Saxon. She did not lie there, a massively huge woman, at the feet of the strangest beast Alaysha had ever seen, letting Theron do his best to tend to her pains when she knew, just knew, that the man she'd saved was dead. And that she was to blame.

No. It was the sun. It had to be. She was certain of it when the ground trembled beneath her feet, nearly imperceptible at first, but when her soles vibrated, she was sure of it. Sun sickness. It made sense.

She stared mutely at Gael for a moment, wondering if he was sharing the delirium.

He twitched his shoulder helplessly. "I'm sorry, Alaysha. I know it's true."

Bodicca groaned quietly and Theron began babbling again in his nonsensical way as he crouched over her. Alaysha didn't understand half of what he said, but then, she rarely did.

"It can't be true." She toed the woman's skin closest to her. "She wouldn't have left Yenic there."

Theron slapped her foot away. "This warrior would have had no choice. No. Not this one." He looked at Alaysha, glaring with unexpected vehemence. "She earned this pain long ago." He ran his hands over the length of her back, never touching the skin, only sweeping the sheerest bit of air currents toward her feet. "You earned it, did you not, warrior?"

Before she could ask what he meant, Aedus crept up next to her and pressed the water skin into her hand. Alaysha glanced down at the dear ferret-like face with its tiny black eyes, and hair in ratty strings of caked and dried mud. She couldn't help a smile.

"You drink, little one," she told her.

Aedus shook her head and Gael shuffled closer. "The girl is right," he said. "You need to drink your fill."

Alaysha's mouth twisted in self-loathing. "Why, because I'm more important?" She thought of the shaman's confession before they'd started this cursed journey that she must be the goddess Liliah.

"No, because I'd rather not end up as a pair of rolling eyeballs on this cracked earth."

"Some humour then, to lighten the load, Gael?"

He shrugged. "I guess you don't know me." Gael grinned and squeezed her shoulder. "No," he admitted. "Because you're more dangerous this thirsty."

"Ah," she said with a sigh. "Lest I drain you all of your life-giving fluid to save my pitiful self." She upended the skin and gulped greedily, forcing herself to pause every now and then so she didn't get sick and waste the fluid. "Barruch," she gasped at last, holding the skin out.

Aedus took the skin from her. "Barruch is already doing better."

Alaysha nodded. "Good." She sighed, loving the feeling of sloshing that took over her belly. She glanced again to the horizon. "We've passed the zenith," she said.

Gael nodded in agreement. "It will get easier for a while." He turned his attention to where Edulph was still sitting, his hands bound in his lap. "Did you water him, Aedus?"

She toed the dirt. "Not enough."

"Come, then," Gael said, reaching for the girl's arm. "I'll protect you while that particular beast drinks his fill."

Alaysha watched them go then reached to feel Barruch's neck beneath her palm "Well, old man," she said. "We live another day."

He snorted at her and shoved his nose beneath her chin. His breath felt hot, but no longer dry and smothering. She gave his nose a pat on the white patch. "I wouldn't have let them do it, you know."

He brought his nose hard against her cheek, bumping it a little more than a loving touch would be.

"Maybe if you were more of a gentle mount I wouldn't have even considered it."

He gave her a baleful stare that made her sigh. He was in a temper. And rightfully so.

"Nothing a few peaches won't cure, old man," she whispered before kissing his white spot, then she turned to the sight she least wanted to face.

"How is she, Theron?"

Without stopping his strange ministrations, he made veiled comment as usual.

"She thought she'd escape it then, but they don't forget. Oh, no."

"Forget what?" Alaysha asked him. "Theron?" Alaysha eased closer and dropped to a squat. She still felt light-headed, but the heat didn't feel so brutal anymore. "Theron?"

He swept his palm over the warrior's back without

being close enough to disturb even a hair. "They will remember us if they remember her, surely." He trailed off mumbling about herbs and broths and twins. None of it made sense to Alaysha, but she did catch one word that made sense: Youngblood.

"Youngblood, Theron? Who is that?" She thought it must mean Yenic, especially when the words around the name seemed to talk of battles and burning flames.

"Do you think she left Yenic to those warriors? Do you really think they'll kill him?" She could barely say the words.

"We have time," he said without looking at her.

"We?" she asked. "Do you mean we or you?" Damn the man and his muddled speech.

He glared up at her, pausing in his movements that seemed to only brush air away from Bodicca's body and no more.

"The moon gives us all time," he said. "But when it meets itself on the other side, he will die."

"No," she heard herself say, not sure what he meant, but sure of one thing. "She can take us there." She looked down at the ravaged warrior, so haughty before, when Alaysha knew her as Yuri's most dedicated warrior, so helpless now as she moaned in what had to be fever. Alaysha knew even as she spoke that the woman was of no use.

She looked over her shoulder at the three others. They sat stretched out on the ground. Bodicca's strange beast rested on its knees beside them. She stole a glance at Barruch, whose belly was twitching in an effort to acclimate the heat. Bodicca was of no use, no. And Theron, deities help him, was needed by the warrior more than with the band.

But the beast. If it had brought Bodicca this far, could

it make it back? Would it know the way?

She reached for Theron's hand. "Can you magic a cool place in the earth for her?" They'd been interrupted in the possibility before, but it seemed prudent to ask it again.

He looked at her, confused, and she had to explain.

"Can you create a deep enough hole to escape the heat, to find water?"

"Such magic needs blood; we told you that," he said and put his palm on the back of Bodicca's neck. She moaned, but not in pain this time. The shaman smiled. "The air steals the pain." He rose and shook his hands. "It is all a poor Clay Arm can do. Yes, sadly, yes it is."

"Theron," she said again. "Can you?"

He quirked his head. "We need blood."

Alaysha said nothing, merely glanced at Edulph as he sat sullen, and the shaman seemed to catch her meaning as he followed her gaze. "That madman may have secrets we need to hear," he said.

"You mean like this madman?" Alaysha asked, touching Theron's chest.

He sighed. "Our witch had that power. Our witch could build monuments with stone. This madman has only residual power; who knows how much left since we lost her. We doubt we can make a hole wide enough to hide in from the sun."

Alaysha huffed. "Then just dig a small hole, far, far down till you reach water." It was desperate, she knew, because if water was within a kubit deep, she'd have been able to draw it. But maybe she'd just been too far gone with fear to try.

"Such magic takes much blood."

She quirked her brow at him.

Gael came forward, overhearing. He looked back over

his shoulder at Edulph as he sat sullenly on the ground. "Then take it from that one," he said.

"That madman--" he began and Gael interrupted him.

"That madman is good as dead eventually, anyway."

Alaysha squeezed her eyes shut. This couldn't be happening. Not after they'd made it this far.

Theron groaned, frustrated. "The blood from such a madman is useless," he sighed sadly.

"Then what, Theron," Gael commanded. "What blood will do?" He stuck out his forearm, poised beneath a blade in his other hand so quickly Alaysha hadn't seen it move.

Again, the shaman shook his head. "If warrior blood was enough for us, we'd bleed the useless one." He eyed Bodicca as she lay in delirium.

Alaysha already knew what blood worked best even before Gael guessed it, his face altering to a storm of fierce rage. She put her hand on the outstretched arm, feeling the hot pulse beneath her palm.

"He means a witch's blood, Gael," she said. "Mine."

Chapter 4

Gael gripped her so suddenly by the shoulders she heard her teeth clack together. "No; we've been through this, Alaysha," he groaned. "No. I won't let you."

He met her eyes with his and held them, trapped by his revulsion. It took effort, but she made herself reach up to touch his jaw, to cup it in her hand. His beard found gaps in her fingers and tickled the webbing.

"No," he mouthed without so much as relaxing his hold or shifting his gaze.

"If we don't find more water, we'll die out here. All of us." She licked her lips, and mercifully, her tongue didn't stick there. The water Bodicca had was enough to begin coursing through all their bodies but it wasn't enough, not nearly enough, to bring them all safely to the other side. "Theron will take what he needs, and that'll be all. I--" she swallowed hard. "I trust him."

Gael's gaze finally unlocked from hers, this time traveling down her face and lingering on her mouth. She knew he was remembering the feel of his lips on hers, the way their tongues danced together, the way she was remembering it now, and he relaxed just enough for his grip to move from her shoulders to face, holding and cupping it so delicately she couldn't believe he was so fierce in his resignation just a moment ago. She felt his fingers kneading the back of her neck, pressing into the hollow her skull made as it connected to her spine. The hilt of the blade on her back touched to her head. She watched as the struggle worked its way across his face and finally, he let go altogether and stepped away.

His chest heaved and, determined, he planted his feet shoulder width apart. He held his blade tightly clenched in his sword hand.

"If a warrior's blood isn't rich enough, then you'll have to have a lot of it," he ground out and even as Alaysha leapt forward to halt the knife in its path to his throat, she thought she heard a croak of surprise come from Theron. She ignored it in favor of throwing all her weight at Gael. He was as solid and as moveable as a mountain and she ended up knocking the wind from her lungs, but at least the blade dropped to the earth. She kicked at it, and caught the end of the hilt between her toes. The pain spread like fire through her foot and she fell to the ground, grasping at her foot.

She rocked back and forth, trying to distract her body from the insult and realized as she did so that the knife was lying next to her, ready to be picked up. She fell onto it so she covered it. If he wanted it, he'd have to move her. Only, don't let it be yet; the pain in her foot was nowhere near ready to let up.

She heard him chuckling.

"What's so funny?"

"You thought I was going to do myself harm."

She peered up at him. "Weren't you?"

He cast his eyes down and shuffled his feet.

"Gael?"

"I was going to kill the she-demon." He peered sideways at where Bodicca was moaning softly.

"Bodicca?" she asked, then it dawned on her. He didn't believe the shaman could save her. And how could he? She was delirious. In obvious pain. It might even be a mercy to kill her. She stopped rocking, the pain subsiding. Gael reached down to help Alaysha up and as he did, he pulled her close, so close she could feel his heart beating against her palms. The earth trembled again, this time enough that she felt it in his chest, and it made her legs quake. He must have felt it as she had; it was too strong a movement not to. She looked up, so far up because he was so large. Then he was leaning over, his mouth against her ear.

"Mark me, Alaysha. Not today, perhaps, but I would die for you if I had to. You were right to think so."

She couldn't speak, only nod, her heart pounding in her ears. He waited until she gathered her footing and her composure and then spun her to face the shaman; when he spoke it was with obvious relief.

"I didn't think he could do it, but he seems to have managed some small magic after all."

Indeed. Bodicca's eyes were open, her mouth working to pull liquid from the ragged edge of Theron's cloak. The shaman pulled the corner from her mouth and dipped it back into the water skin, then pressed it to her lips again.

"This warrior spoke one word," the shaman said, explaining. "More water will lubricate the rest."

"What word?" Alaysha asked, wondering what one thing could make the shaman so happy.

"Well," Gael said for him.

"Well?" She was confused. "Well, what?" And then it dawned on her, the secrets the Enyalia had of crossing the burnt lands. "Dear deities. They have a hidden well." She shouldn't have shouted, she knew she shouldn't, but she was so excited, she couldn't help herself. "That's why she had full skins," Alaysha said. "She filled them."

She looked to Theron for confirmation and his grin broadened. Aedus skipped over, her long hair swinging despite the cakes of dirt in it.

"Water?" she asked. "Do I hear right? Have we found more water?" She looked back at her brother and lowered her voice. "He needs more. He's even madder with the thirst than he was when we took him."

Gael grunted at that and the girl sent him a hurt look.

"He is her brother," Alaysha said, trying to ease the tension, but she felt exactly the same as Gael. Edulph, mad or not, could not be trusted, not even with his little sister.

Gael took his place next to Theron and squatted down. "Where is the well?" he asked Bodicca. She lay half on her side in order to drink but it was obvious from her face that the small contact her sore skin made with the rest of Theron's cloak was painful.

"Halfway," she croaked, then worked to bring her features under control.

"Halfway," Gael mused. "If her skins were full, halfway must be somewhere back where she'd come."

Alaysha groaned. "Halfway. Halfway could be anywhere. In any direction."

Gael gave her a reproachful look. "Halfway is better than you think. It means we've come far enough with the stores we had that we can make it the rest of the way."

"We nearly didn't," she said. "Except for Bodicca."

"But we did," he said stubbornly. "We need to press forward while the sun has lost its power, while the moon is up. We'll rest at the well and rejuvenate ourselves."

"Then what?" She flapped her arms against her thighs, frustrated and hopeless.

"Then we press on. We find the other witch. We kill the woman who wants your pain."

Oh, yes. All of that. She'd been so filled with just the thought of survival, she'd nearly forgotten the reasons she was here in this unforgiving land to begin with. For one sweet moment she could feel pleasure at being nearly in reach of living. Now she had to think again of vengeance and war.

She sighed. "Then find a way to get Bodicca back onto her beast, Theron with her, and let's get moving."

It occurred to Alaysha as they pressed on that she hadn't seen much in the way of life in the burnt lands. A few scorpions scuttled across the plain, one or two snake trails, but no birds flew or called out to each other. Even vultures had abandoned the area. The only sounds she heard were of the shuffling of feet against parched earth and the occasional moan of hunger.

They reached the well just before dawn. The ragtag band, as Alaysha had begun to think of them, had shuffled forward steadily, if not painfully slow for her taste. Theron and Bodicca and Aedus were mounted on the Enyalian's strange beast, Bodicca stretched as delicately as possible across its back in front of a large hump of flesh, and the shaman and girl sat behind it.

Gael had tied Edulph to the beast where he trailed behind, a staggering, reluctant prisoner who occasionally shouted obscenities at nothing. It seemed a bit contrived to Alaysha, who believed, for all he appeared mad, that Edulph was more in control of his faculties than he let on. His madness had the one benefit that she could see, past that of keeping him alive, and that was of Aedus's growing concern for her brother. It all made Alaysha terribly uncomfortable and hyper vigilant. The last thing she needed was for Aedus to suddenly begin trusting her brother again.

Alaysha and Gael walked on either side of Barruch, watching for signs that Bodicca recognized the terrain.

Twice more, the ground shook as they travelled, and the last time, it was enough to make the others leap from their mounts onto the ground, their arms held out to balance themselves. All eyes shifted to her as though she'd somehow managed the magic the shaman couldn't. Alaysha had to admit to herself it had never been delirium; she'd felt it long before they had, her bare feet able to sense the minute tremors through her skin. Something was shifting inside the ground, something that made the shaman send his gaze heavenward and mumble to himself more than usual.

"What is it, Theron?" she asked him.

He blinked at her. "The clay weeps," he said and she could see that his face was smudged from his fingers working at tears that couldn't come. She assumed he too had eyes that burned from the heat, and once more, she hoped the journey to the well would end soon so they could all drink their fill and splash their faces clean.

"If it weeps," she said. "Let's hope the water is fresh."

He gave her a strange look before climbing back onto the Enyalian beast behind Aedus.

When they finally did stop again, Alaysha doubted there was a well at all. Just another encroaching flat plain of cracked earth for what looked like an eternity. Except here and there, a few cacti grew, short and spindly, as though they were exhausted from fighting the battle of drought. Thankfully, it was more than she'd remembered seeing since the first days they'd crossed the boundary into the burnt lands.

"Cactus, yes," she said to Gael. "So there must be water somewhere, but no well."

His grin flashed white at her in the encroaching light. "Look harder."

She strained to see through the gloaming shadows. Theron and Aedus were already easing the warrior from the beast, and Edulph stood kicking at the soil from his spot behind it.

Her nose twitched, tellingly. Yes. Water. Plenty of it. The power started to stretch awake within her breastbone.

"Don't you see it?" Gael poked her with his elbow. "Some water witch," he laughed, and without waiting for an answer, strode to help the shaman with the awkward burden of lowering Bodicca from the beast. Alaysha followed, pulling Aedus away as Gael grunted the woman into his arms and squatted next to a wide and flat piece of earth that was smooth of cracks. Then he eased her onto her side where she braced herself and propped herself up with her arm.

She sighed heavily, as though she'd been holding her breath a long time, then her eyelids fluttered open.

"Thank you, man," she murmured and nodded to the smooth bit of earth just beyond where she lay.

Alaysha crept closer to give it further study. As the sun leaked onto the horizon, bathing the land in blood, she noticed the earth wasn't exactly earth. It was a stone the same color as the ground, smooth and presumably flat. Anyone could stumble past it and take little notice, focusing instead on the cactus, thinking to draw fluid from the flesh, or digging beneath to hope for a small puddle of water.

"The secret of the Enyalia," Alaysha breathed, and Theron smiled at her.

"Shamans such as us always wondered, even traveling with the damned women." He made a face of distaste. "The beasts' innards are not such delectable drink."

Alaysha could swear she saw him shudder, and she wondered what he was even talking about. Then something, a very strong desire, shivered inside her and she found herself licking her lips, not caring about Theron's linguistic mysteries in the least.

"Open it," she said to Gael.

He didn't need telling twice. He pressed his fingers into the ground, feeling around, finding an edge.

It wouldn't budge.

"What's the trouble?" She heard the edge in her voice and knew it was thirst and impatience. "Hurry."

He shook his head. "No purchase."

"Wedge."

It was a croak, but at least a clear croak. Alaysha looked at Bodicca. Of course. They'd need to pry it up. Alaysha reached for her sword from Barruch's back and when she brought it close enough to the stone she could swear she heard the Enyalian grunt condescendingly.

"What?" Alaysha demanded.

"It's sure you're no warrior," the woman answered and rolled her eyes.

Alaysha turned to Gael and lifted her shoulders in question.

He shrugged. "No warrior would use their sword for a wedge."

"You have a better idea? It's pretty big."

Bodicca flailed at Theron. "Shield. Girl. Shield."

Theron hustled Aedus over to the strange beast where she emptied a placard of wood and bronze. The top edge was pointed enough to dig, jab, or stab. The bottom was perfectly straight and flat, but as Alaysha grabbed it, she could feel that the edge was honed like a knife blade, something that could dig in and lift.

She was about to fit it into the groove around the stone when Aedus let go an exclamation.

Alaysha paused even as she was hunched over, Gael at her side ready to help her put her back into it and grab the stone as she pried it up. She felt Aedus nudge her again, this time with Theron's own exclamation.

"What?" Alaysha asked, looking at the girl who pointed to the horizon where black, hulking shapes had come into bare view.

"Sweet deities," Alaysha said. "Saved."

"Not safe, us," Theron said, rushing about to gather everything he could into his pouches and bags. He hurried over to Edulph and stuffed a filthy bit of leather into the man's mouth.

Alaysha searched for Gael's eyes and, finding them, saw steely resolution within the grayish green.

"Who?"

He nodded in Bodicca's direction.

"More of her," Alaysha guessed.

"If they catch us with her, we're as good as dead."

"She'll tell them we saved her, won't she?" Alaysha squatted in front of the woman and saw for the first time how old she really was. Without the typical command of a warrior's stance, or arms, or the haughty knowledge that she could best most men, the woman, in her pain, revealed that she had to be at least the same age as Yuri. Maybe a full season or two younger.

"You'll tell them, Bodicca."

"They won't be happy you saved me," was all the fallen warrior said.

"But you're one of them." Alaysha's confusion deepened even as Theron began rustling about the woman, trying to drag her off somewhere--deities only knew where he thought he would hide. "Theron, what are you--"

Bodicca interrupted her. "I was one of them yes. Many seasons ago. Who do you think did this to me?"

"But--"

"But they are fierce. You don't know, little witch." Bodicca, grimacing and biting her lip, did her best to help Theron, even pushing herself to her hands and knees, and then, staggering to her feet.

The pain must have been nearly insurmountable, even Gael reached out to help her, only to step back when the Enyalian swatted him weakly away. She reached out for the shaman's arm. "It's near Solstice," she said, and the shaman's sharp intake of breath made Alaysha squint at him suspiciously. He covered over the mistake by coughing in a fit but Alaysha knew something dreadful waited in the one word.

She squinted at him suspiciously. "What's solstice?"

"No time, no time, no, none at all," he said and tried to drag at Bodicca's beast, who'd planted padded feet firmly in the earth.

"Leave her," Bodicca said and put her hand out to Aedus. "Come, girl."

Alaysha watched Aedus peer at the horizon, the hulking forms now looming larger, wider, separating into a dozen beasts.

"They'll be coming to the well," Bodicca ground out, her voice was pinched with pain. "Your witch will stay." Bodicca glanced at Alaysha. "You will not want the girl with you." She glanced at Edulph and grinned. "Him--well, you'll see."

Alaysha might not understand what was going on, but she understood urgency, and she understood capture. She began gathering all the water skins she could and slapped Barruch's rump. "You won't have time to get far."

The woman's cracked lips spread in a knowing smile. "Have no fear, witch. When they see you and that one," she nodded at Gael, "We'll suddenly have plenty of time."

Alaysha reached for Aedus and held her arms out. The girl rushed into them and squeezed so hard, Alaysha felt her breath rush from her lungs.

"I'll find you," Alaysha said and felt Aedus' face burrow into her belly, then the girl squirmed to look at where Edulph stood watching her with a keen expression. She blinked and rubbed at her eyes and then peered back up at Alaysha.

"I want to go with you."

Theron stepped closer and peeled Aedus away. "This shaman, we know where to find her, little one."

Aedus went, but reluctantly. She peered back over her shoulder as the three shuffled away, off to find some safety in the distance of a cracked horizon. Alaysha watched them go, leading Barruch away from her, knowing with each step, the Enyalia were drawing closer.

"What will they do, Gael?" she murmured, "When they reach us here, at their well."

He sighed resignedly, "I imagine they will kill us." He chuckled. "Or they will try."

She looked at him, drinking in each feature that the rising sun painted in red, then orange, then yellow. She thought then of his touch on her skin, his breath against her throat. She thought if this was the last moment she would live, then she would think without guilt of the time they spent together. His worship of her body, the heat of his kiss, the feeling of surrender she gave him. She would enjoy it, the entire memory of all aspects of it from the fevered touches to the selfless way he comforted her. It hadn't felt like betrayal of her bond with Yenic--how could it be when Yenic himself had betrayed her. Even so, Gael had respected the bond and asked no more of her than that one moment when he could be hers ultimately and forever. She watched his face as he watched the horizon, tensing, getting ready, and when he glanced at her, she thought she felt a streak of wet running down her cheek, but that couldn't be true. She was exhausted of fluid.

She watched his throat convulse. She knew he was remembering it too. She thought perhaps he'd speak, remind her of that night, but he shook his head, then spread his arms wide, stretching, twisting his torso. He strode to the strange Enyalian beast and pulled out swords and knives and cut Edulph loose and pulled the leather from his mouth.

"You will need to fight for your life. Will you?"

Edulph nodded, grinned, and Alaysha saw for one heartbeat the savage brute who had captured and hurt his sister, then tried to manipulate Alaysha into killing her entire city.

"Fight?" Edulph's voice was hoarse from disuse, but the word was clear. "I'll kill every bitch I see."

The Enyalia took their time; it seemed there was no rush in light of a barren landscape. No need to find an opponent before it disappeared. No reason to hurry a slaughter. Even so, as they drew closer, Alaysha was taken aback by their size. She had but one thought when they drew close enough that she could make out each muscle that tensed and released in gargantuan thighs, hear the rattle of the bracelets around their legs, hips, or ankles. Some of them, the largest, had rows of white marbles wrapped around their thighs and when they leapt from their beasts, those circlets sounded like teeth chattering against the cold.

Gael wasn't surreptitious about it when he passed Alaysha her sword and then pressed her behind him.

She felt a moment of anger, thinking he would coddle her so, but then Edulph took his place next to her and whispered in her ear, and she had no time to think or feel anything, except to agree.

"This is the best way to die."

Chapter 5

When they leapt from their beasts, it was almost as though they did so as one unit. The moon had its near bloat, and the darkness of the desert wasn't as full, as the stars shivered out of their clouds and lent cool white light to the area. Enough that the sight of the immense women struck a sort of dread in Alaysha's chest. The rattling of their movement died and an undercurrent of subtle threat echoed in the air in its place. The largest woman, a redhead as strikingly beautiful as she looked dangerous, strode forward with all the confidence of a panther about to settle in for a languid meal she'd stashed in a tree.

Alaysha watched Gael's shoulders shift subtly, gathering energy from the coils of muscle deep in his spine. She expected an explosion of movement, a flurry of excitement from beside her as Edulph lost the rest of his mind to battle madness.

Neither man moved. Both trained, Alaysha thought, in their own ways, to the warrior's way. Disciplined. Wait for the right time. Wait. Wait.

Alaysha wasn't sure exactly what to expect; she could hear her own breath, finding time with Gael's, with Edulph's finding balance with hers. Everything hummed around her. She felt her heart beat. Filled her legs with air, her fingertips with breath. She became one great lung waiting to exhale.

The leader shouted a word, startling Gael, Alaysha could see. He flinched, but he didn't move to strike, he was that disciplined. Alaysha wanted to steal a look at Edulph, to make sure he wasn't fool enough to engage before time.

The sound came again and Alaysha thought she understood the word. She waited, not sure if she should slip out of line or not. Then it came again.

"Woman."

Gael didn't move so much as a lung to inhale. Edulph stood stock still. Alaysha shuffled, taking a step sideways and those mica colored eyes landed on her.

"Are these yours?" the woman demanded.

"Mine?"

The face hardened impatiently. "These." The woman didn't even drop a look to Gael or Edulph; instead they stayed on Alaysha's face so steadily Alaysha believed they were deliberately ignoring the presence of the two men. That's when she realized they were.

"These are my friends," she admitted. "We're traveling together. Yes."

The woman's gaze narrowed. "Traveling? No one travels the burnt lands." She sent a look to the women on either side of her, and two women stepped forward.

Alaysha only had time to think it was foolish for them to try to defend themselves against such calm command. And then she was sprung like a mechanism too long held taut.

She felt her arm lifting her sword, heard the clang of metal against metal. The jolt of meeting an unrelenting match leapt down her elbow and into some soft tissue beneath her ribcage. She meant to fight with all she had. She meant to meet each thrust with equal fervor, until she fell.

Only she didn't.

She couldn't.

The battle still raged; she could hear the metallic sounds, the grunts of effort. But she herself was impotent.

It took a few heartbeats to realize she was being held.

Two of the mountainous women towered behind her, holding her arms behind her back. One of them should have been enough to seize her, but Alaysha supposed the battle madness had given her enough juice to fight being pinned. And so two now held her tightly against one woman's body, with arms bent back from the shoulders, and her legs trapped between four legs. Alaysha could barely move enough to breathe.

Her shoulder burned deep in the tissues beneath the cuff as the women pulled her arms behind her and pinned them there. She could see Edulph being worn down, and she knew by the way he swung his sword a little too slowly, that he was finding it heavy. Still, the women circling him refused to engage him as anything but one-on-one when they could have made short work of him as a group.

The ground was kicked up in plumes of dust that turned to grit, sanding her eyes and coughing down into her lungs, making breathing difficult. How badly Edulph must be feeling she didn't want to guess, but he fought on anyway.

His opponent took her time, almost lazily playing with him as she blocked his every thrust, lifting her sword at the last moment, twisting it with barely any hip swing. Alaysha realized he was still too dehydrated to stand for long. She wondered why he didn't just give up. It was clear who the better fighter was. Still, Edulph gave it his all and only when it was painfully clear even to him that he would lose, did his opponent leap at him and send him hurtling backwards to the earth, her sword point at his throat. His chest heaved; hers barely moved. Edulph's hair plastered against his head, sweating. Only then, seeing how easily the woman could have taken Edulph did Alaysha breathe easily. The shame she felt at being so quickly dispatched melted away.

"She was playing with him," she heard herself say, and one of the women holding her made a sound of agreement.

Alaysha slumped in their hold. Fighting had been a

futile endeavour, obviously allowed by these women only as a means to demonstrate their strength and superiority. She tried to twist in their grasp, to see if Gael realized it too. To tell him to give it up, not to waste his strength fighting for a life that they obviously didn't plan to take.

Her holders didn't seem to want to allow it at first, but when the sounds of battle didn't stop, even when Edulph was being forced to his knees and his hands bound behind him, Alaysha grew belligerent.

"Pull them off," she growled, thinking it was smarter for Gael to conserve his strength, that to continue to oppose the warriors might well mean his unintentional death--he was a stubborn one, that man.

At first, she felt the women slacken their hold, and then she heard a cry of anguish from beside her. She felt her arm being let go and she spun so she could see around before the other could capture it and pull it taut against its mate again.

Yet the clang of metal continued. Gael, Alaysha thought. He must still be fighting. She needed to twist to see him, but she couldn't. She couldn't move enough, and she prayed she'd not hear the silence descend. That one would fight to the death, she knew.

The moments were few but could have been seasons as Alaysha waited. The sounds of exertion grew more laboured, the sounds of scuffle meant a barrage of warriors rather than two. Alaysha counted quietly; two for Edulph, two for her. That meant at least eight against Gael.

She tried to struggle and heard a harsh command in her ear.

"Be still."

Alaysha tried to catch Edulph's eye as he was forced to his knees. His face was bloody, his cheeks swollen. His beard was cut neatly into two swaths by a long slash. He'd fought with all he had, she thought and sighed heavily. If it weren't for Gael, and for the uncertainty of how far the others had managed to flee, Alaysha would bleed these women of their fluid and be done with it.

The hold on her arms began to twist, and she realized she too was forced to her knees. She swore to herself if Gael was harmed, she would bleed these women. She would, and pray Aedus had gotten far enough away to use the rain that would come after.

As her knees struck the earth, she felt the hold on her lessen, and then she was thrust onto her side, her shoulder painfully ramming the unyielding clay. The point of a sword--her own--was pressed behind her ear as she was left to see the carnage.

Dear deities, there were bodies and body parts everywhere. The ground was soaked with blood.

There, in the midst of three standing, fully engaged women fought Gael. She'd seen him in battle before, and it could be described as beautiful, the way he moved, the way he struck out with such economy of motion it was obvious he treated it with the sense of art he thought it. He fought so now, stepping lightly, face down, arms moving--one with blade, one with sword. Striking only when necessary, waiting with the patience of a cobra for the right moment, except now, his combat was not a thing of beauty.

He was bloodied. Hair clotted with red, arms slashed and bleeding. When he spun to meet the blade of an Enyalian who got too close, Alaysha could see his eyes were swollen nearly shut--he'd been struck by a fist or a sword hilt or elbow.

Someone had got close enough to do him harm.

Alaysha could tell the women had realized one was

not enough to take this warrior down. Several women lay bleeding and sprawled on the ground around him. It was to one of these fallen that one of Alaysha's captors ran, stumbling in a way that told Alaysha the woman was dead, and none of these Enyalia--least of all that weeping and furious woman touching an unmoving face--would let him live for such folly.

Gael was fighting for his life and he knew it. To call to him would be foolish. They were too large, too strong, too disciplined.

Alaysha couldn't feel her lungs expand. She fought to inhale, to feel her heart pump. Once, as he spun and swung, his metal biting into the blade of another, she thought she caught his eye, and she knew what he'd see if indeed he could see at all: her fear. Fear in her face, her posture. Fear in the way she felt her face contorting in an effort to hold back the stinging in her eyes, to sop up the tears that pooled beneath her nose and leaked into her mouth.

And fear of the knowledge that the power was coming despite her best attempt to wait until he was indeed dead and gone, because if he lived through the battle, then she'd drain him as surely as she drained the rest, and she'd never survive the guilt of it.

And then he dropped his blade, let his arms fall to his sides as he halted, facing her, keeping her gaze with his own purpled and bloody one. He surrendered for her, she knew that. He would've died fighting but for the guilt she'd have to live with if he didn't. He chose instead the blades of his opponents as his death, all three of them darting for him at the same moment he gave in.

Alaysha braced herself for the strike, telling herself she would unleash the coiled power the moment the blades went in. She did her best to hold it back, knowing that if she let go too late, it would be she who took Gael's life.

But it was too late.

The power was unready unfurling.

Chapter 6

One heartbeat, two. Before ten, and she knew the mist would gather as it drained and psyched every bit of fluid it could detect. All the tears and sweat from these women--Alaysha could already taste the salt. Edulph's blood drying in his veins, Gael's. But first the most available: the water skins filled and bloated on the beasts' backs. The water from the well as it rose from the crack Gael had managed to create as he'd hefted the stone lid.

Fury had hold of her, and it wanted--no, needed--to see the mist gather. She wanted these women to dry to leathered husks and drift on the wind like dried brush at the weather's whim, and she couldn't care less what happened to their seeds as they fell from their sockets, unliving forever, never to be released. Never to take root and inhabit any other savage world ever again.

She thought she heard her name, but it didn't matter. The woman standing next to her fell, not dead--not yet, but the skin was already drying. Alaysha looked past her, thinking to let the rain burst over Gael when it bloated to its limit, thinking she'd give him back the fullness of his flesh after she'd taken it so he would still be beautiful, so his eyes could stay where they belonged. His eyes. So gray green, so filled with the soul of his body.

His eyes. Open. Staring at her, reminding her he wasn't dead, that it wasn't time for vengeance.

Alive. Alive, Alaysha. Let it go, let the power go. She forced herself to think of nohma again, the love she felt for the gentle woman seep into her being and fill her hands, her feet, her moisture as it raced through her veins. Nohma. Aedus. Saxa: all those she loved without question or doubt or fear. She pictured their faces; reached out to them with her mind.

And the power went. She felt it evaporate and leave her panting, sobbing, from the effort to control it. The water she'd psyched from the well, from the skins, the minute amount she'd gathered from the dead around her, the living too, all burst with all the power of the fury she'd used to drain it. She couldn't stop herself from weeping in relief. The shivering made her thighs quake as she knelt, and she couldn't keep herself from collapsing.

The leader squinted at her suspiciously and motioned to the others next to her to truss up the man she'd scored with her blade. She moved to Alaysha and fell to her haunches, grabbing Alaysha's chin and twisting her head this way and that. Her thumb pressed painfully into the tattau.

"You are a witch," she said flatly. Alaysha sent the woman a scathing look.

The warrior seemed unaffected even with the new flush of rain running down her cheeks and pooling on her breastbone.

"This man was yours?"

What did she mean 'was'? Surely Gael still lived, she'd seen his eyes. She knew he was alive. He had to be.

"That man killed several of my best." The woman looked backwards over her shoulder, then she twisted back to face Alaysha. The eyes she'd thought were black as mica stones were dark, deep green. There was the unmistakable air of respect on the Enyalian's face. She grunted thoughtfully.

"He will be well fought over, little maga," the Enyalian said. "We thank you." She stood, then, and with a quick motion, the rain sluicing down her body unheeded, she had the remaining warriors heft Gael onto one of the strange beasts.

Edulph was lifted and deposited onto another.

Two women hoisted the cover of the well and peered in. Alaysha could tell by their reaction that it was empty.

The leader glared at Alaysha. "It will take at least three moons to refill, even with all this rain."

Alaysha shrugged but said nothing. She knew the warrior understood what had happened to it by the way she'd called her witch. There was no need to answer with words. The woman broke into a grin.

"I could leave you here to enjoy your downpour, little maga." Her gaze trailed to the horizon where Alaysha could make out a huddled bulge on the horizon that she knew were the others lying flat. She hoped the Enyalian would see it as a shadow and no more.

Alaysha tried not to let her face give away her fear of losing Gael to these women, and as she worked to appear composed, she realized what the woman meant by asking if Gael was hers.

Was hers.

But no longer. He was theirs now, and Alaysha understood all at once that the warrior knew she'd unleashed her power only when she'd thought him as good as dead. This woman, this cunning woman understood the crux of the power all at once, that she'd not use it if the ones she wanted to protect were alive. She knew Alaysha posed no threat as long as they had Gael.

It seemed once again she'd given herself away. They knew how to manipulate her even as Edulph had, as Yuri had. And then she understood the silent message in Gael's eyes--it wasn't for death or for salvation. It was begging her not to use her power because then they'd understand the most important thing about it, that she had a weakness that could be exploited.

And now she'd done it--she'd shown these warriors the same thing she'd shown Yuri, and in his turn, Edulph. That she could be manipulated by her love for others.

Chapter 7

It poured all night and Alaysha hoped that the steady onslaught would at least rejuvenate the companions she'd had to leave behind her. It also left her wondering just how deep the Enyalian well had been. Surely to psych so much fluid that the heavens could drip for so long, the well had to be leaguas deep, not hand spans as most were.

They plodded along for hours on the strange beasts, the long necks of the things swaying in a rhythm that would put a weary traveler to sleep. At times the ground quaked, stronger than before, but if the warriors noted it, they said nothing to each other about it. They stopped when the sun met the lip of the horizon in a kiss so wet it seemed the entire world had flooded. Alaysha's leather tunic was soaked through and her hair stuck behind her ears, leaking water into the crevice between her breasts and trickling down to her belly button.

The Enyalia seemed to take it in stride. The one who had called her maga, the largest and the one who sat her beast at the front of the queue, turned her face repeatedly toward the sky, letting the rain pool into her open mouth. Her hair, a shade that resembled the kind of reddish brown that dying leaves turned in the more frigid lands past Sarum, was twisted into lengths that sent the rain into miniature rivers down her back. What water the woman didn't swallow, she spat into her water skin. Seeing this, the others did the same. Alaysha made note not to share from those skins unless she had nothing left to drink.

The leathers they wore, brief things on their torsos that stretched up in separate halters to cover their breasts and tie behind their necks also splayed downward into strips at the waist for easy movement. All the skins must have been tanned in a way that made them supple, and coated with grease because they had a way of sluicing the fluid into rivulets that traveled the creases. They all wore leather belts that hoarded any number of tools and pouches, a blade, rope, even. Alaysha guessed the weight of them alone was enough to keep their legs strong.

At one point, each of them pulled out some sort of hollowed out root that they then tied to their waists and used to catch the water that ran down their backs. They repeatedly upended this into their skins. When the rain slackened, they pulled from their packs flax-woven bedrolls and draped them over their backs, letting the material grow sopping wet and collect in small narrow gourds they'd tied to a corner.

Resourceful women, women used to traveling in the burnt lands, wasting no drop of precious fluid. Her heart sank, thinking it must mean they were still far off from the end.

As the sun began to set again, the Enyalia halted the caravan and leapt from the beasts in nearly one fluid motion. They pulled Edulph and Gael from the backs of the beasts and set them apart from each other, then dropped dried apples and nuts onto their laps. The large red-haired Enyalian passed some fruit to Alaysha, her green gaze flicking over her in silent assessment.

"Eat," the woman said in a voice that sounded loaded with the gritty earth beneath her feet. Too much time spent in the dried lands, Alaysha supposed; her vocal cords were undoubtedly little strings of baked sinew. "Walk. But don't wander."

Alaysha looked out over the distance they had yet to cover, at the ground that was cold but hard, without vegetation or grazing beast to relieve the eye of earth. "Where would I go?"

That seemed to satisfy the warrior and she marched off, chewing a mouthful of nuts and apple. Alaysha edged her way over to where Gael had been dumped. He slumped down into himself, and if his eyes were open, he stared broodily off into the distance. She settled next to him, touching him on the arm; she felt it tremor beneath her fingers and sensed an echo in her own chest. He refused to look at her.

"I'm sorry, Gael," she whispered. It was obvious that past his grievous injuries sustained in battle, she'd also made him sick and weak from the power that leaked from her when she'd been afraid. She wondered how much she had dehydrated him and whether he could recover easily enough to make the rest of the journey safely. She recalled the way she'd made Saxa sick when the power had unleashed itself because of fear, nearly taking all the fluid from the healer as she'd nursed Alaysha back to health. It seemed so long ago that she'd nearly died of wounds to her side, wounds inflicted by her father's favoured scout--a lifetime ago rather than a few fortnights. Theron had to help replenish Saxa's fluids then, feeding them to her constantly with additional herbs to help her body distribute it quickly. There was no such help here. No herbs.

"Gael," she tried again. "I'm sorry I hurt you. I thought--"

"You thought I was as good as dead. I know," he said. The normally strong voice was thready.

She let go her breath. At least he was speaking, even if he sounded flat and morose. She tried again, not sure why she needed his forgiveness, but realizing she did. "It came too quickly, Gael. I couldn't stop it."

"I know, Alaysha," he said in dismissal and she could

feel her cheeks burn.

She sought Edulph's form in the encroaching darkness, making sure he wasn't within earshot just in case the brutal man decided to take his revenge on them while they rested. He'd fought with them against the Enyalia, but he still couldn't be trusted. He'd come along quietly with them on the journey, happy enough to leave the well Aislin had left him in deep in the mountains of Sarum. That didn't mean he wasn't planning something with the fire witch. It wasn't but a few short days ago that she and Gael both believed he was sent by Aislin to spy on them and to help her locate Yenic.

Alaysha found Edulph in short order. They'd placed him next to the beasts, making him squeeze the bedrolls until the water sopped into the fibres let go and streamed into the open water skins. Strange, how the Enyalia had selected him to perform the menial task while they let Gael rest. It made her wonder if the warrior could be forced to such tasks at all.

Perhaps the Enyalia were more discerning than she'd given them credit for.

She studied the way the women strode about, feeding the beasts, chewing their dried fruit without pause, never once sitting down or taking a break. None seemed concerned about their captives escaping. But then, where would they run to? And besides that, they needed the Enyalia to help them get safely past the burnt lands. Surely the women knew that too.

Gael hunched too sullenly to appear a threat to them anymore, she supposed.

She reached out to him. No leather bonds about his wrists, nor on hers. The Enyalia were cocky, thinking once beaten, the captives wouldn't dare rise again in vengeance. Alaysha had only to look at the unmoving bundles lain reverently across several beasts to know they *could* be beaten.

"Gael," she whispered, hoping the tension she felt in his forearm would ease. "Gael."

He said nothing, but at least his arm snaked around her shoulders, and she felt at once reassured and something else she couldn't name, but it sent her a quick flash of memory of the both of them in the darkness of a close, hot tunnel, the sweetness of intimate touch flushing her cheeks. She should have felt as though she was betraying Yenic, but the truth was she still wasn't sure he hadn't already betrayed her to his mother. It was something she had to know: if Yenic loved her enough, if he would side with her to release Sarum from his mother's mad takeover, or from whatever else she had in mind and according to Theron, there was plenty of it.

She didn't know how much of that she believed either. Gods and goddesses fighting each other, following each other to a garden created for the safety of a few children. Those things seemed remote compared to the very real issue of the people she loved being murdered by a woman who could control her power a little too well and who couldn't be manipulated by anyone or anything. Except maybe Yenic.

There were so many things about Yenic that she didn't know, and yet she loved him still. Deities help her, she doubted whether it was the bond alone that drove her feelings for him. She looked askance at the warrior who sat next her. So little did she know of herself and of her own world, and yet she knew this one thing: that this man next to her would die for her. And she'd nearly killed him.

"I thought you--I mean," she floundered. "I thought--"

"You thought I'd given up." His voice sounded tired. She didn't blame him. He'd fought like a madman. And now his fluids were low. He must be struggling just to speak.

"I did. Sorry." She felt ashamed that he was able to guess how she felt, that she remembered a day when he had given up, when he'd admitted that he didn't want to live anymore. She'd nearly killed him that day too, and brought the rain when she managed to pull back the power. But that too was fortnights ago. So much had happened since then.

He chuckled. "No apology needed, Witch," he said, and she almost gasped in pleasure at the return of his mocking term for her, the one that had changed to endearment so subtly over the weeks that she'd grown to miss it when he stopped. He pulled her in closer, easing her head onto his chest, and sending a burst of warmth down her side. He was terribly hot; too hot for even these lands.

"If I can fool you, think what these women must think."

"So we'll beat them by being docile?"

"Not beat," he said. "There's no need to fight a warrior who believes he--I mean, she--has already won. We'll use them."

"To get to Yenic if he still lives."

"Yes, and through Yenic, Saxon."

Alaysha hadn't forgotten Gael's nephew--her own half-brother, truth be told. Yuri's heir. The one he died to protect even as he was confronted to make the choice to save Alaysha instead. But then it hadn't really been Alaysha, either, that the fire witch planned to kill in front of Yuri, was it? No, it was Alaysha's twin, and her father had known that too, even if Alaysha had no idea she even had a sister.

She almost wished she hadn't let her mind travel down that complex path of her father's devious machinations. There were far too many pains from small thorns on the sides of those pathways, but she couldn't stop the memories that flooded in. Memory. Curse of the temptress bloodline, to remember so clearly and so lengthily. Her nohma had said it was long memory that allowed the power to work so well through her, to find and remember the fluid pathways so intimately it could pull the water in mere heartbeats.

Except there were so many holes in that memory, a very ordinary mechanism her mind put to use to protect her from the tragedies she'd suffered: the pain of her mother's death, her nohma's, the torture she'd suffered at Corrin's hand, the neglect of a father she loved.

Too many holes, and thank the deities she'd been spared them so long. Now, though, things were different. She knew too much, and that knowledge made her angry.

She heard her own sigh of frustration and felt Gael's finger on her lips. A little shock tremored through her in response.

"They're coming," he said and resumed his previously sullen and defeated posture. It was such a good act that Alaysha found herself doubting it was all feigned.

Two of the brutishly tall women towered over them, their arms and leathers still slick from the rain that had stopped by the time the group had. The small marbles around her legs clacked together with each movement.

One of them kicked Gael's outstretched foot, but he made no sound.

"Get up, man. Cai wants you to kneel when she comes." The voice was almost too lyrical sounding for such a large frame. Alaysha peered up at the face, trying to see what she looked like.

When Gael didn't move right away, the woman reached down, and with a short grunt of effort pulled him to his feet. It took Alaysha by surprise that even a woman of her size could force Gael to his feet. At least until she remembered he was playing along. At least, she hoped that was the case.

"What about me?" Alaysha asked and the woman eyed her with some speculation. Even in the approaching gloom, Alaysha could see the woman was thinking.

"You may stand or sit as you please."

There was a sort of grudging respect in her voice, Alaysha thought. She chose to stand. "Who is Cai?"

The woman's look of speculation disappeared. In its place came annoyance. She gripped Gael by the arm and twisted him toward where the sun was setting, facing away from the group, then forced him to his knees. After that, both warriors took their places on either side of him.

Alaysha noted that none of the others even bothered to stop to watch what was happening; they merely went about their business, collecting water skins, attaching them to the beasts, wrapping up their food stores.

The ground had gone slick from the rain, and Alaysha could see Edulph doing his best not to slip in the mud as he hefted the skins and packed the bedrolls back onto the beasts. He was working without complaint, Alaysha noticed, and she remembered Aedus's words when she'd first met her, that her people were used to work, used to brutality. Not for the first time, she wondered about the girl and her brother, their past, their people. A tribe Yuri had obviously wanted to enslave for his own uses.

It was long moments before the woman Alaysha assumed to be Cai came forward. The Enyalian, obviously their leader, strode toward them without rushing. The same woman who had gripped her chin and called her maga when she'd inspected the tattaus. The woman stopped in front of Alaysha, rattling hazelnuts around in her palm.

The way the shadows crept across her face, the aquiline nose, the speed her cxpression shifted, all looked vaguely familiar. Despite her startling beauty, Alaysha shivered instinctively.

Just when Alaysha thought the warrior wouldn't speak, she addressed Alaysha impassively. "We're nearly home. I need you to relinquish these men to me."

"Relinquish? You already took them."

The woman smiled slowly, quietly. "Indeed. They are ours now, but you must know this too."

"Why? What will it change?"

Cai cocked her head thoughtfully and her eyes lingered on Alaysha's tattau. She really did have striking eyes, a dark shade of green but outlined in an almost translucent yellow. Set like almonds in skin that resembled young milk pudding.

"They're no longer yours, maga," she said. "They belong to the Enyalia now." She spoke slowly, working hard to pronounce the words so Alaysha could understand. But it was the meaning beneath that Alaysha thought Cai wanted her to grasp.

"If you do them no harm, I won't psych your land dry," she said in return and grinned spitefully at the woman.

"Our bone witch will want to see you," Cai said, ignoring the threat in the air.

"Bone witch?" Alaysha was instantly wary.

"Our healer." Cai waved the question away as though it was an obvious one, and Alaysha silly to ask it. "When she's done with you, you will leave these men. They belong--"

"To Enyalia, yes." Alaysha thought she heard Gael let go a bark of anger, but since none of the women reacted, she supposed it was just her own wishful thinking. Still, she wouldn't agree. She couldn't agree. She didn't own anyone.

"Maga?" Cai prodded.

Alaysha shook her head. "They're not mine to relinquish."

Cai shifted subtly from one foot to the other, and Alaysha felt a brief moment where she thought the warrior would change her mind. She dared to believe the woman would let them go. Then the moment was over and Alaysha thought the Enyalian looked pleased, but certainly not enough to let them go.

"If they belong to no one, then so now even more they're ours, and you have no reason to remain when Thera is done with you."

Cai stepped away even as Alaysha was trying to decipher exactly what deal had been struck without her consent. The woman stepped behind Gael and looked down at him, saying nothing for long moments. Finally, she edged sideways so that she faced the warrior standing on his left. The blur she created the next instant took Alaysha by surprise; the woman spun hard, the velocity behind her body lending enough energy that when her foot shot out sideways, it landed on the back of Gael's neck and he fell forward without a sound. He lay, unmoving, while Cai looked down at him unemotionally.

Alaysha was already sprinting forward as he fell, but she wasn't fast enough to catch him. Even with the full weight of her anxiety propelling her forward, she landed against the flat of Cai's palm, held outstretched almost lazily.

"He murdered five of my best, little maga." There was a subtle pressure from Cai's hand as she pushed Alaysha away. Her hair was in her face, but she did nothing to sweep it aside. What Alaysha could see of the green gaze beneath was as cold as the waters of the broad sea. "When he wakes, he'll find himself tied to my beast by his ankles."

"You can't do that."

Cai motioned to the two guards who pulled hemp rope coiled around the leather belts that hung on their waists and began wrapping Gael's feet together.

"I can do whatever I like with him. He belongs to Enyalia." She whistled with fingers in her mouth and the rest of the women went into action almost as though they were connected mind to mind. Cai set Alaysha away easily.

"You may ride," she said.

Alaysha watched as Gael was tied to Cai's beast. Thankfully, he was tall enough that even being strapped to the animal by his feet, it was only his shoulders that took most of the ground. Still, who knew how long he'd be dragged along behind before they reached their destination.

"If he belongs to Enyalia, then Enyalia will end up with nothing but a useless bloody mess."

Cai merely shrugged.

"His back will be torn to shreds."

"It's not his back I need to concern myself with, maga."

"You should," Alaysha said, fully aware she was pleading, bargaining. "He'll die."

"All men die eventually, little maga. But we have a very skilled bone witch who will heal any--troublesome--wounds." Cai crawled onto her beast and looked back at her. "You may ride," she said again and indicated the spot behind her.

Alaysha scanned the group. Edulph had been hoisted like a sack onto another beast with two humps and he lay across it facedown. Undignified for a man who a few fortnights ago commanded an admittedly bedraggled but dedicated group of soldiers, and uncomfortable for any conscious person.

Gael still hadn't come to. At least he hadn't seemed to. Alaysha took some comfort in that.

She took note of Gael as he lay on the ground and crossed her arms stubbornly. There was no way she'd let him be dragged while she sat on a beast for the rest of the trip. She either got him untied or she carried him.

"Untie him," she said to the leader.

The woman turned her back on Alaysha and made a short movement with her hand; the beasts nudged forward. Alaysha scrambled to grab for Gael's shoulders and missed as he moved inches ahead. She shouted, begging the woman to stop and was rewarded. The redhead turned again but with a smirk.

"You want on, little maga?"

Alaysha shook her head and grappled for Gael's torso. It took several grunting moments but at last she managed to heft Gael's weight onto her shoulder. The woman pursed her lips and waved her comrades on; the shambling motion of the beast started again and as Alaysha staggered forward she realized something Cai said that had struck a quiet niggling part of her mind.

She'd called the bone witch Thera.

She knew well that Saxa's people named their sons for the mother. Saxa had named her son Saxon even though he was Yuri's heir. And Theron himself was from Saxa's tribe. And Theron had been this way before. It had to be coincidence. Had to be.

Alaysha worked to get at the pivot point of Gael's body as she considered the bone witch, twisting and working beneath his deadweight frame so that she managed to get him draped across both of her shoulders and upper back rather than just on one. Even getting him successfully hefted, she didn't think she could take one step with him let alone an entire journey. She wanted to sob in frustration and indeed thought she let go a brief gasp of breath before she caught herself. She had opted for this and she would do her best to see it through. She knew Gael would do the same for her. Except, she thought sourly, Gael was at least three hands taller and weighed at least double Alaysha's nine stone. He could carry her over one arm, draped like a piece of rag and still walk a leagua.

"Put me down."

Gael's voice, groggy, but most definitely aware. They hadn't taken two staggering steps and her thighs were begging her to do as he asked. She couldn't find the energy to answer and hold him at the same time.

She forced her feet to move, commanded her knees to hold her. Her legs trembled, but she made some progress. Three steps at least. The beast he was tied to never faltered, it's rhythm a shuffling, shambling kind of movement that made each step torture.

"Drop me."

"I won't." There. Another step. Now that he was better balanced, she found she could move, even if it was incredibly difficult. She began to hope.

"You'll kill yourself trying to carry me," he said.

She didn't answer. He was likely right, but what choice did she have. There. Ten steps, ten faltering, painful steps.

The pace of the beast kept on without stopping. She bit the fear back.

A grunt came from behind her left ear and then she was stumbling, falling to her knees; the line went taut and she was free of her burden before she realized she was in danger of losing it. Gael, on his side, and then on his back, slid along the ground--no, was drug along the ground behind Cai's beast, his heels in the air and his shoulders making a sickening line in the hard earth. She watched his head bobbing away from her as he tried to keep it held aloft.

If she only had her full control as Aislin did, that cursed witch of flame who could contain fire to a man's own body, these Enyalia would be nothing but husks of leathered flesh. But she didn't; the power leak during the battle proved that she didn't have control. She would have to continue; she couldn't harm these women without harming Gael. And they knew it.

So she might not be able to bear all of his weight, but she might be able to pace herself closely enough with Cai's beast that the animal could do the biggest part of the work. Much like two people carrying a large sack, one on each end. If she kept the line taut enough, yet slack enough, the animal would do the greatest share.

She stumbled to her feet and rushed to catch up. She grabbed for Gael's shoulders and, with a great deal of effort, managed to hoist him. She grinned down at him in victory, only to see he'd passed out again.

By now the light was nearly gone, the sun laying pools of crimson across everything it touched. His face, where the sunset bathed it, showed bruises and swelling. She swallowed hard. It would be a long trek, but she'd see he got there as undamaged as possible.

Six times, she had to let go, but she did so as easily as she could so that he didn't suffer the jolt of falling. It was a blessing for him, she thought, that he was unconscious most of the journey. He'd taken a bad hit from Cai, and even before that, had fought fiercely against at least half a dozen of the Enyalia. There was no telling if he was injured from his fall, or even if most of his injuries had come from the original fight.

It was also a blessing that the terrain had begun to shift. Gradually, the ground became thick with brush and grass and made dragging him any farther more trouble than it was worth. The caravan halted.

Alaysha eased his shoulders onto the ground. Her own shoulder blades felt as though they'd stretched out a fathom, that her knuckles would touch the ground if she stretched them out. She was sweating, she was exhausted; she wished she could just collapse, but she wasn't sure her knees would remember any other state but straining to keep her legs from breaking.

She had to force herself to sit, to gather Gael's head onto her lap while she reached to untie his wrists. She didn't have the energy to go for his ankles and his feet still hung off the ground until the great beast itself groaned to its own knees.

Cai came back to her with a water skin. She looked composed and rested. Alaysha wanted to swat the skin out of her hands.

"Drink," Cai said and held the skin out.

Alaysha accepted it without a word. She remembered her vow not to drink from it, but she knew by now she couldn't be so picky. She pulled at the leathers tying it closed and worked Gael's mouth open, tipped his head up from his chin.

"It's for you, not the man," Cai said, reaching to take it back.

Alaysha bared her teeth at her. "He will drink," she growled and dribbled what she could into his mouth. The bruises showed already on his neck, stretching onto his collarbone from behind, and there was blood caked in his hair. She wished Theron was with them: he'd know what to do. She ran her fingers through Gael's hair, close against his scalp to feel for cuts and bumps. There was one huge knot at the base of his skull, and an abrasion on his forehead just at the hairline that had already coated itself closed with blood.

For one heartbeat, Alaysha wished him dead. She wished him gone and left his body so she could drain each and every one of these women of their water. Then she felt a knot of grief twist into her belly and took it back before the power could realize she'd thought it. She reached again for the water and took a large pull from the mouth of the skin. She gulped three times, swallowing with purpose, giving herself a moment to calm down. When she had, she peered up at the Enyalian.

"You better hope he lives," she said quietly.

A twitch of a russet eyebrow, not much more than that, but the woman responded at least. "Oh, I do hope he lives, little maga."

"Then I suggest you send for your bone witch. He'll never make it to your village."

"Oh, no?" The Enyalian looked surprised even as she managed to sound teasing. "I think he'll make it; won't you, man?" She toed Gael in the ribs a little too hard for Alaysha's liking, but when she saw an involuntary flinch streak across his face, she knew what the Enyalian had guessed.

Gael was hurt, yes, but not unconscious, not at the moment. He might have been for the past few, but not now. The woman chuckled and strode off, leaving Alaysha to dig into the packs for a blade to cut his ties. She did his ankles first, then returned to his side to cut the ones on his wrists. She peered down at him as she rubbed blood back into the fingers. He was looking up at her.

Without thinking, she leaned forward and kissed him full on the dry, cracked, and swollen lips. They burned her mouth, and his breath had no vapour. She felt the tip of his tongue dart in between hers and touch her palette playfully just behind her front teeth.

"I'm dead," he said into her mouth. "I've died and received my warrior's due." He sighed in contentment, and she could feel a quick tremor run down to his chest. She flung her arms around him in relief to hear him speak, pressing closer until she realized she was undoubtedly covering over his face--his nose and mouth and that he probably couldn't breathe.

"Sorry," she said.

"Don't be." His voice held a soft rattle.

"How do you feel?" she asked.

"Like I've been drug behind a horse." He coughed but tried a weak smile on her.

Lifting the water skin for him, she said as he drank, "You need Theron."

He coughed on a bit of fluid. "Yes."

"How bad do you think it is?"

She could tell he was trying to shrug. "Bad enough. I think I might've cracked a rib or two. It hurts. But it could have been worse--except for you."

She looked away, unable to meet the bald gratitude in his gaze. She was weary. Every muscle in her body ached and burned simultaneously. The thought of facing his gratitude when she knew she'd not been able to keep him aloft the whole time, that she dropped him at all when she knew he needed her--that alone was more painful than any soreness. She felt him try to shift to his side, realized his cheek had burrowed into her lap. His breath was hot on her thigh, then his lips, burning against her skin in a kiss as delicate as a moth landing.

"My goddess," she thought he said before his body tensed briefly and he passed out again. She searched the group frantically, thinking there must be someone who could help her. One woman, smaller than the others, more squat than tall with only a double circlet around her left thigh, leaned against a pack, chewing a piece of dried fruit. She was eyeing them carefully. Alaysha thought she recognized the grief-stricken warrior from the battle.

"Help me," Alaysha shouted her. "Something's wrong with him. He keeps passing out."

The woman shrugged indifferently. "Then he'll be less trouble." She popped the rest of the fruit into her mouth, lazily, but at least she got up. When she stood over Gael, it was with an inspecting toe prodding him here and there. Finally, she made a smacking noise and sent Alaysha a hopeless look.

"His head swells." She pressed her bottom lip into the top, thoughtfully. "I've seen it before. He won't make it." Then she smiled.

"Won't make it? He has to."

The woman lifted a shoulder. "No, he doesn't. We'll use what we have. If he dies, we'll leave him to the vultures."

"Use? What are you talking about? He has to live."

The woman's face grew hard and for the first time, Alaysha could see true brutality there and something else she didn't expect or understand: hatred.

"Then your man shouldn't have killed my sword sisters. He deserves death." She kicked him in the ribs and he let out a soft groan. "A small shot for Yoliri," she grumbled. "Would that it were more."

Alaysha didn't have time to argue the finer points of

defending oneself against attack. She went straight to the one tactic she thought she had.

"I tell you, for your sake, and the sake of all your remaining *living* sword sisters, this man needs to survive or I swear to you, I will take great pleasure in drinking your every drop of moisture from every tiny hole in your skin until you are nothing but a leathered husk."

"The Enyalia does not threaten easily."

"Then they are fools. If this man dies, you will have no time to pull a sword. Trust me."

The woman glared at her, and in her stoic expression, Alaysha knew she was plotting something; she gave in far too easily. She had the shifty look of someone who wasn't done arguing.

"I will tell Cai." The woman gave him a scrutinous examination with eyes hooded by something Alaysha thought was cold assessment.

"You'd better hurry, woman," Alaysha told her, letting the inflection of the word show her revulsion. The soldier said nothing more, but at least she headed toward Cai's beast where the redhead was inspecting her packs. Alaysha let her fingers run again through Gael's thicket of tangled and bloodied hair.

"Hold on, Gael," she said to him. "Please hold on."

In the end, Cai herself hoisted Gael onto her beast and bid Alaysha sit behind him to hold onto him. Enud, the warrior who had fetched Cai, insisted on following, with the excuse that if the warrior was faking, she wanted the leave to kill him. Cai said nothing to the affirmative; Enud acted as though it was a foregone conclusion. With Cai in the back, and with the animal loping awkwardly through the brush, Alaysha had time to reflect on things. It was obvious the Enyalian didn't trust leaving Alaysha with the others; she must have realized that her tribe's safety meant Gael's life, and that if she removed Gael altogether she couldn't be certain Alaysha wouldn't retaliate on those left behind.

So it seemed manipulating a witch had its benefits and limitations--something her father had discovered long ago and used to his advantage. Alaysha finally understood she could use it to hers as well.

Trees began to appear as the silver light of a thumbnail moon shifted quietly to a waking sun, becoming more and more frequent. The farther they travelled, the stronger the quakes were when they came. Three times, the beast stumbled and Alaysha had to grip the woman's waist to keep from falling. The warrior's stoic posture told Alaysha it was a common thing to feel the earth move so, and she wondered at how such a thing might form a woman into a hard and cold thing in the face of such loveliness she was beginning to see.

She could smell balsam and lavender and what she thought were peach blossoms. Her heart ached for Barruch. How he loved peaches. She hoped, not for the first time, that her comrades had made good use of the rain she'd psyched from the well. She prayed to the deities they were well, and that they'd follow and find them before whatever these women planned to do with them could be done.

As the trees and wildlife grew thicker, she began to realize how breathtaking the land was: lush and heady with fragrance. Birds called to each other in the early morning. Twice, she saw deer race across the path. And then she caught sight of a village. Through the trees, only a few almost natural type formations for lodgings, and then as they drew closer, lodges made of animal hide and some of wood. Finally, the dwellings stretched as wide as they seemed long. A large smouldering fire pit sat in the middle, hides being tanned across racks beside it. She thought she could make out an open-air forge far to the right, a bread oven being stuffed with dough by young boys. There were people within, too, but no one rushing or bustling about. Each step they took seemed purposeful and planned.

Eventually someone caught sight of them and hooted loudly, sending dozens of women finally bustling about. Several small children, boys it looked like, hustled toward the fire pit, seeming intent on scooping broth into a beaten metal bowl. Alaysha could smell spices and broiled meat even from this distance and it made her mouth water instinctively.

Cai reined in her beast and a boy with long white hair and owlish blue eyes took them without comment. The Enyalian leapt from her beast and hoisted Gael over her shoulder, barking at the boy all the while.

"Get me the bone witch," she growled. "And be quick."

The boy darted off as quickly as he'd come. He disappeared into a squarish lodge tucked into a lush garden of herbs and strange flowers. When he returned, it was with a wiry woman about the same age as Cai, her black hair twisted into ropes that piled on top of her head, held there with bits of twig and bone. The hands that wiped themselves on a flax rag were marked with black pictures very much like a tattau. Above the delicate nose, sat two wickedly black eyes that rested on Alaysha in an expression that put Alaysha in mind of Theron; the rest, the face, the width of the woman, her hawkish nose and arched brows reminded her of someone else, but no woman she knew. Rather, she thought she could detect a bit of Yuri to her posture and deportment; her profile certainly had that haughtiness her father wore so often.

But that was the least shocking thing: that this woman reminded her of two people she knew. It was the other quality to her features that made Alaysha's mouth gape and her speech escape her. This bone witch had a tattau on her chin, sloppily done, perhaps, with much less finesse than Alaysha's, and a few uneven symbols, but that was only a fraction of what made her speechless.

Because only a witch with similar powers to Alaysha's would have a mark like that, and that had to mean that Theron's clay witch was right here in Enyalia.

Chapter 8

The bone witch wasted no time in her attempt to help Gael, which meant anything Alaysha wanted to ask was of lower priority; she sent a scurry of boys to fetch a litter made of woven thatch and tied by aged sinew to some sort of hollow poles. She was probing Gael's body with deft black-marked fingers even before the litter was settled next to him.

"His ribs are cracked in three places," she said to no one. "A few wounds that could use threading." She continued her examination and made a small sound of discovery. "The other wounds will heal with attention, the swelling will retreat." She eyed Cai suspiciously, her furrowed brow an indicator that she thought Cai responsible and she wasn't the least bit pleased. "But this knot needs draining."

Alaysha already liked her.

Cai shrugged as though an answer to a question was left hanging in the air without being voiced. Her leathers creaked as she leaned over him. "He would be worth saving." It sounded to Alaysha like an admission.

Thera gave an almost imperceptible nod, Alaysha caught it, believing she knew what they were thinking.

"You can save him, then?"

The witch moved closer to Gael, leaning in so that she could listen to his heart, then feel for his breath. She inhaled deeply, exhaled very slowly as though she had become part of Gael's breath. Then she squeezed her eyes shut pensively.

The wait was unbearable.

"Please," Alaysha said. The pleading was in stark contrast to her threat of before, but she didn't care. She watched his chest move, his eyelids with their smoky lashes resting like smudges at the top of his cheeks, and she thought if she lost him too, she wouldn't be able to keep the peace within herself long enough to care if Aedus and Theron had crept within power's distance of the camp. Or if Yenic was here, somewhere. She knew better than anyone that the threat of unleashing the power was not an idle one.

Without answering, the bone witch grunted in satisfaction. She looked up at Cai. "He'll be ready."

Cai nodded, looking pleased. "Good enough. Take him."

The boys who stood around quietly made to grab for the litter but couldn't lift him. One of them ran off and came back with another half dozen and they struggled their way to the witch's lodge. Alaysha watched them go with trepidation. She waited to see if someone would explain what Gael would be ready for, and ended up having to ask.

In reply, Cai put a massive palm on Alaysha's shoulder, leading her away even as Thera led the litter across the compound and disappeared behind the leather flap. Alaysha watched over her shoulder as Gael disappeared inside behind her, then she turned to Cai, who had been talking all the while. Alaysha must have missed most of it, but she caught one word now: solstice.

"What does that mean?" She'd heard Theron say it in the burnt lands when the Enyalia was but a mere threat.

Cai extended her arm, sweeping the air in front of her to draw Alaysha's attention to the village. The dwellings were a mishmash of styles from animal skin to stone and thatch, to mud bricks. The trees on the outskirts formed a border where beyond lay such beauty and lushness, Alaysha immediately thought of her oasis where she'd first met Yenic.

"Yes," she said, thinking she understood what the woman was trying to tell her. "It's beautiful."

"Beautiful, yes, but do you not notice anything else?"

Alaysha pursed her lips, considering. "You have a forge. An oven. Your people are tall, broad." She shrugged. "A village like any other except for your stature, of course."

Indeed, there was a tiltyard were soldiers practiced. Young boys came through the trees from gathering wood, the smell of roasted meat hung in the air. But for knowing these women were the best fighters she'd ever seen, she couldn't imagine what the secret might be. She pulled away from Cai, who was obviously the chief here. Too many of the women avoided her eye--all but the warriors, at least. Those met Cai's gaze with respect and deference. Each woman who rattled past as they strode through the village, their thigh circlets dancing together like teeth. Each woman--

And then she realized what it was that was different about the Enyalia. She watched as a slow smile spread across the woman's full mouth as she saw Alaysha's comprehension.

"Are *all* your warriors women?"

"You are observant, little maga."

"Don't you worry about attack?"

Cai seemed to want to avoid the question but offered an answer eventually. "Who would attack the Enyalia?"

"Anyone."

The woman shrugged. "Generations ago, I suppose. Every now and then, now. But most of those who know of the Enyalia also know our ferocity. Once, more than a dozen full seasons ago, a man did come with warriors. I was young myself, then. Nowhere near old enough to take up a sword."

"And?"

"And we lost a good deal of women. One or two warriors. He was said to have come from here, but who knows the real truth of it."

Alaysha found this intriguing. "You didn't kill him?"

"He should have died several deaths at our hands." Cai's expression turned stormy. Alaysha didn't dare press her further. Instead, she scanned the village, mentally counting the faces she saw, the number of weapons, all things she did instinctively because of Yuri. There were plenty of women who didn't look like warriors, and she knew at least a handful were behind them by at least a day. Still, not so many Enyalia that the village couldn't be taken by a large army. Assuming a person had a large army. Which she didn't. If she was careful, that could work in her favor. If she was careful.

"Your numbers--"

Cai nodded. "Not as plentiful as of late. And with the solstice coming and us not being able to complete the raid--"

Alaysha wasn't sure which word was more surprising, but she thought one would be more likely answered than the other. "Unable?"

The woman had a habit of tapping her fingers along her biceps when she was considering how much to reveal. She was doing it now. "We counted three men for solstice."

"Three?"

Two more taps against her bicep, and this time the woman's lips tightened into a long thin line. Alaysha waited.

"You risked yourself for your large man," Cai said finally.

Alaysha hadn't thought about it that way; it hadn't been that much of a risk. Riskier would have been to let him die, but she couldn't explain that to this woman. What she could explain was the real truth.

"There was no other choice for me."

Cai halted at the tree line where a gaggle of young girls fought each other to the point of bringing blood. Alaysha made to stop them when Cai held her back. She eyed Alaysha with some speculation, the deep green seemed to move as the pupil kept adjusting to the variance of light, the thick russet lashes like a dying flame. Alaysha was lost for a moment, brought back from her worry about Gael and her sense that this warrior's eyes were more soulful than she let on, by the voice that was as emotionless as Yuri's could be when he wanted something difficult.

"I see you care for your man, little maga, but you must let him go."

Alaysha stomach grew tight. "I told you; if he dies--"

"I believe you. Trust me. I know your power. But that's not why."

"Why then?"

The woman sighed and turned back to the girls where one still stood, but surrounded by others sitting, nursing sore knees, bloody noses. "We are not all Enyalia from birth. Our madres consume the sister flesh that worms its way from between her legs along with us. When we first suckle, she ensures we taste the death of our own weakling sustenance and so it shows us that we must find a way to live without her. The only women who would do such a thing are warriors. Warriors beget warriors."

Alaysha held onto her gurgling stomach at the description.

"The Enyalia war like we breathe. No man, no one-man, no dozen men, can stand against us and live. No one man against one Enyalian. No ten men against one Enyalian."

"But Gael did."

"Gael? What is this word?"

"His name. Like you are Cai, he is Gael."

"Oh," she murmured thoughtfully. "You name your

males?" Then she swatted away the question and smiled down at Alaysha. "It doesn't matter. Your man stood against us. He killed. He very nearly won." There was something strange moving behind those eyes: respect, perhaps. Desire? Maybe. Whatever it was, it was quickly replaced by the implacable composure again and the moment was gone. "Rest assured, your man will not be cast for."

"Cast for?"

"The reason for the solstice. Every warrior who wishes to, has the right to choose a man."

Alaysha let her eyes wander toward the girls who had risen again to best the winner. None of them made a sound as they struck out. Their movements were fluid even as children.

"And you have only three men to cast for?"

Cai's green eyes settled on Alaysha. "It's not every woman who would risk her life for a man. No woman that I know of. No Enyalian. And yet you carried your man at great risk of exhaustion and fatigue. It speaks more of you than it does of him. Only an Enyalian would have suffered so greatly without complaint."

Alaysha had the brief sense she was being complemented. The woman's palm ran down the length of her arm and Alaysha had to work not to pull it away.

"And so, while we have three for solstice, which would already be a pitiful lot, we have two to cast for. As I said, your man will not be included."

Alaysha floundered about, trying to subtract Gael and add an invisible man to Edulph in order to come up with two. It was an impossible task. She didn't dare hope. She didn't, but Bodicca had mentioned the solstice. She had taken Yenic from Aislin to save him.

"Who is this second?"

Cai spoke carefully, as though she wasn't sure how much to reveal. "A sister came with another. Not as fierce as your man, but still very capable. He, too, had marks like these." She touched Alaysha's chin so tenderly, she barely felt the thumb run along her jaw and flick over her earlobe. "He must also be yours, little maga. It's only fair to warn you that he *will* be cast for. The lesser warriors who want to, will fight for him."

"So he lives?" Her stomach clenched, waiting for the answer, bracing against the negative possibility.

Cai nodded. "He lives. Any other time of the year and he would not." She made a face. "Nor would your men today have lived. We meant to take them alive and hale, but--well, they spoke to the Enyalia soul."

Alaysha's mind was racing. Yenic was here. Safe. Gael had been certain he'd be dead, but he was here, right now. Alive and well.

"Might I see this marked man?"

Cai shrugged impassively. "It's not forbidden, but then no woman has wanted to visit a man before the quarter solstice before." She furled her russet brow in thought. "Nor has an outlander woman visited us before. He is free in a sense, to do as he wishes while he's here. But that doesn't mean it would be a good idea."

"But you're their leader, surely--"

"I am the komandiri. Together with the bone witch, I lead. Not alone. Never alone."

The bone witch. Clay witch, to Alaysha. The other one of her own kind. She must have recognized Alaysha's tattaus the same as Alaysha knew hers for what they were. Had she been hiding here all along, deep within the land no man could penetrate? It was clever. Very clever. Now it made sense why

Theron said he'd been this way before, why he'd worked to get through the burnt lands: his witch was here.

"May I meet with your witch?" Alaysha asked and touched her own markings absently.

Cai noticed and nodded. "I'll see to it."

"Good." Alaysha felt the small padding of hope creeping along her spine. So much to do, and all finally within her grasp. Cai turned to walk away, Alaysha presumed to bring her to Thera, but it wasn't the time. Gael needed the witch. Right now, the best thing was to tend to the other matter.

"Can you take me instead to the man? The one with markings like me."

"Little maga," the Enyalian said, almost affectionately. "There is no other man capable of moving but the marked one. And we don't go to a man. We bid him come." She nodded toward the clearing to the left of the girls where the fire pit sat, sooty and black.

"You'll find a good spot there," she said. "I'll have the young ones send him to you." She began to leave but halted. "First, if I do this for you, you must promise not to use your power when the large one dies."

Alaysha ignored the phrase: *when he dies*, choosing instead to believe Thera would manage to save him. "Of course," she said. "I promise."

"Good," Cai said, showing very even and perfectly white teeth in a smile that would have enraptured a dozen men. "I would hate to have to kill you."

Chapter 9

Alaysha found the glade easily enough and waited uneasily. What would she say to Yenic, how would she react? His inaction against his mother, which led to both her father and her sister's death, had been the single moment of true betrayal after several long days of mistrust and doubt, when she'd stubbornly stuck to the belief that he loved her. The moment she knew she even had a sister, that she wasn't alone; the moment she remembered, her long memory releasing its stronghold, allowing her to recall touching the heel of her twin as they slipped from their mother's womb, that moment was the one when Aislin chose to send her power dancing in flame through the girl's body.

That was the moment of her sister's death and Yenic had watched it happen.

A step sounded, crushing dead leaf litter and she turned to meet him. The time had arrived and whether she was ready or not, she had to face him.

The moment she saw him, all doubt washed away.

"Yenic," she said, unable to keep his name from her lips. She wasn't prepared for his shock, for the way he fell to his knees, his head bowed. He still had the same broadness to his chest, the same beautiful skin, but the arrogance was gone.

"Not again," he mumbled. He rocked back and forth, hugging his chest, refusing to look up. "There's no need to torture me so."

She hurried to kneel next to him, gathering him against her. "Yenic, love."

A gasp. "Alaysha?" He sounded uncertain, but hopeful.

"Yes. Who else?"

He buried his face in her neck and inhaled deeply. "Deities save me," he murmured over and over. "It smells like you."

Then she realized that he'd believed her dead, killed by his own mother. The last time she'd seen him, he'd been horrified, watching her twin burn before his very eyes into a pile of ash. Things had certainly escalated then. Bodicca stole him away to maintain the surety that Aislin would not also kill Yuri's son, Saxon. It occurred to her that he hadn't known it was her twin that died.

"How?" he said. "Is this, too, some trick?" He cast about, searching for something that obviously wasn't there.

"Trick?" Alaysha reached for his cheeks and pulled his face out where she could see it. She searched the honey of his eyes, trying to find the spark within that looked like liquid flame. It too was gone. "No trick. It's me."

He searched hers, and seeming to find what he was searching for, scrambled to his feet uncertainly.

"It's a good likeness, for sure." He backed away carefully. "But you won't fool me again."

"Fool you? No. Yenic. You're confused. The journey, the stress, it's addled your mind."

"My mind is addled by your magic, Mother; but no more."

"Your mother, Yenic," Alaysha said, confused at his rambling. "My--father. They used us. I know it's impossible, but I had a sister," she choked on the words, trying not to take in his haggard form; it was well fed, yes, but also drawn and fatigued.

"My sister died beneath your mother's power that day. It wasn't me."

"Not you?" He looked wary. "The flame, where is the

flame?"

She shook her head. "No flame. The fire is out and smoking only. How can I convince you when your eyes can't?"

He raked a hand through his hair. "My eyes have deceived me before."

"I had only one twin; they can't deceive you again."

"Can't they?" He laughed but without humour. "Tell me how we are bonded." He hid his careful scrutiny beneath hooded eyelids, waiting.

She couldn't help smiling. "Such an easy test, Yenic." She reached for him and when he would have avoided her touch, she ran a finger beneath his eye. "My tears. You consumed them and only then did I have reason to live again."

"She would know that." He looked at her in panic. "Tell me more."

"My nohma thought you young to carry the burden of being an Arm, and you thought yourself too young to be bonded."

Something within him seemed to be battling his instincts. Finally, one side won over the other.

"Sweet Deities." He fell against her, pulling her so close she felt his heart, the length of his thighs, the muscles trembling against her. Then he was kissing her neck; his hands were rough as they searched her hair, pressed against her neck, washed down her shoulders. His mouth commanded hers, and she returned his kiss with the same hunger. She couldn't feel enough of him against her body, couldn't taste enough of his tongue, feel enough beneath her hands.

She didn't care that the trees had eyes or if they cared to look; she only cared that he touch her, enflame her, take her and erase all the doubts she had, the fears of his betrayal. She wanted him and more, she wanted to trust him. She'd give herself over if she could let the bond have its way.

When the earth shook this time, it was enough to break them apart and for Alaysha to scan the ground, fearing it would crack and pull them in. She clung to Yenic's elbow as it moved like a giant, groaning awake then shuddering itself back to sleep. This time, when it quieted, the earth felt different to her feet. The tremors ran through her like her blood did, making a cycle that she could swear hummed beneath her skin. Then it was over, and the earth felt as though it relaxed into submission.

They stared at each other, breathless. The life had crept back into his eyes.

"It's been happening all during my journey here," he said. "It was worse before."

She looked at her toes, wiggling them to test the current in case it wasn't over. She wanted to process how it felt, consider the possibilities that it had to do with Thera, who most undoubtedly was Theron's clay witch, and question why she would make the ground tremble so if she wanted to keep a low profile. It was bewildering.

"Does my mother live?"

It hit her like a slap.

"You can't truly be asking that of me."

"I have to. I know nothing more of that day; only the things after Bodicca took me. Sweet Deities, the things they did to her." He shuddered.

It was obvious his mind was racing as much as hers. She worked to remember that he'd had no contact, knew nothing of what had happened after he'd been taken. He must be starved for information. Alaysha chose to ignore the first question and instead spoke to the statement. "We saw what they did."

"We?"

"Yes, Theron and Aedus have her in the burnt lands. She saved us."

Yenic eased his eyes closed. "She was in no shape to save anyone last I saw her."

"No, and yet she did." She told him about how Bodicca led them to the well, and how Theron and Aedus stayed behind to look after her until she was well enough to travel, hoping to heal her. Alaysha spoke of the battle, how she'd unleashed her power, the breaking of it to bring rain. By the time she'd expanded on the whole story, they were sitting together on the grass, their hands clasped. She had the feeling things could be all right. Then she remembered Aislin.

"What's wrong?" he asked. She wasn't sure how long they'd sat together, but there were shadows beneath his eyes.

"No matter how I run through it, Yenic, I can't understand why you chose to deceive me. You hid Edulph, letting us think he was still out there somewhere when all along you were feeding him, keeping him for your mother; you knew Aislin had Saxon while we searched for him. You let me think we--that you--"

"I do love you, Alaysha. I never lied about that."

"But you lied about other things. Too many things. Our bond isn't enough for me to forgive that."

"Yet, you forgave your father many things worse."

"He was my father." It pained her to say it, but she still loved Yuri, no matter what he'd done. That she couldn't help that love.

"And Aislin is my mother."

"Who is both cruel and greedy."

"As was Yuri."

"The difference is that Yuri never wanted me dead."

"You don't understand the power of the bond, Alaysha."

"What of our bond? Doesn't it matter to you?"

He didn't answer for a long time. "You wouldn't ask me that if you had an Arm."

"Then explain it. Tell me how you can betray the woman you love for the sake of a woman who would murder hundreds of innocent people."

He grinned wryly. "And you've not killed an innocent." His voice took on a nasty tone.

"I was different then. I'm not the same thoughtless weapon I once was."

He shrugged. "She's my mother, Alaysha. And I'm her Arm. I'm bound to protect her. Past my life if need be."

"Past even me?"

He looked down, ashamed. "I don't want to have to test it. Please don't ask it of me. When I thought you were dead, I couldn't stand it."

"But you watched as I died and did nothing to stop Aislin."

He plucked at a blade of grass. "It wasn't you."

"But you thought it was."

"Again. You don't have an Arm. You can't know."

"And if I did. If I had a bond with someone else so strong I chose him over you--how would you feel about that?"

"Don't." His expression grew hard, hurt.

"Why not? It's what you're telling me."

"I'm telling you it's not the same, Alaysha. I love you. I don't want you to have to suffer the agony of choice. It's too horrible."

"So I should go without the same protection you offer your mother--the woman who would see me dead."

"Please. It's not that simple."

"It is that simple, Yenic. Am I to do all this alone? I don't even understand my own power, where I came from, what I'm meant to do--and the man I love won't work with me." She was breaking down, she knew she was.

"I didn't say that. I can work with you. I can teach you the things I know. Please, Alaysha." He reached out to touch her and for a heartbeat she wanted nothing more than to let him. She wanted to forget everything and just be the woman he could love without the added pains of the machinations of power: hers, Yuri's, his mother's.

His fingers trailed down her arm, then found place at the small of her back. She felt herself arch into him even as he gently pulled her forward. His mouth found hers, but only for a breath, then it was roaming freely over her throat, down to the cleft between her breasts where he grew impatient with the tunic covering too much of her skin.

"I've dreamt of this for so many nights," he said, pulling her shift to one side, exposing her nipple to the air and to his fingers. "I thought I'd never see you again. Never feel your skin, hear your voice."

She gasped as he pinched a little too hard and he smiled up at her, the honey shifted in his eyes like it was moving in heated waves. "If this is a dream, it's the best yet."

His fingers moved from her breast to her waist, and finally, easing over the skin of her thighs, rose up under the tunic and joined with her in a way that made her breath move fast, faster, as his did, until she clung to him, tight against his body, her heart racing.

"A good dream for you, too, Alaysha?"

She didn't trust her voice to speak for her and he smiled at her silent nod.

"The bond *is* strong," he said. "Never doubt it."

She eased her eyes closed, all the better to catch her breath and find her voice.

"So what do we do now, Yenic?"

"You tread carefully, Alaysha. Trust me, but only so far. Question me. Doubt me where you need to. I won't lie to you, I swear."

"But you won't endanger your mother."

"I can't. I'm joined to her through her magic. But I'm also joined to you through yours." He kissed her fingers.

"And so you must balance as if on a knife's edge." Alaysha heard the frustration in her own voice, but could do nothing to offer him any comfort.

"Your nohma knew that, Alaysha. She understood that to protect you, she needed to find a way to join you to Aislin. Her strengths can be yours that way."

"And that strength is you."

"It's me."

Alaysha thought for a moment. She suspected he knew more but could only say so much. She had to ask him the right questions, so he could balance the knife edge. "But Aislin should have known what that connection would mean."

"I suppose she thought it would be worth it."

"How so?"

"That connection should work both ways, should it not? It would be a price worth paying, to let me love you so she can have that visceral connection to you. Have you never felt that, Alaysha?"

"A connection to Aislin? No."

"Never? Not once? She would have used it, I know she would have. Fire and water. So opposite but so connected to each other. If it existed--"

It took a moment for the realization to strike, but when it did, it took Alaysha's breath. "The desert. The flood. She came to me in the flames."

"Pyromancy," he said thoughtfully. "The same as she's used on me all these days" he broke off in a choke and regained his composure when she looked confused. "It's a form of scrying, of seeing past your own state to another's." His amber eyes turned to hers excitedly. "Surely if she initiated the connection, Alaysha, then so can you."

Yenic took her hand and pulled her to her feet. "They keep me at night in a lodge past the village. Now I have you, I don't want to let you go."

"Keep you?"

He rubbed his biceps absently. "I'm not a prisoner, but they watch me. I imagine we're being watched now."

She felt her face flush. "Please say that's not true."

He shrugged playfully. "Maybe not that closely, but someone is near. They're always near."

"So how will I come to you?"

"You'll find a way."

There was no sound to warn them someone was near, but Alaysha knew it when her skin crawled up her back. She swung around to see Enud.

"Thera calls for you, witch," Enud said. "She wants to ask you a question about your large man."

Yenic's face went from surprise to sullenness and Alaysha glowered at the Enyalian in thanks.

"Gael is here," he said.

Alaysha reached for the hand he'd let drop from hers. "Yes. And Edulph will be very soon. At least, I hope so."

"Edulph? You hope?" He didn't sound convinced.

She shrugged. "They captured us in the burnt lands.

It's a long story."

He sighed almost unhappily. "Then I suppose you can tell me later. It seems Gael has need of you." He tried to wink but she noticed his eye made more of a furrowed glare than playful wink and an obvious sense of victory fleeted across Enud's face. She wondered what the woman would care if Alaysha had to defend herself. She put on an implacable expression and turned to the warrior.

"Can you take us to him?" She asked, then turned her attention to Yenic. "He's terribly hurt. He's with the bone witch." She put emphasis on her next words. "The witch's name is Thera. Have you seen her?"

Yenic gave a short nod. "When I first arrived. She--" he sent a look at Enud. "She was with the other who drove Bodicca out."

"The other?"

"A long tale of my own," he said with a sad half smile.

Alaysha sighed. "We'll swap, then. But first: Gael." She stepped closer to Enud, expecting the woman to show them back to Thera's dwelling. Enud didn't move.

"The man may not go."

"That's ludicrous. He is--he is mine as is the large one. I need him with me."

"He *was* yours. He belongs to Enyalia now. He can wander, if he so desires, but in view of my sword sisters only."

"I want him with me," Alaysha demanded.

"You don't matter, silly witch. You are not Enyalia."

It stung, especially after being called as good as one just a short while ago by the komandiri of this awful outpost. It stung, and Alaysha wanted to retaliate. She glared at the woman, taking in her height, her brutish width and muscled thighs. She sneered at the bracelets around the woman's thigh.

"Your komandiri thinks otherwise. She as much as gave this man back to me until your quarter solstice. He goes where I go. You have no authority over him. None of you do."

The woman was unaffected. She merely quirked a blonde eyebrow. "Is that true, witch? And do you know about our quarter solstice and what happens to the brood men?"

Yenic stepped closer to Alaysha, putting his arm around her waist, reassuring her. Unconsciously, she moved closer to him.

"I know they are--cast for." She had a hard time with that, with knowing the two--yes, two--men she loved would be given to another woman, be expected to procreate. But if it was necessary to get them set free of this place, then so be it.

Enud crossed her massive arms across her chest and chuckled. "Yes. Indeed they will service our warriors quite well for a short time."

"But that time is not now." Alaysha pulled Yenic with her and as she picked her way across the clearing, Enud's cold voice stopped her.

"So, did Komandiri Cai fail to tell you what happens to the men when the quarter is over, when their deeds are done and their seeds are sown?" She looked at Yenic and pursed her lips. "Did you fail to tell her?"

Alaysha spun on her heel, feeling a pebble lodge itself in her arch. "And what would your komandiri fail to reveal when this young witch can drain the entire village dry."

A quirked, but pleased, brow in answer. "Enyalia would welcome the battle, little woman."

"Believe me when I say there will be no battle."

"Have you not noticed our village? Such poor powers for a witch, to ignore the fact that over half our tribe is populated by the stronger sex only. A few male children like pups scurrying about."

Two men in the village, Cai had said. Two. And it hadn't occurred to her to ask why only those two. Only to ask whether the second could truly be Yenic.

"You have no men, I know this," she heard herself say and the Enyalian grinned nastily in answer.

"Only at the quarter solstice."

"And then?" Alaysha's stomach began to hurt.

"And then we grind their bones to make our blades." Enud chortled and started past them, slapping Yenic on the shoulder as she passed. "We rid our land of them as we would any vermin."

Chapter 10

Enud disappeared through the trees leaving Alaysha gaping after her. She swung on Yenic.

"Did you know?"

He looked sheepish.

"Yenic, you knew they'd require you to, to--and then they'd kill you?"

"They can try to kill me," he said, his sheepish grin leapt to light his eyes. "Bodicca told me there could be but one chance for me, and that was the solstice." He shrugged. "We talked of lots of things, really. You have to admit these women would squash any enemy who thought to enter."

"Even your mother?"

"My mother will send men first; she won't try to cross the burnt lands; only a fool would." He toed the moss and gave her a teasing look that melted her resolve to scold him. "Lucky for me, you're a fool."

She chuckled. "So say many of these Enyalia."

"I had no idea the price she'd pay for bringing me here."

Alaysha thought of the state of the warrior's back and shuddered. "And yet she paid it."

"I owe her," Yenic said.

"I think we all do," Alaysha murmured but something else ran through her mind besides the debt she owed the woman and Yenic caught her hesitation.

"What's wrong?"

"Nothing."

"Now who's keeping secrets?"

"It's not a secret; it's just, I don't understand why she did this. Would she place herself in such harm's way for a vow she made my father, to keep Saxon safe?"

"A vow can be a powerful thing." He took her hand and let his fingers roam hers. "You have to trust someone sometime."

She chewed her cheek. "Trust has proven a bad companion for me. Everyone I've trusted has betrayed me in some way."

"Surely not everyone." He looked hurt.

"Gael. Aedus." She took in his face and the way the names sent a shiver of pain through it. "I'm sorry, Yenic. But those two only. And it's only a matter of time before they do, too." She hated the sound of disappointment in her own voice and she forced herself to brighten.

She tugged at his hand, taking steps from the glade. "Come," she said. "This Thera asks for me and I don't care what Enud says. What would they do to you--kill you?" She smiled uneasily.

"Why didn't you tell me Gael and Edulph were with you?"

"I don't really care about Edulph," she said to him. "Not really. He hurt Aedus. He threatened me. He nearly had the whole of Sarum murdered."

"But you care about Gael."

She couldn't lie. "Yes. Of course I do. He has--" she was about to go through each of Gael's virtues but remembered how much the men hated each other. Yenic would never care why Gael should be saved.

They had left the clearing, were out of sight of the young girls training to hurt each other; all the better to hunt others when the time came for them to be true Enyalia. Still, they were far enough from the village proper that Alaysha felt she could speak.

"If Thera is asking for me, she might want to reveal herself. I need to make use of the opportunity."

"You think she's the witch of clay?"

She nodded. "Theron must have brought her here. It would explain why he knows of this place."

"You heard Enud. Men don't leave Enyalia."

"But what if he did?"

Yenic squeezed her fingers. "But Alaysha, you would have--removed Theron's clay witch. In the village."

She stopped short. "Oh." She turned to him, deflated. "Of course. I killed her. Didn't I?"

His face seemed to be trying to settle into something between agreement and encouragement. "I'm afraid that witch is long gone."

"But she would have had a daughter."

He blinked. "Yes. Yes, she would. And maybe Theron's part was to travel her here where she'd be safe."

"So, it's possible. You think so?"

"I do."

She grew excited again. "Then the path is clear. We need to get her and you and Gael out of here before these brutish women do something I'll regret." She glowered at the ground, trying to think of some way to accomplish it all but all she could think about was what was going to happen to Yenic and Gael if she didn't succeed. "To think they're healing Gael just to--"

"Don't think of it."

She nodded. To think that meant she'd have to think of Yenic in the same trouble. "I shouldn't think of it. Thinking of it makes me want to drain the village dry."

"Alaysha."

"I'll thirst their water and when it's gone, I'll bring it

back down on their dried out husks."

"Alaysha."

"I'll float them to the broad river where the fish will pick at their skin, and swallow their eyes."

"Alaysha, don't," he said, gathering her finally into an embrace where she wept silently, trying not to let her shoulders shake, trying to keep him from knowing her despair. She felt his palm on her hair, smoothing it. His lips warmed her ear, his breath heating her neck as he nuzzled her closely. His voice lowered as he caught sight of a few women milling about as they gained the village proper. He talked into her ear, careful to lean close so nobody could hear.

"All is not lost, Alaysha. We have time yet to formulate a plan. I don't plan to go to this easily or passively. Enyalian or no."

Her throat burned too much to speak, the effort of trying to stem the anxiety and fear too great. She let him talk on, encouraged as he spoke.

"I'm sure Gael has no plans to be a broodmare either. Do you really think we'd let a few warriors take us so without a fight?"

"No," she squeaked. An image of Gael in the burnt lands, hair matted with blood: his attackers and that of the half-dozen Enyalia dead at his hands. "No," she said, feeling stronger now, more certain. "You, me, Gael, Edulph. They'll truly have a war to contend with."

"There's my girl." He eased away far enough to touch her lightly on the forehead with his lips, and she felt calmer the moment he did. "There's hope yet we can get out of this place with our dignities intact."

"They're strong, though. It'll take all we have."

"Yes. Maybe more."

"A plan," she said.

"A good plan."

They arrived outside Thera's hut, only to notice a boy sprinting from the door, headed past the fire pit and off into a lodge that was both wide and squat. Alaysha recognized Cai's tackle next to the beast tethered outside. Thera's frame filled the doorframe in front of them, and another woman, old, with chalk etched all over her face followed her, taking her place as though she commanded fealty.

"What's wrong," Alaysha asked Thera.

Thera levelled her with a look that made Alaysha nervous. "Your man has the mark." She didn't sound pleased with the information. Whatever The Mark was, it had made the witch beside Thera angry; that much was obvious from the way she glared at Thera as though the younger woman had put the mark there herself.

"What mark are you talking about?" Alaysha asked, suddenly afraid it would be something that could ruin the already tenuous plans.

"What does it matter?"

Thera's black eyes nearly disappeared behind her squinting eyelids. "The Mark of the Enyalia. Under his chin." She pointed to the hollow where her throat met her jaw. Alaysha noted the brand burned into the flesh there. "Only an Enyalian can receive this mark." She squinted suspiciously at Alaysha.

"What have you done, foolish witch?" The old chalky woman came forward and stabbed a finger into Alaysha's chest.

"I don't understand."

"The Mark." She slapped Thera beneath her own chin with the back of her fingers.

Alaysha looked to Yenic for help explaining something that shouldn't require lengthy explanation but that seemed to have offended the old woman terribly. "It's his warrior's brand," she explained. "All my father's soldiers have them."

"Your father? What is this word?"

Now was Alaysha's turn to be frustrated. "The man who sired me. He is--was--a great leader. A--a conqueror."

The old woman nodded to herself. "Yes. I know the type of man." It sounded as though she was choking back a laugh. "But who is he that would he know our Mark? And why would it be on your man?"

"I have no idea how your Mark came to be so similar to ours."

"It's not similar. It's the same." The crone's impatience showed through and Alaysha noted Thera shuffled foot to foot, anxious to speak.

"It can't be the same," Alaysha said.

The old woman spat on the ground. "I know our Mark, woman; I make it. I burned it into her skin." She grabbed Thera's chin and tilted her head to show Alaysha. "No one knows of this practice. No one but an Enyalian and her bone witch."

"So *you* are the bone witch?" Alaysha was disappointed at the thought.

The crone glared at her. "I *was* the bone witch. Now I mentor this one, whose forging arts are even weaker than her healing arts." She sounded disgusted, but Thera merely looked smug, as though she had a secret the old crone wouldn't approve of.

Alaysha pursed her lips, chewing the inside of her cheek thoughtfully. She didn't want to answer right away, but with the crone staring her down, she had no choice.

"I had nothing to do with the mark. Gael was marked by Corrin. The same as all my father's warriors were--any who made it through the training."

"This Corrin is your father's bone witch?"

"Was. And no, he had no magic."

"He?" The crone looked indignant. "A 'he' does not deliver a mark."

"And yet, he did." Alaysha wanted to goad her now, just because of the indignant way the woman looked and the way she felt at the woman's patronizing tone.

"And without magic?" The woman huffed. "Impossible. What gave him the right?"

Alaysha shrugged. "My father gave him the right."

The woman threw up her hands in disgust and eyed Thera eyed thoughtfully. "A man does not give rights to anyone." She shouted for the boy who had run toward Cai's cottage and who was now sprinting back. "Where is Komandiri Cai? You should know better than to return without her."

The boy sprinted off again and Thera turned to Alaysha. "We best hear more about this father of yours. Uta will want to know all of it."

Uta sent a scathing glance Yenic's way who had stood quietly during the entire exchange but who eyed the old woman thoughtfully nonetheless.

"Find a place away from here, man. This is woman's business."

Instead of acting as though dismissed, Yenic sent her a broad, bright smile. "Your merest desire is my command." He sauntered away, whistling a lark's tune, but Alaysha knew it was all show. His arrogance would never allow him to be brow beaten. He'd take a fight, but not much else.

Cai passed him in the compound, but she neither looked at him or swerved to avoid him. It was as though he simply wasn't there. In fact, every woman in the village treated him as if he were invisible. Cai took her elbow when she got close enough and, with Thera, steered her toward the back of Thera's garden where privacy from passers-by could be found; to a hewn log meant as a resting place for a weary gardener. The trees surrounding the garden stood about a dozen paces away and framed it like a border, its dense underbrush masking it effectively from peekers-in.

"Sit, Alaysha. There's no reason we can't talk without fear."

"I don't fear you."

Alaysha caught the look Cai sent Thera, one that said she thought she was foolish, but to her credit, the warrior never said it. What she did was stretch her legs out in front of her, letting the circlets she wore rattle against each other. Alaysha couldn't take her eyes off them as Cai flexed her thigh muscles. They weren't stones, not exactly. Not even shells. Fragments of bones, perhaps, but far too regular. She tasted sour bile when she realized what they actually were.

"Those are teeth," Alaysha said.

"Taken from our enemies. I told you this."

"No. You told me a girl earns a circlet in war."

Cai nodded. "And takes the teeth of each man she kills. Yes."

"And what of the women?"

Thera answered, looking Alaysha up and down. "The women are allowed to come here."

"To be slaves."

"No. Never slaves. To be part of us. To breed our children, to nurse our young. They're welcome. Never chattel."

"And if they refuse?"

Cai chuckled. "It has been many seasons, and at least a generation, since the Enyalia have been refused such sanctuary. In truth, we don't need to war so often, either." She rattled her circlets. "Young ones have less teeth for their circlets these days. These are becoming as thin as our tribe." She looked up at Alaysha with a piercing gaze. "We don't seek war--it comes to us. Men have always wanted to win Enyalia. Imagine a world where the women are alone. Where they have no men to compete for attention. Where a single woman is as good as ten regular females. It's an intoxicating notion for them." She shrugged. "And they come."

"And you kill them."

"Wouldn't you?"

Yes. Alaysha would, she had to admit. "Then why raid for men at all?"

Again, the shrug. "We choose what is best for Enyalia, not simply take what comes calling. Enough of this." She leaned forward, her elbows on her knees.

"I don't know any more about Gael's Mark. I swear."

Cai nodded. "I know. I believe you. You believe her too, don't you, Thera?"

Theron neither nodded nor shook her head and Cai continued. "You see, it makes perfect sense that you don't know--no one should, but it doesn't explain how he came by it. So you must instead tell me about your--father--is it? Do I pronounce that right?"

Alaysha bit her tongue at the comment that wanted out. "Why is it so precious to you?"

"Because it's ours. When an Enyalian meets her first battle, she enters it with a blade forged here, especially for her, by our own bone witch. Thera, most recently; Uta in the time past. The handle tip of each sword hilt contains a bit of shaped metal."

"That you heat in the fire--"

"And press into the warrior's skin, yes." Cai looked pleased. "It bonds her to the blade and through the blade to all of her ancestors and from them comes her strength."

Thera shuffled about. "We temper the steel with the ashes of our greatest komandirae."

"And you want to know what leader Gael is bound to by his mark? I don't know. My father--Corrin--neither of them would have known of such a ritual."

Cai and Thera passed a look between them that made Alaysha think there was more than what they were admitting to.

"What? Then you must think Gael is an escaped brood man, or an escaped slave."

"No. No one has escaped and lived."

"Then what?"

Cai tapped her fingers against the outsides of her thighs. "A young Enyalia cast for a boy once. He wasn't a brood man, you understand. He was born here." The woman inspected a few teeth on her right circlet, turning it this way and that fastidiously. Alaysha wasn't fooled.

"I thought only warriors could cast."

"Not perfectly true," Thera said. "Some stock women may throw down a spoon--her offspring would only ever become a citizen, never a warrior. But still, allowing it keeps the tribe diverse. Except this girl was most definitely a warrior. Young, though. She had just received her own mark."

"And?"

Cai eyed her. "And she was allowed to have him. Thera and I would be born seasons later, but we are all told the story. Every Enyalian is told the story."

"Why?"

"Because the girl refused to do her duty at the end of the solstice. She refused to do that part of the right that she throws down for."

Alaysha was beginning to grow even more anxious. "And what happened to her?"

Cai shrugged. "She was forced to leave the village. Exiled from her sisters forever. Never to return but on the sure pain of penalty."

Alaysha tried to swallow and found her throat choked up. "What is this penalty?"

Cai held her gaze. "I think you know it."

"How would I?"

"Because I believe you saw this woman."

Alaysha imagined a large, arrogant Enyalian, the only large woman she could ever recall outside of this border, suffering pain without complaint. Expecting to die, not caring if she lived. Her back a mess of stripped and melted flesh.

"Bodicca," she murmured.

Chapter 11

Alaysha quickly snapped her mouth closed. So, the scouts had known Bodicca was there in the desert after all. How much more did they know, she wondered. She cast about for something to say, unsure where all this disclosure was coming from, but knowing she could never let these women realize Theron and Aedus were out there too, working to save Bodicca's life.

She was spared further comment when Thera leaned towards her. Alaysha couldn't help inspecting the tattau symbols on the woman's chin and thinking how poorly done they were compared to the beautiful ones her nohma had created.

"Tell us. Does Bodicca live?" Thera's eyes were very black, nearly no pupils at all. Alaysha could see the age in her eyes at that moment.

"She may," she hesitated to answer, trying to decide how to reply.

"May."

"Yes. She told us about the well because she knew we were dying. Then we left her to find it. She was pretty bad off." It was true, at least the first and last half. What did the middle matter?

Thera's face didn't so much as shift expression, but Alaysha knew the witch suspected there was more.

"Does she live?" Thera asked again.

"What does it matter? Surely the burnt lands will take her if the wounds don't."

Cai started to speak, but Thera held up her hand, silencing her. "You've had your turn, Komandiri." The witch leaned back, studying Alaysha, letting whatever things turned over in her mind travel her face. Alaysha had the feeling the woman could read her every thought but that was ridiculous, wasn't it?

"Tell me," Alaysha said finally, thinking to turn the tables. "Why does it matter?"

"She left us your man, knowing it was quarter solstice, perhaps thinking to buy her way back to her sister land after all these seasons, but knowing she would have to pay the price."

"Yes, Yenic," Alaysha said, grasping at the only thing she understood. "His name is Yenic."

"And this Yenic also has my symbols." Thera's black brow quirked. "Same as you do."

"Yes." Alaysha gave the wary answer but watched the bone witch's face and thought there might be even more behind her questions than even Cai suspected. The witch wouldn't look the warrior's way; her torso was turned away from her co-leader, almost absently saying there were things in her face she didn't want Cai to see.

"And this other man of yours," Cai said. "He has the Enyalian Mark."

Alaysha noted that Thera's expression grew impatient as Cai spoke, as though the Enyalian Mark was less important to her than Yenic's marks. Her hand even went up as though to swat the warrior's question away.

Thera captured Alaysha's gaze with her own black one. "You met our sister upon the journey."

Alaysha nodded, her mouth dry.

"A woman who brought that marked man into our village."

Alaysha smiled, thinking perversely that she'd force them to speak either Gael's or Yenic's name. "And which marked man do we speak of now?" She wasn't prepared for

Cai's slow, understanding smile.

"The large one, of course," she said, and Thera groaned under her breath as though it was not the name she wanted to hear. Alaysha turned her attention to the witch.

"You want to know of Yenic's mark or Gael's?"

"Uta wants them," she said, dodging the point.

"The deaths take Uta," Cai said and faced Thera who glowered silently. "It's not Uta who wants them. Uta knows more than she tells us; no doubt she has the answers already and lets us flounder here like babes trying to wield warriors' swords. No doubt she grins at us in secret as we piece it together." She shuffled her feet absently. "Since the quaking you have not been yourself, and I tire of it."

Thera's glance fell to her feet and Cai pressed on. "A man is brought to this village just at quarter solstice by a sword sister in exile and he wears your marks so you give him shelter and food and a solid watch, but a man with our mark--*my* mark is brought in by me and this little maga--who also wears your mark, and you leave him to Uta. Uta, Thera. Think on it." Cai turned fully to the bone witch, touching the woman's chin. "You are the bone witch now, Thera. Not Uta. You give her too much power."

A moment of silence descended and Alaysha used it to grapple the one thing she'd thought she understood. "Quaking?"

Thera turned away quickly, but not before Alaysha saw the way she closed her eyes in alarm; she'd struck a chord, surely. "Cai?"

The warrior's russet brow rose. "Little maga, surely you've felt the trembling."

"I have," she said thoughtfully. Could it be that Thera was releasing power without realizing it? Could she not know what she was and be wielding her power unconsciously out of some fear for the solstice?

It was time to test it, see what the woman knew. She touched her tattaus and caught Thera's eye. "And what is this?" she asked. "I could ask you the same. It's obvious my and Yenic's marks are more striking than yours. Why don't you tell me how you came to carry *my* marks. Why don't you tell me what you know of Etlantium."

She'd struck something, she knew, but she didn't have time to assess it. Both women clasped at their necks as though bitten, first Thera, then Cai, and then in unison they fell forward, landing heavily on the forest floor.

Alaysha's body went into high alert. She leapt to her feet and spun this way and that, searching for an attacker. She could see nothing through the trees, and stepped closer to Cai, all the while watching the foliage. She tried to kick the huge Enyalian over with her foot, but the woman in dead weight was too much for her.

Alaysha let her gaze leave the forest for a fraction of a moment, darting down to the woman's neck. She checked for signs of attack.

She heard her breath leave her lungs in relief. There, about a fingernail apart were twin quills leaking a purple viscous liquid onto the woman's skin.

She turned back to the woods, a smile playing on her lips.

"They're bigger than your average enemy, Aedus," she said, spinning slowly. "You don't know how long they'll be out."

The trees to the right of her seemed to shift and Alaysha was surprised she even recognized the spindly frame that showed itself--even if it was just barely. Aedus had spread mud all over her body, not just in her hair as usual, and then stuck moss and leaves and detritus to it.

"The bird nest is a nice touch," Alaysha told her, grinning.

Aedus came forward, craning her neck sideways to peer down at the nest she had tied onto her shoulder with dry grass.

"I ate the eggs," she said then blinked at Alaysha, seeming to be thinking. A moment later, she rushed headlong across the clearing, and flung her scrawny arms around Alaysha's waist as they met. It was the best thing Alaysha had felt in days.

Sweet as it was to see the girl, there were others to worry about. "Theron?" Alaysha had to ask.

Aedus mumbled into Alaysha's belly. "Tending to Bodicca a day's journey from here."

"And Bodicca?"

Aedus peered up. "Getting better." She swallowed as her eyes left Alaysha's face and traveled to the warriors she'd felled so quietly and efficiently. "And what of my brother?"

Alaysha shook her head. "Edulph's captors haven't returned yet."

The girl said nothing and Alaysha's heart ached for her. No matter what he'd done, the man was still her brother. And she loved him.

"I'm sure he's fine. After all, he's with the Enyalia. Unless he's angered them, he's safer with them than anywhere else."

Aedus let out a dry grumble. "If," she said. She peered off into the woods as though something waited there, and Alaysha followed her gaze, squinting into the dense brush.

"Is there something else, Aedus? Is someone with

you?"

"No. No one," Aedus said, and if Alaysha didn't know the girl better, she'd swear the shuffling that took over the girl's feet were from guilt. But that couldn't be. No doubt the girl was anxious for her brother, for Yenic, for Gael.

Best to shift things, Alaysha thought. "Yenic is here. And Gael."

The girl squeezed and let go, stepping back quickly. "He's all right?"

Alaysha couldn't help but smile. "Yes. Both of them. Well. Gael *will* be." She didn't know how to explain why and for how long.

"But there's something else?"

Alaysha touched the girl's chin because everything else was too covered in filth for her to reach any skin. "You don't miss much."

"What else is there?"

Alaysha sighed. "I'm not sure I can get them out of here."

"I'll help."

"No. I just need time to think."

The nest quivered as Aedus stomped her foot. "I can help."

"I know you can."

The girl fleeted a look over her shoulder and turned back, the guilty look resting again on her face. "I know things, Alaysha. I can help. And my beetles--"

"Are untested on such large foes. Remember Gael?"

The girl hung her head. She'd darted Gael with enough to put two men down because he was so large, but he didn't stay out as long as she'd thought.

A soft groan came from behind them and before

Alaysha could even warn Aedus to run, the girl had already disappeared into the foliage so completely Alaysha couldn't say which direction she'd gone. She turned toward the two still lying on the ground. She knelt next to Cai and swiped away the quills, then moved to Thera to do the same. Just as she was wiping her palm on the moss to get rid of the dye, she had the eerie sense she was being watched. Prickles went up her neck to her hairline and she sent a casual look around the glade, expecting Enud, poised for battle.

There was no one.

Still, the wariness remained. She checked her palm to be sure the purple was gone, and when she did she caught out of the side of her eye, a flutter of movement. Cai, sitting up, her gaze hard and suspicious on Alaysha's hands.

"What happened?" Alaysha asked her, thinking misdirection was the best tactic.

Cai 's eyelids shuttered down suspiciously. "You tell me."

Alaysha eased to her feet, offering the Enyalian her hand. "We were talking, and then you just fell. Both of you." It was the truth, and Alaysha had no trouble keeping the warrior's suspicious gaze, even when Cai brushed the offered help away and stood, her circlets chattering.

"Thera?" she said.

Alaysha turned to the witch who is still on the ground. "Still out, I'm afraid, but breathing as you were." It was hard not to chew on the insides of her cheeks, especially when Cai began a grid-like search of the surrounding foliage for the attacker. Alaysha watched her, feeling her heart racing like a bird's. She hoped Aedus had been smart enough to leave. When Cai finished, she strode back to the glade and stopped in front of Alaysha. The assessing stare reminded her of

Yuri--and how he could deliver a threat without saying a word.

Alaysha tried to make her posture seem less fidgety. "What do you think it is?" she asked the woman.

She thought Cai would never answer then was spared the silent examination when Thera gave a short groan of exertion. She was on her feet as quickly as the warrior had been.

"What happened?" she asked; Cai squared her shoulders and held a hand toward Alaysha. "Ask our witch."

"I'm not your witch," Alaysha said, using the chance to continue leading them away from the real question.

Neither fell for it. Cai sucked on her front teeth thoughtfully then said, "Apparently we simply passed out simultaneously."

Thera's arched brow quirked. "Indeed?" she said, but she didn't question any further. Instead, a look passed between them that sent a shiver down Alaysha's back.

She could swear the two massive Enyalian looked afraid.

Chapter 12

They wasted no further time in the glade. Whatever the women wanted of Alaysha, they'd obviously gotten it. Both were careful to keep the conversation light, and although Alaysha knew it was deliberate, she didn't care. All she could think about was getting back to Yenic, Gael, and finding a way to get out of this cursed village.

And to think at one time, Alaysha believed the worst she had to concern herself with was Edulph finding the wind witch and manipulating her much the same as Yuri had his water witch--his own daughter. Now, knowing the complexities of the elemental magic, it meant even more was at stake.

According to Theron, it all had to do with sibling gods from another time. Alaysha grinned at that one. If that was true, it meant Alaysha was one of them: the sister god, whose twin brother wanted her finally, ultimately dead--so dead her very soul would cease to exist.

But that was only if Theron was right and in his right mind at all. She didn't doubt the power of the elemental legend to move men to desperate acts, but she doubted the source. In truth, she didn't really care; she had enough to concern herself with worrying about Aedus and Saxa and all the others she'd come to love. She needed to see them safe, and if it meant running a fool's errand for a mad shaman, so be it.

In the end, she only knew that if one single person could control all the elements, then the result would be more catastrophic than some fairy tale Etlantium god using witches to threaten others into subservience.

No. To control earth, wind, water, and fire could mean the destruction of everything, and had those who had ever thought to wield that power ever failed to use it unwisely?

So she needed to find the two unknown witches: earth and air. Undoubtedly Thera was the earth temptress as Theron called her, despite her sloppy tattaus. She snuck a look at Thera as they strode back to the village proper, wondering why she would reveal herself in the mud village by opening the earth to swallow the multitude of rain Alaysha had unleashed, and why that same witch failed to recognize her now. It could be that she didn't know her own power, but released it the same as Alaysha did, without control when afraid or under threat.

Not for the first time, Alaysha cursed her ignorance. Growing up alone without love or support, put to training by Corrin, being separated from her own heritage by her father's decree that she live outside his city walls--all compounded her ignorance. Discovering pieces of the mosaic and putting them together without knowing the pattern was exhausting. It made her head hurt.

By now, they had entered the village proper, where young boys kept busy, where girls fought beside huts and tents, where stock women and Enyalia alike did everyday, ordinary things like eating or talking. It could look like a regular village except for the striking absence of grown men.

"Has the remainder of your party returned?" she asked Cai.

The warrior pursed her lips, tapping her fingers on her bicep, but said nothing. She nodded briefly to Thera who headed back toward her lodge.

"Cai? Have they brought Edulph yet?"

The woman didn't answer.

"What is this Edulph?"

"A name. You know that by now."

Cai looked innocently surprised. "You mean the third

man?" she said again.

"Yes. The third man. Have they returned yet?"

"They are here if they are here."

Alaysha crossed her arms, frustrated that she wouldn't get a straight answer. "Then I want to see Gael."

Cai's face brightened. "Thera says he heals almost as if by magic."

"She has no magic." Alaysha thought to test her.

"Oh, but you're wrong, little maga." Cai grinned. "She was made by magic, so the chalk witch before her was and the chalk witch before her."

Alaysha's heart skipped. So it was true; now Cai's easy acceptance of Alaysha's own power made sense. "You mean Uta?" Alaysha scanned the village quickly. She saw young, very young, and mature women. She did not see old.

"Yes. You saw her; she's old, for sure, but she still lives." Cai noticed her scrutiny and interpreted it correctly. "Our witches live as long as they like."

Strange statement, but useful in its way, Alaysha thought. "I want to see Gael."

Cai shook her head and tucked her auburn plait into one of her halters. "His warrior's mark is very distinct, pretty maga. You saw how it upset Uta, but you can't know what it means to us, and so Thera and Uta will be very busy deciphering this puzzle."

The warrior sniffed the air and a slow, languid sort of smile spread across her face. "Come with me."

They stopped at the fire pit, where a spit had been stretched over the coals. Several hares, skinned and brown, were impaled along the pole. The smell of honey and unknown spices made Alaysha's stomach rumble.

"I thought you said you would take me to Gael."

Alaysha watched a young boy ladle broth into a copper bowl and pass it to a stock woman, then pull a strip of meat from a roasting hare.

"I said so?" Cai shrugged. "I don't remember it." The warrior made a motion to the boy who hurried over with a roasted leg and a savoury type of mush mixed with flatbread and chestnuts.

He fell to his knees, head bowed, arms held out to proffer the fare. Alaysha had this disquieting sense she was back on campaign with her father, Bodicca roasting honeyed rabbit and chattel making tables of themselves so Yuri could eat and sit. Her head swam and she lost focus for a moment.

"You're hungry," Cai said.

The water in Alaysha's mouth kept her from denying the truth of the statement. The Enyalian scooped a finger full of the mush and pressed it against Alaysha's mouth. She opened without hesitation and rolled the stuffing around her tongue, savouring the flavour.

"Good, isn't it?"

Alaysha nodded and discovered a strip of meat pressed into her lips as well. "Eat," the woman said.

Alaysha's belly gurgled and she obliged Cai happily, thinking how strangely intimate it was for this woman to be feeding her this way, like a pet.

Or a lover.

She caught the woman's green eyes at the same moment the thought struck. Her fingers went to her mouth, pressing in the last of the meat, chewing quickly, swallowing, then she stepped abruptly backwards.

"Gael," she said to Cai, doing her best to tear her gaze away from the magnets that were the Enyalian's eyes. She stammered a repeat of her order, hoping to cover over her fluster. "You said--"

"I did not say, young maga."

"Well, perhaps if I see him, I can help you solve this puzzle."

Cai looked over her shoulder where boys were piling tinder and straw into an oddly familiar shape. "The moon will come soon."

"You wanted to know about Gael's mark."

The green magnets turned on Alaysha again. "You said you know nothing, and so I believe you."

"I don't know, but perhaps if I met with your witch, with Thera--"

"She will have nothing more to say to you."

"How do you know?"

"She would have said it."

Alaysha watched the boys retreating into the woods, presumably for more wood, and she felt the frustration so keenly she couldn't stop herself from chewing her cheeks. "What are they collecting for?" It was far too much tinder to be used for roasting fires.

"I told you, the quarter solstice is coming."

"Do you celebrate it with fire?"

Cai looked surprised for an instant, but then gathered herself and clapped a large hand on Alaysha's shoulder. "You're clever, little maga."

"Will Thera harm him?" She recalled Cai's coldness to him in the burnt lands and worried suddenly for his safety.

"Oh, no. He's meant for the solstice, remember?"

Yes. She did remember. As were Yenic and Edulph if he ever returned. The sole three grown men in the village. Even with the few warriors she saw here, Alaysha couldn't see how they'd all escape before the solstice. Watching the boys gather wood, thinking of the coming foreign ceremony, Alaysha's stomach gurgled for entirely different reasons than hunger.

"You said Gael would not be cast for," she said.

"Indeed, I did."

"But that Yenic would be."

"Yes."

"And Edulph."

Cai's finger tapped against her bicep. "When my sword sisters come, yes."

Alaysha watched the warrior's expression, wondering if Cai could somehow follow the direction of her thoughts, but the Enyalian face remained unchanged. So much like Yuri, Alaysha thought. No betrayal of his thoughts or emotions through his body or face. None here either. Alaysha had to believe the woman was so caught in the foregone conclusion that Yenic and Edulph would enter and exit the ceremony as men always did that she expected nothing amiss. Still, she was a soldier and soldiers left little to chance.

She didn't care what happened to Edulph. But she knew Aedus would.

Getting Gael out in his injured state would be a tough feat. She'd need Yenic for that. And she'd need to distract the two witches unless Alaysha could get to Thera and somehow make the kind of connection she needed, to gain her trust...

"Where are you, little maga?" Cai said. There was a note of playfulness in her voice, but her eyes revealed nothing.

"Thinking," Alaysha told her.

"A dangerous activity," Cai said. "Best left to the witches."

Alaysha tilted her head provocatively and Cai finally smiled. "Yes. As you are. Of course. So what does a witch think about?"

"How to stay alive," Alaysha said honestly.

"Oh, little maga," Cai gave a soft chuckle. "Have you no fear. I will keep you from danger." She put her arm out, gathering Alaysha in despite her hesitation. "Women have nothing to fear from any Enyalian warrior."

Alaysha could smell the honeyed meat and smoke on the warrior's skin; she made an effort to wrest herself from beneath the warrior's arm and with a soft chuckle the woman let her go. They strode side-by-side toward the Thera's lodge; Alaysha dared hope Cai would use her influence to get her inside to check on Gael. They were a few paces away, almost close enough to make out the noises coming from inside. She had begun to unwind them from the clamour of actual language and, further, into words when Enud came sprinting across the village from the trees. She made no shout, nor any noise of startlement as she sped, but the way she looked and the great, rushed strides she took told Alaysha something was wrong.

Cai was off before Alaysha could think to follow, and she watched as the two met mid-compound and went immediately into focused conversation.

It was obvious this didn't happen often. The boys, the stock woman, even the young girls halted whatever activity they were involved in to watch. All of the few remaining Enyalia--a couple of handfuls of them--took note of the exchange and hastened to where the two warriors stood. Whatever it was that had sent Enud into the village like a blaze was at her back was not a common occurrence. Cai looked back toward Alaysha once, perhaps to check that she was still there, Alaysha wasn't sure, but she was certain she was close enough to Gael to take a chance while everyone was occupied.

She gave a brief thought to Yenic and where he might have gone when Uta ordered him away, then she inhaled a bracing breath, knowing at least one of the Enyalia witches was in with Gael. Without further deliberation, she pushed open the leather flap.

She could have stepped into a past, not so far long gone. She imagined three leathered crones hunched over a dead fire, with their eyes dried seeds on the ground in front of them. The fragrance of this room was the same as then. The spices, the brimstone. The tendrils of smoke like fingers reached almost consciously to the ceiling. Alaysha could have been back in the mud hut where she'd killed three powerful witches at her father's command.

The breath she took seemed trapped in her lungs. She didn't want to remember that battle, and besides, the woman in this lodge was very much alive.

And she was gaping at her in fury.

Chapter 13

When Thera spoke, there was no hint of the anger on her face. Instead, she stepped sideways, seeming to block something from Alaysha's view "He's there," she nodded toward a sleeping figure, nude, on top of a bed made of rushes, and if Alaysha was right, softened by cattail seeds and goose down. The fluff of them must have taken thousands of plants to harvest to make such a bedding. Lucky Gael. Alaysha started toward him and stopped a few paces from the bed. Gael was most definitely sleeping. The bruises on his ribs were clearing and already turning yellow.

"He must be cold," she said to no one in particular.

"In this heat?" Thera said, taking the opportunity to work her way past the smouldering fire she'd been kneeling over when Alaysha had entered. "Don't be foolish."

Alaysha had the nearly irresistible desire to cover Gael's hips. She had nothing but her own tunic to do so. "At least cover him, give him some dignity."

"A man needs no such consideration," Uta said, holding the flap of the door high enough to enter. The breeze danced through the space, picking up scents of balsam and wild onion. Thera stepped backwards again, moving so as to distract or attract attention, close enough now that Alaysha could smell the myrrh on her. What had she been doing, Alaysha wondered. And why didn't she want Uta to know.

Alaysha dared turn to examine the face of the crone and was instantly sorry she did.

The woman's hair must have been white, but it was too full of wet chalk blended into ropes that reached down to bare sagging breasts with nipples coated in chalk residue. The face creased itself in hundreds of wrinkles caked with the same chalk. It was almost as though she'd painted her face so often into the same pattern that the wrinkles traced the lines for her now. It was the eyes that frightened Alaysha the most. She expected them to be filming with age but they snapped with life and vigour. Vigorous they might be, but they were not good-humoured. They narrowed as they bored into Alaysha.

"You and this large man came for the boy Bodicca brought."

"We did."

"You know of her fate, then?"

Alaysha nodded, deciding she wouldn't think of the mess Bodicca's back had been in, that this Uta had made of it.

The crone eased her way to a doddering stand at Gael's bedside. "Best to leave, young one," she said. "We'll see you laden with beast and bounty."

Alaysha meant to push the woman away from Gael, but when she moved, so too did Thera, side stepping as though there was something behind her that she didn't want Alaysha to see, but there was nothing but shadows in the gloom of the lodge. A few furs and covers on a cot at the other end. Perhaps it moved, that pile, rising slowly, falling again like a sleeper breathing during light dreams. She thought to take a step toward it but caught Thera's eye; she could swear her legs had somehow got stuck in mud. Her feet, always bare, had muck seeping out between the toes; she could actually feel it squishing between them until she looked down to confirm it and nothing was there.

She darted a look at Thera. Alaysha could feel it already letting go, the sense of capture easing. Light flooded the lodge and a current of air washed over her arms.

"Leave," Cai said to her as she entered. "Find your

young man and--do whatever it is you do with your men."

Thera took an almost conscious step forward; the look that passed between them earlier had returned. "The party--"

Cai glared at Alaysha, but nothing short of death could move her. The raiding party meant Edulph, and though he wasn't exactly an ally, he was much too much of an enemy for Alaysha to be ignorant of his welfare. Alaysha stiffened her back stubbornly.

The magnets never left Alaysha's face even when she answered Thera. "Only one remains. The man is gone."

Gone? Only one?

"I don't understand," Alaysha heard herself say."

Cai crossed her arms and the playfulness, the flirtation, the easiness of before was gone. Back again was the impassive stare, the trained face of the warrior. Oh, how well Alaysha knew it.

"One Enyalian has returned," Cai said. "The rest are dead. Your man is nowhere to be found."

Edulph couldn't have killed them. Alaysha knew it; she also knew Cai didn't believe Edulph had killed them either. In fact, she thought everyone in the room believed him completely innocent and that left one very big problem.

Because no Enyalian she'd met so far seemed the least bit worried about attack. Until now.

Chapter 14

Alaysha looked from one woman to the next, thinking someone would break the tension, but ended up doing it herself when none of the Enyalia spoke.

"What of the survivor?"

The three looked at each other, then Cai strode toward her, with the obvious intention of herding her out. Alaysha planted her feet. "If she lives, where is she? She can tell us who attacked them."

Cai's hand rested on Alaysha's back; she felt it there, pressing gently, but the woman was strong enough to move her. "There is no us, little maga."

Alaysha stumbled along, doing her best to resist the woman's more raw strength.

"Don't make me pick you up and carry you--my sword sisters would not look at you the same if they saw me do such a thing."

Alaysha grabbed onto the only solid thing she could; the wooden bench just along the door next to the wall. "Maybe I can help."

"How? You will knit her another hand?"

The hand. So, that was the peculiar reaction. "Her sword hand?" Alaysha forced herself on the bench, sitting down hard and wrapping her toes around the leg. She wasn't sure why she cared, except the woman's reactions were entirely unexpected. Cai reached for her hand to pull her off the bench and despite the best efforts to stay put, Alaysha sailed over the woman's broad shoulder.

"I gave you a choice," Cai said and impassively made for the door.

Only Uta's voice stopped the warrior, and it was a

thoughtful, familiar tone that she'd heard hundreds of times in her life. Her stomach sent bile up her throat when she understood the words.

"Perhaps we could use a powerful witch," Uta said.

Without letting her down, Cai spun to face the old woman. "No," she said. "We have no need of such magic."

Alaysha couldn't see Uta's reaction, but she understood the harrumph plainly enough.

"This magic is different, Cai," Thera said. "It's of the land. It's brown, not black. Maybe we can use it."

Alaysha wasn't sure how she felt about being talked about as if her very nature was wrong, but she had no chance to argue it. Thera and the chalk witch took to speaking, both at once. Cai had to shout to get them to quiet down.

"I know the power, sisters. Do you?"

It seemed only Uta moved to answer. She slunk toward Cai. "You know I know it."

Alaysha felt Cai's hands tighten against her hips. "Yes, Uta. The witch past the burnt lands who could move stone and earth. I know you *think* you know the power." She tapped once, twice. "It's for Thera and I to decide now, Uta; your turn is done."

The old woman didn't complain so much as threaten when she responded. "My turn saw more power than you even believe exists."

"Then what will happen if the little witch extends her full power? What then?"

Talked about as an object again. So, so familiar. Alaysha hated the way Cai was speaking of her, hated the way her tone revealed how she really thought, of Alaysha being a dangerous liability. Alaysha didn't want to stop herself when her fists began pummelling the warrior's kidneys as she hung over her shoulders.

Cai set her down and spun her around to face the magnets of her eyes. She didn't seem hurt, only annoyed. "Stop. Stop it all. You don't know what they ask of you."

Alaysha heard the impassive tone again, but this time it was coming from her own mouth. "I do know."

Thera was next to her in an instant. "You know and yet you don't argue it."

Alaysha faced her. "You want me to drain your enemies for you." She gave the witch a weary shrug as much to say she'd journeyed often on the same path. It was obvious now, Thera was not the witch she sought. If she was, even if she was and didn't know it, she would still feel the power, see the results. She'd know to move the earth would be as useful as moving water. No. Thera was not the clay witch. The clay witch had been past the burnt lands in Uta's time; this Thera would not--could not--be her daughter.

Thera's silent appraisal unnerved her at first, but the woman seemed to make up her mind about something.

"You will want your men in return."

It wasn't what Alaysha expected; it was leaguas better.

"I want both of them." Alaysha said it, not planning to keep her bargain, only seeing it as a way to get around the tricky business of escape.

The discussion seemed to be running down to agreement when Alaysha held up her hand. After all, she was nowhere near done.

"And I want the third one when he's found."

"That's much to ask for."

"My power is worth much more." She counted on the innate greed of any person to want more than they could afford. She expected a quick agreement: at the same time worried she'd get it. No one that she knew of had been able to have such power at their command and yet not take it.

She didn't expect Cai to step forward. "No," she stated to Thera. "You can't make this decision alone." Cai was unmoved, as impassive as Alaysha had yet seen her except when she was punishing Gael.

"The quarter solstice is one sunrise away." Thera said. "Our warriors will be occupied and then by all hope, they will be unfit for battle."

"The Enyalia is never unfit."

"Would you risk our future by sending them to battle, then?"

"There is no risk. We are superior."

Thera's eyes flashed in anger and Alaysha could see she was doing her best to keep her tongue.

"Then we will cast tomorrow as tradition dictates, and the outcome of all of this will be on your shoulders." Thera turned, dismissing Cai, and Cai just as impassive as before, took Alaysha's arm to pull her from the lodge.

Alaysha looked over her shoulder at Gael, certain she heard a sound come from somewhere in the back of the gloom; he lay perfectly still. Asleep. Unconscious.

More than likely pretending. Awaiting the prime time to act, if she knew him well. And now she'd been shut down from making a bargain that could see them all free, she'd need him awake when she came for him. She'd find a way. She and Yenic.

She caught Uta's eye and what she saw there made her uneasy; *a witch past the burnt lands who could move stone and earth* Cai had said to her. The real temptress of clay, not Thera at all.

"You mentioned a witch," Alaysha asked her.

Uta nodded. "From past the burnt lands. A woman of

incredible power." She sounded impressed.

A woman of incredible power from past the burnt lands. It didn't matter who the witch was, all those witches had encountered the same fate and telling this crone of that fate just might force a little fear into the old bones.

"I think you should know," Alaysha said to her. "That woman of incredible power you speak of--I killed her."

Chapter 15

She left with Cai on her heels. The warrior was too disciplined to ask what was burning in her throat, Alaysha knew, and with luck, she could use the information to get some of her own. She intended to do so immediately.

Once outside, she spun on the warrior before they even made it a dozen paces from the lodge. Young boys hustled about, carrying water and tinder, and the occasional tinder bundle.

"Who is it that has your people so afraid?"

If she expected a straight answer she was more foolish than she'd been accused of.

"The Enyalia aren't afraid. We don't fear death."

"Looked like fear to me."

"Resignation. Exhaustion. Nothing more."

"From what? Who?"

"I don't owe you an explanation, little maga."

"You have two of my men prisoner. You owe me more than an explanation."

"By your admission they are not your men. We won them in battle." Cai gave her a peculiar look. "We own you as well."

It was a shock to hear it. Alaysha hadn't for one moment thought of herself as a possession.

"No one owns me."

"You're wrong." Cai's mouth turned up at the edges ever so slightly but Alaysha couldn't have called it a smile.

"I said no one owns me. Have you forgotten what you saw in the burnt lands?"

"I saw a witch afraid to use her power for fear of killing a man." Cai lifted one broad shoulder. "That alone makes you ours. You'll stay because your men live. Only remember your promise and I'll let you live in return."

The commander's mask had gone up again. Cai was impossible this way.

"Don't you want to know why I killed that witch Uta so revered?"

Cai waited as a young boy passed her a flatbread. It smelled of char. She sniffed at it. "I already know why."

"You couldn't."

"But I do. You killed for the same reason we all do: survival, greed, hatred. Love."

It was Alaysha's turn to smile. "No. I killed her because a man asked me to."

"Then you are a foolish witch." Cai bit into the bread and chewed thoughtfully. "We have plenty of enemies. We always have, but this one Uta wants to be free of is an enemy generations old."

"You took their men," Alaysha guessed.

"Some, yes. But there's more to it than that. We thought them weak because they were so accepting of the fate. Every komandiri thought so. But the witch you killed was not the only one of her kind."

Alaysha's heart raced. Did she dare say more or just wait. She opted to wait and was rewarded with Cai's further reflections.

"The komandiri of Uta's time pressed into many lands in search of the solstice men. Her komandiri before her, too. We've seen many peoples, but nothing like the witch we met past the burnt lands. She was very powerful, so Uta says. She grew to hate a woman she'd never met. A woman who was powerful enough to change everything we knew about ourselves without so much as stepping on our soil."

Alaysha fidgeted, wanting to ask a thousand questions, but she realized to prod the woman might be to stop the well.

Cai tore a piece from the flatbread and offered it; when Alaysha shook her head, the woman continued. "The people from the frozen lands rose against us before, during Uta's time. Very early, you understand. Alkaia was very young then. They both were."

"Alkaia?"

"An incredibly fierce komandiri. She is legend, even now, besides being one in her own time. Uta's time. She took many teeth from many men. She also took from women. The only komandiri ever to do so. Men, you see, their only value lies in their teeth, and only as war trophies. But when the people from the frozen lands came, we had to fight. They were not content to have us use their men and so sought to rescue them."

Alaysha thought the story had more to do with the men who were here now, warning Alaysha in subtle ways to be careful, more so than the men of yesteryear. She kept her own counsel, though. Let the woman continue.

"Those women fought fiercely enough, but of course they were slaughtered. Alkaia took their teeth in memory of their bravery. Those who did survive didn't go back to their lands. They spread out, letting us think them wiped out. Some of them went to the highlands and stoked the fires of vengeance."

"And they've returned."

"Yes. And much more able to do damage."

"What could be such a challenge to the Enyalia?"

Cai gave her a knowing look and when Alaysha didn't seem to understand, finally answered the question. "They have a witch of your making in their arsenal."

"That can't be."

Cai swallowed the last bit of flatbread. "But it is."

"I tell you it can't be true."

"And why do you feel so certain?"

"Because I killed her too."

Cai quirked her brow to show her surprise but no more. "So much killing for one from the other lands."

"It's true."

"Then it is you who are wrong, little maga."

"I tell you, I killed them both. At the same time. Both old women were nothing but leather when I stood over them at the end." Alaysha decided not to speak of the third; that would be a secret she could use later. If she needed it.

At this, Cai laughed. "So now we both know that the woman you killed is not who you think it was. This witch I speak of is but a mere babe and already powerful enough to suck the wind from a dozen Enyalia."

Alaysha tried not to betray her thoughts at the revelation. She hoped she succeeded but the warrior watched her face with keen interest even so.

It was true the wind witch could have died at Alaysha's hand and still, there be a witch in her place. It was obvious Cai had no idea what created a witch of her kind, that it was passed down through her mother and initiated only at the mother's death. Alaysha did some quick processing. She'd killed all three of the other witches by order of her father, not knowing who it was or why she was doing battle. All three were old women even by the time Alaysha had taken their lives. That meant each passed down their full power to the daughters they had somewhere in hiding. The crones sacrificed themselves in order to pass their powers on to a daughter somewhere too far for Alaysha to reach. One of those women was Aislin who had murdered Alaysha's sister and abducted Saxon and now held Sarum in her grip.

Now to know that the wind witch was somewhere near, was being used already as a weapon the way Alaysha had been most of her life both excited her and repulsed her.

Cai interrupted her thoughts, pointing out a fur-lined hut with smoke rising from the top.

"Come, little maga. Best we rest. The casting can be difficult and the day will be long. You should sleep." She headed off, assuming Alaysha would follow.

Alaysha made her feet move, but she knew she'd never sleep. The wind witch so close.

Too close, really, because as long as Alaysha stayed in the camp of the wind witch's enemy, she too was in danger.

Chapter 16

Inside, the hut smelled of rushes and sage. Two young boys scuttled to the corners when Cai entered, Alaysha but one pace behind her. She watched as they pulled fur blankets from a chest made of cedar. In moments they had a comfortable, almost decadent bed made for Alaysha, thankfully across the room from Cai. They never once showed their faces, rather kept their eyes and heads tilted down at their feet. She had no idea how they could manage to do so many things without looking ahead at where they were going, but she supposed a few seasons of forced practice could do wonders for a person's skills.

She thanked the boys profusely and touched one of them gently on the forearm. He let out a squeal and then went rigid, apparently working hard to keep from running away.

"I don't bite," she said and grinned, hoping to ease the boy's fear. The other looked wary, but seemed less apt to bolt than the first.

Two sharp claps sounded, catching Alaysha's attention. She looked up to see Cai glowering at her. "You have much to learn, little maga."

"You don't thank the boys?"

"There is nothing to be grateful for."

"Everyone likes to be appreciated; even an Enyalian boy."

"Another thing you must learn. There is no Enyalian boy. Not everyone who seeks shelter here is Enyalia."

"I thought--"

"I understand that's what you thought. But Enyalian is our word for warrior. A woman must earn the word. As for the boys, they aren't used to being addressed without purpose.

They must think you mean to kill them."

"With kindness?"

"They are kind to the sheep before the slaughter."

Alaysha nodded silently. She tried to offer the boys a look of apology, but they had scuttled to another corner where a pile of straw afforded them some sort of bedding. Alaysha was grateful that they at least had something to sleep on; she wouldn't put it past these women to make children sleep on hard ground. Her own childhood wanted to worm its way back into her memory, but she squashed it down determinedly. She would learn from those hard lessons, but she would not be broken by them.

Cai stood in the middle of the room and for a second seemed to be trying to make a decision, then shrugged her shoulders and fell into a series of stretches and squats the like of which Alaysha had never seen. The hand movements alone were a thing of beauty, but when she combined them into fluid motions of her feet and arms, and all those worked with her sword and blade, Alaysha could see that it wasn't just brute strength that gave the Enyalia an edge, but the combination of every sense that made up their body. She had the feeling she was watching something very sacred and when the woman stretched finally, the tips of her fingers scrabbling at the thatch of the ceiling, Alaysha squeezed her eyes closed just in case the woman looked her way and caught her watching.

Alaysha waited for what seemed like hours for the woman to fall asleep. The boys had gone under seemingly as soon as their heads touched the straw, and in the small amount of light from the fire that burned in a hollow in the ground, and sent its smoke through a makeshift chimney, she could see that they were wrapped around each other, one of them sucking his thumb.

After what seemed an eternity, Alaysha got up and fed the fire with peat just in case any of them grew cold and thought to rise through the night. She wanted to get to Yenic before morning came. She wasn't sure where he was being held, or if he was being held somewhere at all. It was this realization that made her decide to wake one of the boys.

She chose the one sucking his thumb because he was the one who hadn't jumped when she'd thanked the other. She touched his shoulder gently and his eyes flew open immediately. She put a finger against her lips to indicate she needed him to be quiet. "I need you to gather some herbs for me. My belly hurts and I need to make it better."

It wasn't true, of course, but she couldn't very well ask him where Yenic was, not here in Cai's Lodge. The last thing she wanted to do was alert the woman, or to get this boy in trouble. He got up quickly and without bothering to wipe the sleep from his eyes, trudged toward the door. Alaysha followed him and lifted the flap to the sound of frogs calling for mates in the distance. They had cleared the Lodge and were making their way into the forest when she caught up to him and put her hand on his shoulder.

"I don't need herbs," she admitted. "I need to know where they keep the solstice men."

He had an intelligent face, eyes that showed deep thought processes beneath his brow. The moon was turning full, offering plenty of light to see by, and Alaysha realized why tomorrow would be the beginning of the solstice, set by the rhythms of the moon and the coming of warmer nights, longer days. She could see the boy was afraid to speak, obviously uncertain of what would happen to him if he told.

"It's okay," she told him. "I won't tell anyone. I'll tell them you gathered me some herbs for my sore stomach and then went back to bed."

He looked back over his shoulder to where several of the warriors were tending the fire and keeping watch.

"Never mind them. They'll be my problem."

He bent over and leaned towards a short bush where a few spindly flowers clung. They must have been bright pink during the daylight, but looked more like the color of a sick ear now. He picked a few and pressed them into her hands. "There's a small hut just past the tiltyard. He will be there."

Alaysha made a show of rubbing her stomach, just in case the women were watching, and she whispered a thank you to the boy. He reminded her of Aedus, not scrawny-looking or as ill-fed, but with that furtive kind of fidget to his posture that she'd had when they'd first met. He said nothing in return, merely shuffled back off toward the lodge and disappeared behind the flap. She hadn't expected him to say anything, actually, and in truth thought it was very smart of him to act as though he had done exactly what she'd asked.

She stole a glance towards the women around the fire; they were looking in her direction as she expected, but they paid subtle attention without making a great show of it. Even so, they didn't seem overly worried or concerned that one of the newcomers was up and about in the middle of the night.

She wasn't foolish enough to think that Yenic would be alone. She moved toward the trees, working her way into the few shadows the tree trunks made with the shrubberies, hoping the warriors around the fire had assumed she'd gone back to bed. It was interesting that at night there was more fragrance in the air than during the day; she noted several whitish blooms spread open, stretching toward the moon. The smell was almost intoxicating. Without thinking, she brushed her hand along a row of them and lifted her fingers to her nose, inhaled deeply. But for the circumstance, she could have enjoyed this quiet evening.

She picked her way along from shadow to shadow, finding her way even farther into the woods surrounding the village. She'd begun to think she had veered off into the completely wrong direction when she caught a lick of flame off toward her left. A small fire, certainly, but enough that she realized she had indeed gone too far left as well as too far ahead. She backtracked, keeping her eye on the bit of flame that showed through the trees. She got close enough that she could see a single warrior squatted directly in front of the lodging made entirely of spindly poles and animal skin. A makeshift lodging if she'd ever seen one, able to be erected quickly and taken down without much effort. Several of these could be made, she realized, depending on how many were needed, and then disassembled without leaving a trace.

She'd undoubtedly found Yenic, but how would she ever get inside with this brute of a woman sitting in front? She'd have to get around to the back, maybe slip beneath. But of course, if she could slip in, then it was very possible the occupant could slip out. There had to be something more keeping him here than just the single woman in front of the fire.

She studied the area carefully, scanning it in small blocks moving from one grid to the other with painstaking care. It took long, exhausting moments that frustrated and tested her patience; she went over the area three times before she saw it: two seemingly naturally occurring bits of debris at the back of the dwelling. They both pointed distinctly toward each other, but far enough apart that an unsuspecting eye would never notice they were a pair. Alaysha worked her way backwards from the lodging, taking great care to study anything that looked out of the ordinary. When she saw the thin bleached ligament stretching from the edge of the animal hide up into the trees, she realized what the danger was to an unsuspecting eye. The Enyalia had assumed that anyone wishing to rescue a man from that tent would be in enough of a rush not to take the time to check for traps.

She smiled to herself and crept through the trees, hoping the woman in front wouldn't decide to do a check. Instead of the back, Alaysha would move slightly to the side. Since the side closest to her had too much noise-making leaf litter, she opted for the one farthest away. She was so focused on making as little noise as possible, and keeping her eyes out for the sentry, that she didn't see the nearly invisible ligament stretched chest high from tent to tree. When it brushed her shoulders, it rattled what Alaysha took for nut casings just above her in the trees.

She cursed to herself and froze. It was useless, however. The sentry came around with her hands on her massive hips, staring directly at Alaysha as she stood midstep with one foot in the air.

Just her fortune, the sentry was Enud, and the Enyalian looked incredibly pleased to see her.

"No doubt you saw the whip trap," she said grinning.

Rather than answering, Alaysha's eye went to the tree. Now that she looked closer, she could see several sharpened stakes attached to the top of the thin sapling.

"We always make that one easy to spot; then the other one becomes much more effective."

"And what if I'd not spotted the first?"

The woman sent her fingers trailing across the circlet on her thigh, making the teeth rattle. "Then I suppose you would be dead."

A chill went up the back of Alaysha's spine. "I want to see Yenic."

"What is a Yenic?" The woman pronounced the words carefully.

"Yenic. The man inside. I want to see him."

"Plenty of time tomorrow. Plenty of time, plenty to see, tomorrow."

Alaysha heard a sound come from inside and then Yenic was peering around the side, looking sleep deprived and haggard. Even though she'd seen him just that afternoon, she drank in the look of him.

"I'm all right Alaysha," he said. "Except for being unable to sleep, I'm fine."

"Big day tomorrow."

"Something like that." He grinned.

Enud watched the exchange in seeming boredom until Alaysha stepped toward him. Then she came to life like a sun-heated serpent that'd just found its dinner within striking distance.

"I think not," she said, crossing her arms and using her considerable breadth to bar Alaysha's way. "Your little man is mine now."

Alaysha didn't want to think about Yenic belonging to anyone, least of all this snake of a woman. She had to think of a way to let him know she would find a way out.

"I'll be there for you," she said.

Enud made a sound somewhere between a grunt and a chuckle. "It will do him as much good as it will do you," she said.

Alaysha ignored her. "I will be there."

"I know what's going to happen," he said. "On my journey here Bodicca told me."

This time Enud spat on the ground. "Traitor," she mumbled.

Alaysha turned her. "Without the traitor you wouldn't have this fine man to cast for tomorrow," she said.

Enud leered at Yenic but not with a look of desire, at least not sexual desire, the emotion that burned in her face was one Alaysha understood well, having seen it on Corrin's face as he tortured her, on Yuri's face when he learned of Saxon's kidnapping. It was one of revenge, and Alaysha couldn't help wondering what Yenic might have done to make the Enyalian hate him so.

She spoke to Yenic without taking her eyes off Enud's. "Just know that I'll be there. Cai has promised me that Gael will not be cast for. That just leaves you. And I'll be there."

Enud had apparently tired of the exchange and stepped forward so that she towered over Alaysha, looking down at her. She'd eaten onions, Alaysha could tell, and she seemed quite pleased to wash Alaysha from head to toe with her breath. "Komandiri Cai is a woman of her word."

"I believe you." Alaysha stepped away, her shoulder catching again in the ligament line, making the nut casings rattle in the tree. She gave one last look toward Yenic as he backed up and disappeared behind the dwelling. She heard a small scuffle coming from inside and imagined he was settling into bed, thinking about how things would go the next day. Alaysha spared a thought herself for it. She had no idea what it would entail, but she would do what it took to win him away from these warriors, and when she was at last able to have him to herself without interference, they would secret Gael away and rendezvous somewhere in the woods with Aedus. They'd be on their way.

But one thing niggled at her conscience as she made her way back to Cai's Lodge. It was the way Enud had so heartily agreed that Cai was a woman of her word. It made her wonder exactly what had been behind those words that Alaysha didn't understand.

Chapter 17

Birdsong woke Alaysha. She rolled over on the makeshift bed and stared at the thatch of the ceiling. The boys were already up it seemed; she could hear them scuttling around the room. She propped herself up on her elbow and scanned for Cai. The Enyalian was nowhere to be seen.

Alaysha shot out of bed in a panic. How long had she slept? Had she missed the casting already? Apparently even as on edge as she was, exhaustion and fatigue had been quite able to steal her body and lull her to sleep. The battle in the burnt lands, the draining of her power, carrying Gael. Enough to make her sleep for days. Even sprinting to the door, she could feel the effects deep in her tissues as they practically begged her to stop moving. She lifted the flap and stared outside. Plenty of activity, more than she'd ever seen in the hours she'd been here.

Several warriors were sharpening blades, spitting on the edge and rubbing fingers to test sharpness. Warriors who weren't sharpening blades were performing the same strange ritual she'd watched Cai complete before sleep. A couple of stock women stood silently with their arms crossed, spoons sticking up between their bosoms. She spotted Cai standing outside of Thera's hut, both of them in focused conversation. The door flap was open, and women streamed in and out.

Not a perfect development.

She strode across the compound and toward Cai with all the defiance she could muster. "Where's Gael?"

Cai looked at her the way one would look at a bothersome child. "Gael? You mean the man?"

"Yes, you know I mean the man. Where is he?"

A woman bumped into her as she exited and knocked

Alaysha a couple of feet away from the door. Cai moved to catch her and gathered her beneath her arm, pulling her close. Alaysha could feel the teeth of the woman's circlet digging into her thigh.

"The man is no concern of yours, little maga. I thought you understood that."

"You said he wouldn't be cast for."

"And he won't be."

"Then what is all this?" Alaysha took a swipe at a particularly large Enyalian, ending up backhanding her across the tricep. The woman spun on her quickly, her hand poised to encircle her neck when she noticed Alaysha was under Cai's obvious protection.

"Komandiri," was all the woman said and strode away.

"What is all this?" Alaysha said again.

"Have you more to say to our bone witch?" Cai said, changing the subject.

"About his mark? You know I don't."

Cai turned to Thera. "Have you more to say to this little witch?"

Thera looked to be considering. She sent her gaze up and down Alaysha's form from foot to face, lingering on the tattaus, and then shook her head. "I think she has nothing to tell me."

Cai's hand went around the back of Alaysha's head, her fingers trailing beneath her hair, tickling just behind her ear lobe. "Then I'm afraid, little maga, it is time for you to be off."

"No," she said. She thought of Yenic, of her promise. She thought of Gael inside, probably still suffering from his injuries, about to suffer whatever indecencies these women planned for him. "I told you. You know what I can do."

Cai shrugged. "I do. And I also know you won't do

anything."

"That's a big risk. But you're not counting on the men themselves. You don't think they'll let themselves be subjected to your whims."

"Many men before them have. You must know little of men."

"You know little of *these* men."

"Look around you, little maga. Look at how many Enyalia are here still. Your man inside is barely able to lift his head to drink, let alone heft a sword. And your Yenic, whom you esteem so highly, was brought in by a single Enyalian, so docilely he could have been her pet. I doubt we'll have any trouble."

"I won't go."

Thera tired of the exchange and started to say something when she paused, mouth open, hand already lifted to wrest her away from Cai. But her face changed so quickly, so drastically, Alaysha knew something had to be going on. She pulled away from Cai, who also turned to face what Thera found so intriguing she couldn't even close her mouth.

At first, Alaysha expected it meant they were under attack from the young wind witch. Instinctively, she drew her self together, readying her body and mind to harness the power that she could already feel tingling beneath her skin. She'd do her best, everything she could to keep the power from draining Gael, from draining Yenic, but she had no guarantee she could control the thirst that well. They might well die this day. She swallowed, thinking she'd have to let go before the air began to thin and she couldn't breathe, but when she saw that the bedraggled forms stumbling into the village, her mouth went dry in surprise.

It was Cai who spoke. "Bodicca," she said in obvious

confusion.

"And Theron," Alaysha heard herself say.

She was about to rush forward to help him with the still hunched and wounded Bodicca when two warriors stepped toward them from behind, blades in hand and to the ready. They grabbed for both in unison, and pulled them sharply to their backs, meaning to slice the throats of the uninvited interlopers.

Chapter 18

It was Uta's command that saved them from certain death. The chalk witch had stepped from behind Thera's lodge, her arms filled with herbs. She shouted one word: no. Cai made a short motion with her head that indicated the warriors were to bring the two of them forward, then she turned to Uta .

"You put the boar grease to her back yourself, Uta. Why do you save her now?"

"It's not for her I wait."

Alaysha was surprised to see Cai gape at the chalk witch. "The man? Surely not."

"You're too much of a young bitch yet to understand." Uta shuffled forward the few steps to meet with the warriors who brought both captives forward. Alaysha caught Theron's eye as they drew closer, his expression was pinched and determined. Something in his black eyes made her think he was forcing his feet to move step-by-step into what he thought was certain danger. Indeed, it was. But there was something more behind his gaze. Something that made Alaysha bite her tongue so that it wouldn't ask the question that was right on her lips. She had to trust him.

He faced the chalk witch, pointing all the while at Bodicca's still healing back. "Is such a horrible thing as this what was done to Alkaia? Tell us, you cruel woman."

"Careful, man."

He laughed with something almost akin to true humour. "The woman knows our name, she does; oh, we know she does because Alkaia used it, and this woman heard her use it."

Alaysha could see that everyone was as dumbfounded as she. Something was happening that rooted each set of feet to the ground: some in disbelief, some in confusion. It seemed the mere mention of Alkaia turned their backs to stone.

"I heard her use your name, man," Uta agreed. "What is that to me?"

"She knows who we are. A shaman such as Theron is recalled after all and would have thought to find his death here in this forsaken village. Why not let us die at your warrior's hands, woman, as you would have let your own, this sister of yours, die."

"She is no sister of mine." Uta made a show of turning away from Bodicca as though ashamed she knew her. "But I thought you could see the fruits of your labours here before you die, man."

She held her hand toward Thera and Theron's black eyes flicked over the bone witch for the first time. Alaysha heard his sharp intake of breath, watched him swallow repeatedly, either trying to get water down or bring water to his mouth.

"You look like her," he finally said and his words came out in a croak. "You have Alkaia's skin, her mouth." He made a motion to reach out, but before his fingers touched her face, Thera had pulled a blade from one of the warrior's hands and plunged toward her father's neck. Cai reached out almost lazily and grabbed the woman by her shoulder.

"Stand down," she said and turned to Uta. "Why would you shame her like this in the face of her sisters?"

Uta didn't flinch in the face of that magnetic stare. "For the same reason I put those marks on her when she was born. For the same reason her sisters wouldn't let her train to Enyalia."

"I *am* Enyalian," Thera insisted. "I have the mark." She lifted her chin but Alaysha noted that even Cai tried to avoid looking at it.

Instead, the komandiri nodded quietly and then turned to Alaysha. "She was born of the only man freed from this land. We can never forget."

"You said no one escaped."

Cai shrugged. "No one did."

Alaysha spun to face Cai, mustering all the disgust she could onto her face to show the crone what she thought of her. "You marked her?" Alaysha asked Uta in disbelief. "Why?"

"It's a mark of her shame."

"It's a mark of great power," Alaysha argued, realizing for certain these women knew nothing of the clay witch and her true power. "You have no idea."

"I do, witch," Uta said. "I know very well." She turned to Theron again. "How do the marks look, man? Are they correct?"

Theron wouldn't answer.

"I had only Alkaia's description to go by you see."

Theron swallowed hard and shook his head.

Uta's voice was mocking. "Why do you return? I thought you dead."

"This shaman very nearly died, but then a witch such as this one would know that since despite the bargain Alkaia made to keep me alive, it's the other that nearly took me."

Uta chuckled quietly. "So her pre-man whelp didn't hold to his oath, then?"

"Oh, he tried; yes, yes he did. It just took much longer than you expected for him to do his ugly deed."

Thera had pulled herself from Cai's hold and stepped in front of Uta. "This small man is who you would have me believe sired me?" She cast a disgusted look Theron's way. "He's nothing. My madre would not have risked her back for such a one."

Uta didn't back away. "And yet she did."

Alaysha was doing her best to make sense of it all. Theron had been here before, she knew that. She also knew he had somehow escaped. But to be a solstice mate of their most revered komandiri? It seemed impossible the shaman had kept such a secret.

Cai flicked her wrist toward them, initiating the warrior's clamping down on both of their arms. "He may live for the moment, but he will have his time as will the others. Find a place to put them for now."

Alaysha heard herself protest. "But Bodicca needs treatment. She's hurt."

"She's hurt of her own accord, even if it is a generation later. Enyalia have a long memory. She knew that when she entered the village again."

Alaysha thought there was nothing she could do but let them go and was willing to lose the small battle to win the larger war when Theron spoke up again.

"Ask them what they mean to do with Yenic and Gael when they're finished with them. Ask them, young witch."

Uta spoke when Cai seemed reluctant to. "It's no secret, man. They die. They always die."

Theron grinned broadly. "Ah, but men don't always die. Sometimes they sire children and are then freed. Sometimes men are born here and are similarly freed to do damage where they can. To create an army. To gather the magics of witches the like you've never seen. Sometimes they seek vengeance."

His words chilled Alaysha to the bone, not just because of the threat, but because he was eerily clear for once. She could tell that it disturbed the others as well. She turned to see Cai, whose face had blanched. The woman tried her best to retain her composure but Alaysha could see she was struggling.

"What is he talking about?" Alaysha asked her.

"Yuri." Theron said. "Fierce Leader of a thousand: he was the only man except for this poor shaman to escape this place alive."

"No man escapes," Cai said, turning to Alaysha with fresh eyes. Comprehension spread across her face in a way that made Alaysha uncomfortable.

"The man you call Yuri, your father," Cai said thoughtfully. "The pre-man Bodicca freed in her youth, the reason she wears the boar grease and suffers the shame of exile. These two are the same man. He lives?"

Alaysha shook her head. "No. He's dead."

She thought she heard Bodicca sob, but she couldn't be sure; the woman's face was as impassive as always.

"Then all is as it should be," Cai said decisively and clapped her hands together as though done with a distasteful task. "The pre-man is dead despite the love of a foolish would-be warrior who thought to save him; Alkaia's man will now die despite her shameful act of granting him freedom. The natural order is restored." She explored the shaman with scrutinous eyes. "I don't think any warrior will cast for you, man, but you will do well to feed the fires."

Theron took to mumbling again and Alaysha wouldn't have given his words credence except she caught a word that she recognized, that normally wouldn't matter to her but for reasons of late made her super sensitive.

"What about a twin, Theron?"

"The other man who lives." He eyed Uta speculatively, waiting for a reaction. "And not that filthy urchin Yuri bargained out of here. I see she has forgotten that one, hadn't she? Oh yes, we see she did. How delightful to know she can forget some things. But alas, he too, is dead, that vile creature." He grinned broadly. "No." He nodded at Thera. "I'm talking about *her* twin."

"She has a brother?" Alaysha couldn't keep the surprise from her tone and was relieved to see the others were just as shocked. All but Uta. Uta merely see-sawed her jaw back and forth.

"Uta?" Thera said, taking a step backwards, nearly stumbling. She sent a quick glance toward her lodge and a host of expressions ran across her face. Alaysha didn't have time to assess them all, but they ended up with one bald look of seeming comprehension that made her fidget nervously.

"The babe perished in the wild. The man lies." Uta's chin set itself stubbornly.

Alaysha could see she'd have to press the point to get the information; no one else seemed inclined or informed enough to do so. "How do you know this, Theron? What does it have to do with my father?"

Theron's black eyes met Alaysha's. "Oh dear, this shaman named Theron does know things, though he keeps some secrets. Yes. Yes, he does. But this one secret is too delicious to savour alone. That babe the cruel woman sought to kill became my Neve's Arm. My Ellison."

Thera made a sound like a swallow and a groan at the same time. Alaysha watched her, the beads of sweat forming on her brow.

"Your Neve? Her Arm?" The pieces were falling; Alaysha had only to assemble them.

He nodded. "Alkaia's son, yes, oh dear me, yes. Ellison: named by my clay witch in the old tradition. For her. My Ellissa." His voice broke and with it realization struck

Alaysha. She'd killed that old crone along with the others, and all this time Theron knew it.

"Your Ellissa was the witch?" Alaysha felt sick.

He pressed his chest out, proudly, at Uta. "She raised that infant as her own. Yuri brought him to us, thinking to bargain for our knowledge. He was ever a greedy pup, that one."

Bodicca spun towards him impassioned. "You know nothing, Shaman. Yuri loved that boy," she said, turning to Alaysha. "We have a word for two sword sisters who share a madre, but none for two males who do. Yet he felt for that boy the way a sister does to a sister. He brought him to the shaman in promise."

"Whose promise, foolish girl?" Uta asked, seeming to lay more shame on her with the term when Bodicca was obviously anything but a girl.

"Komandiri Alkaia's promise. She wanted him to live."

"Absurd. Our Alkaia wouldn't wrest such a promise from a whelp she didn't speak to, for a whelp she cared nothing for." Uta stepped menacingly in front of Bodicca, who met the woman's eye just as menacingly. "What could you know of it?"

"You sent us to kill the boy, and then to kill Theron. You *know* this."

"And yet, you speak as though I've forgotten it. Do you think the sisters will be shocked at such a thing? They were but males." Uta shrugged.

"But Komandiri was our best. Was she not?"

Uta had the grace to nod.

"Yuri killed her in the wild. That's what I know. She begged him to take the infant to Theron and then she let Yuri take her life."

There was a collective murmur that made Alaysha's skin crawl.

"It can't be true" Uta murmured. "I left her back unmarked. She would have lived. She wouldn't have let a man take her life. "

"Yuri killed her. I know this. We burned her the way a warrior should be, hot and high, and we collected her ashes and he took her sword."

This time the murmur became straight out shouting. Alaysha missed the reasoning and touched Cai on the arm for explanation.

"Our swords," the warrior said. "Our bone witch forges our swords--"

"With the ashes of your leaders. Oh my God, Cai. It is true. He killed that woman."

"What makes you certain?"

"Gael's mark. Alkaia's sword. My father must have used her ashes to mark his warriors and forge their steel." She turned to search for Thera, thinking the bone witch would want to know the truth, but Thera was gone. The leather flap of her lodge moved quietly.

Theron chuckled and Alaysha wanted to throttle him for his insensitivity. He shut off the chuckle, but kept Alaysha's eye. "The poor pup, never able to re-enter the bitch's den; how it pained him."

She didn't feel sorry for him, then; she felt afraid, wondering what else the man knew that he was keeping to himself.

Chapter 19

In the fracas that followed, no one seemed to care that Alaysha was present. In fact, with the amount of people hanging about, she was able to slip into the witch's lodge without being noticed, thinking to check on Gael. Two other warriors stood next to his bed, holding the blanket away from him, running their hands down his bare legs, cupping his calves and other parts that made Alaysha's face burn with shame for him. They were clearly inspecting goods, and when one of them tilted his chin and spied the mark, the other noticed and made a curious sound of shocked pleasure.

He was so still. He'd been barely conscious when they arrived, yes, but not this completely still. She would've thought him dead except for the poking and prodding of the other two women that indicated their interest in him. She waited until they were finished, both of them coming to some agreement with each other as they left the dwelling. Neither of them looked directly at her as they left. Alaysha moved close, laying her palm on his chest. Heat came off of him and waves; his heart thrummed in his chest. Alive, and most definitely drugged.

She did a careful inspection with her fingers, testing behind his neck where he'd been struck by Cai, feeling for scabs that might indicate a good amount of healing. What she felt at the base of his skull was a small bandage that she slipped off and probed tenderly with her fingers. The knot on the back of his head had gone down and in its place was a hole about the size of her fingernail. When she touched it, he groaned and tried to twist away. It must still be sensitive. She had the feeling there'd been more to his healing than magic; she heard about shamans who drilled holes in people skulls to make them docile, but she'd not heard of them doing so to heal. A little flutter went through her chest. What if the bone witch had done this to Gael so they could use him and then murder him without trouble.

She watched his eyes roll about beneath his lids, dreaming. She hoped they were pleasant, but the way his arms were twitching, she doubted it. She ran her hands down his chest, holding the blankets off of him with her forearms and peering beneath. Bruising where his ribs were; so he had indeed broken at least one of them. His clavicle might have been slipped as well; it showed a fair amount of bruising that had already turned yellow. She didn't want to look at his back. She only hoped they'd put some ointment on his contusions and scrapings.

She laid the blanket down gently and reached for his jaw, letting her fingers trail to the back of his ear. "I'll get you out of here, Gael," she said to him.

"I doubt you'll be able to," said a voice from behind her.

Bodicca. She'd expected Cai or Thera. Alaysha didn't bother to turn around. The reality of all she now knew was almost too much to process. "You loved my father?"

"Always."

"And you knew of his connection to this place?"

"Of course. It's both of our connections."

It explained so much to Alaysha, Yuri's cold manner, his brutal method of decision-making. "And Corrin?" Alaysha's voice almost broke on the name.

She heard Bodicca moving, coming closer, but with obvious effort. Theron had done a wonderful job of getting her mobile, maybe even of healing her back to some degree, but it was obvious from the way she moved that the only thing keeping her upright was incredible concentration.

"I know that's what he named him, but I had no use for him. He had no honour."

Alaysha turned on her finally. "And honour means something to you? You who helped my father kill his own mother, who probably helped him murder mine, and my nohma, and how many others, Bodicca? How many lives have you taken for my father?"

"I would have taken all I needed to and no more. Same as you."

Alaysha grunted at that but the woman wasn't satisfied.

"I would think after spending time in this village, you would understand. It's obvious you know nothing." Bodicca showed her a back still raw and weeping, but covered in honey to contain the fluid within the sores. Theron hadn't even put linen on it to protect it, but then where would he have gotten linen in the burnt lands? The woman headed toward the door, but Alaysha wasn't done with her yet.

"You brought Yenic here to what I now discover is certain death; Gael will die as well."

Bodicca spoke over her shoulder, twisting just enough that Alaysha could see her face and the haggard tiredness that ringed her eyes. "Bringing your lover here was the safest place for him. In the end, you'll see that." She turned her attention to Gael. "A warrior is a ready and willing sacrifice for the people they have committed to." She shrugged. "Better to focus on Yenic. Leave that man's fate to himself."

It was long moments before Alaysha could breathe again, and when she could, she pulled the air of the lodge in slowly, trying to gather strength from it. The fragrances of myrrh and sulphur mingled, stinging her nostrils. She heard a sound behind her and turned to see Thera laying yet another fur atop the mound on the cot. The witch said nothing, merely strode toward her and cast another handful of rubble onto the smouldering fire. More sulphur. The stink became unbearable.

She lifted the flap and went into the sunshine. Alaysha could see the crowds of the Enyalia becoming more scattered throughout the courtyard. Stock women pooled together, tapping their spoons against their biceps. The sense of something coming, the tension in the air, was palpable even from inside.

Yenic. He was probably even now being brought to the square. She inhaled deeply and reached down to kiss Gael on his cheek. The prickle of new grown beard took her by surprise. He was always clean-shaven. Her throat tightened up. And even if she wanted to say goodbye, she couldn't.

She let Thera pass her by and said nothing. The woman was preoccupied, even in her duty. But it wasn't the solstice that had her mind; it was something Uta had said, something Theron had said. The twin. Could Thera really care about a brother she'd never met? Could she be concerned that she had a twin at all?

The entire village seemed to be focused on the youth standing on a broad stump that had been drug from the forest and set to rest against the backdrop of luscious foliage. The flowers that drooped from the stems called to mind a rainbow, and a variety of leaves with every color and shade from dark green to moss, with every texture from spongy to spiked, could have given a viewer pleasure. It might well offer pleasure to the women of Enyalia, but for Alaysha, it only brought anxiety.

Yenic himself was naked, and she could see someone had gone to the trouble of smudging the shadows of his muscles with soot, making them stand out more plainly. He projected his usual arrogance, but Alaysha could see in his features the shade of distaste. He would show them he didn't care, but beneath she could tell he was silently planning their deaths.

Several Enyalia were circling him, going about much the same routine as the women inside had been doing to Gael. The inspection was thorough. For long moments the Enyalia examined the potential and a handful of stock women had begun to grow impatient. Alaysha could hear them complaining, the mumbling becoming louder. Finally, Cai stood in front of him and indicated for Thera to stand next to her. Both women divided the crowd into several distinct groups: one of stock women, all who held onto spoons; one of very large, very broad and almost mannish Enyalia, and a final group of shorter, more squat Enyalia, whom Alaysha noticed had far fewer circlets on their forearms and thighs than the first group. As she scanned the groups, she realized that the hardier warriors, obviously the strongest, with the same ones who had been inspecting Gael as he lay unconscious.

The remainder were to cast for Yenic. She had the ludicrous thought that Gael would be impressed that he was being saved for only the best of the Enyalia while Yenic was getting the leavings. The thought didn't last long. If she was to act, she had to act now.

She stepped in front of Cai and threw down the only thing she had on her person that she could use to show she was a warrior: the small blade she used for scoring apples. She been allowed to keep it as a token of respect while her sword had been spirited away somewhere during the initial journey.

"What is this, little maga?"

"I wish to cast for the man," she said, hoping she was using the right terminology.

Cai shook her head while Thera just glared at her. Alaysha thought she heard Bodicca somewhere to her left chuckling heartily. She didn't spare anyone else a glance, rather kept Cai's gaze as directly as she could.

"Not possible."

"Why not?"

"You're not Enyalia."

"You told me Enyalia is your word for a warrior. Do you disagree that I'm a warrior?"

Cai said nothing for a moment and in the space of time it took for her to consider, Enud stepped forward, the circlets on her thigh chattering loudly. In one thrust, she had pulled them free of her leg and threw them down next to Alaysha's blade. "If the woman wants to cast, let her cast."

Cai looked at the group of Enyalia that Enud had come from. Most of them shrugged indifferently, others made no motion of protest. It seemed none felt challenged enough to care. Then from the group, she turned to Thera. The bone witch shrugged indifferently. Alaysha noticed Enud stealing a look at Uta who stood to the side, her face a careful mask of disinterest.

"Because the solstice has so few men, we will spare only five of our warriors to cast for this man. Understood?"

Some of the Enyalia began to grumble then, but Enud's hard glare stopped some of the smaller ones immediately. "We understand."

Cai sent Alaysha a look of sadness. "It seems it's done, little maga. Fight well."

Three other Enyalia came forward, their circlets in hand, and threw them into the same pile, making a grotesque lump of teeth and sinew. Cai turned to Thera and extended her arm, touching the bone witch's fingers briefly, and then joining with her hand. The bone witch let out a series of undulating shrieks that brought the hair on Alaysha's arms to a full stand.

The whole of the village backed off as though they'd been given a command. Both Cai and Thera linked hands. In one voice they declared the solstice.

"This man has been cast for. The woman who remains when the battle is done shall have the right to this man, to his seed, his life, and finally his death."

It was only when two of the warriors came forward and knelt before both leaders, kissing their feet, taking their leave of their Enyalian oaths that Alaysha realized that these women planned to battle to the death.

And that in casting, she had pledged the same.

Chapter 20

There was time, evidently, to also take your leave of the people you loved, just in case you lost. Alaysha couldn't stop chewing on her lip; four of the women strode off to what Alaysha assumed where their homes while Enud merely stood with arms folded, feet planted shoulder width apart, with her face an impassive mask of purpose. Once, she caught the woman exchange a silent glance with Uta who had taken to collecting bits of leaves from young barley plants. Why she'd do it herself when she so obviously preferred the chattel labor of the boys was a mystery.

For the first time, Alaysha realized her plan was foolish, but then, what else could she have done? She had her doubts the Enyalia would let her leave peacefully; Cai and the witches knew her power. They surely understood the risks to their village if both Yenic and Gael were to die. She'd promised Cai she'd not bring the power, but she had no intention of keeping the vow; it had been made when she didn't understand the breadth of it. It would be impossible to spirit the men away now; with Theron and Bodicca in the village, the Enyalia were hyper vigilant.

While Alaysha had been relatively safe in the village, she wasn't foolish enough to think she was free. Casting for Yenic would buy her time, as well as Gael. Time just might mean Alaysha would be able to use their solstice against them.

"He's not safe, yet," Cai said from behind her.

Alaysha waited for the woman to stand next to her before she spoke. "At least he has a chance."

"Don't you realize you've not bought him any time but wasted yours?"

Alaysha ran a toe across the grass, watching the blades

fold over and spring back upright. "If I win then your village is safe from my power."

"It is safe at any rate."

The oath Alaysha had made or just arrogance? It didn't matter in the end.

She felt Cai's hands on her shoulders and she was spun to face the warrior who pulled her close, lifting her just a bit so that her face upturned. "Foolish maga, you have no chance of winning."

"Then you have a problem."

"Do you think Uta or Thera will let you live long enough to test your powers? That threat is weak by now, and I would think more a problem for you than us."

Alaysha studied her bare foot. "How so?"

"What if by some miracle you do win--what then? You'll have to take his life. It's what you cast for."

Alaysha met the pull of Cai's green eyes, so much like Yuri's she realized now, except a softer shade than Yuri's icy blue, somehow more emotive. "I'll refuse. Like Bodicca did. Like Alkaia."

"Little maga, they were true Enyalia." There was a chuckle in Cai's tone, but it wasn't mocking. Her palm traveled down Alaysha's back, pressing gently. "Your flesh is not nearly so hardened. Your spirit isn't made of the same steel."

Alaysha licked her lips. "I'm his only chance."

"And what happens to his chance when your power, in its fear, drains the fluid from the entire village, including your man?"

Alaysha shrugged in the woman's hold and her eyes moved to the pulse in the woman's neck; she couldn't hold Cai's gaze anymore. It was probing far too deeply for her liking. "That won't happen. I'm not afraid."

Cai let her arms fall and folded them across her chest. She seemed to want to say more, to be searching for words that might change the outcome. Instead, she settled on ordering Enud away from Yenic. When Enud went storming across the compound and into a small hut made purely of animal skin and wooden poles, Cai nodded to Yenic. "There's no need to stand there longer, man," she said. "Go find a boy to feed you."

"And dress him," Alaysha said.

Cai gave her a queer look. "No reason not to," she said. She flicked her wrist, and a young boy came running, the same boy from the previous night. He stole a quick peek at Alaysha and the small tremor that crossed his face could have been meant as a smile if she cared to interpret it. "Get the man food and clothes," she told the boy.

Alaysha made to follow behind the two of them, thinking she could spend some time talking to Yenic, work out a plan that had them disappearing through the night, but Cai stopped her.

"You asked me what I would do for the person I cared for."

"Yes," Alaysha said.

"If I couldn't save them, I would do what Enud is doing. I would find a way to hurt the person who harmed her."

"I've done nothing to Enud."

Cai smiled slowly. "No, but your man in Thera's Lodge did. And he loves you."

The realization struck Alaysha in the middle of her solar plexus. The woman Enud had wept over: not a sister, a lover.

"Enud will kill you, little maga. She will not let the others win the chance to fight you."

"I won't let that happen. I have skill, yes; but I know I can't win against the likes of Enud. Except my father taught me not to fear, not feel." She met the warrior's gaze stubbornly. "Trust me. I can take this whole village if I need to without a single care."

"There's no need for threats," Cai said. "I told you that if I couldn't save the woman I cared for, I'd do what Enud is doing. But if I could, the person I loved would not feel one moment of pain. And so there is also no need for fear."

She left Alaysha standing alone, watching her back as she strode away through the crowds of stock women chattering noisily and threatening young boys with their spoons.

Chapter 21

The battles began with much less ceremony than the casting. Alaysha wasn't able to spend even a few moments with Yenic; he'd been dressed by the boys and fed, obviously. He sat next to the fire, untethered, but guarded by several large warriors. Alaysha remembered the story Edulph had told her about Yenic taking on three of his best soldiers without so much as a blade. Yenic had used anything he could put his hands to, and in the end he used his powers over fire to scatter them. She tried to catch his eye, thinking he could use the flame even now to cause bewilderment; that they could run. But she knew it would be a waste of time.

He wouldn't use his connection to his mother for fear it would reveal them, and even if it might mean his escape, Alaysha knew he wouldn't risk it. Too close, he'd said, and she hadn't understood, but she decided to trust his decision. Whatever too close meant, in the end it meant he feared it. Aislin might never cross the burnt lands herself, but she obviously had some skill Yenic feared.

Alaysha began to understand why Cai said it would be a long day. She could imagine in Theron's time when there were a dozen men to cast for and fight over, that the solstice battles must have gone on for weeks. With one man and only five fighters, it would certainly go faster, but these were no ordinary soldiers. Each Enyalian, whether blonde or brunette, whether thin or squat, had skills that would surpass most warriors Alaysha had met. The only person she'd seen with such natural gifts for battle was Gael, and even he didn't possess the coldness it needed to take a comrade's life so mercilessly.

These women had grown together, trained together,

and yet here they were fighting against each other, to their ultimate demise, over a man whom none of them found desirable. They fought for the right to continue their line, and obviously saw each sword sister as secondary to that duty.

The lots had been drawn by small stones scratched on by soot from the fire. By some odd chance, neither Enud nor Alaysha's stone was selected first. Rather, two women of equal size drew their blades against each other.

It began when the Sun was at its zenith, and that battle still drug on now far past that.

Alaysha was as entranced as if she was watching a dance and no more. Without the emotional connection to the assailants, she could study their movements, examine any habits that were born of the same training bidding them to move with instinct. She wasn't certain that all of the women would fight the same way, but she was confident they would have similar battle habits.

What she noticed was that the women used both arms equally skilfully. Sword in one hand, blade in the other, those lengths of steel were extensions of their arms and where they bid them strike, they struck. The muscles in their thighs never quivered with effort even when they squatted to avoid a blow, or when they leapt to advance. She expected to see movements like Cai had practiced in her lodge, but if those were movements of battle, they were not put to use during this fight. There was very little of beauty in the battle, and more of pure brutality.

At first, Alaysha believed she could watch each movement and study every minute swing, but when the fight wore on into the early evening with no seeming victor in sight, she actually grew bored. She scanned the crowds, hoping to see Bodicca or Theron. She was surprised to see Enud and Uta in deep conversation, seemingly oblivious to the battle unfolding. A tap on her shoulder startled her.

"They conspire," a voice said.

Theron. The wrinkles in his face were dirt filled and the alert black eyes were red rimmed.

"I thought they--"

"Hid this poor shaman away; yes, yes. But they have more to concern themselves with than the activities of a weak-willed man." He seemed entirely pleased with himself.

Alaysha wasted no time. "When it's my turn to fight," she said. "I need you and Bodicca to retrieve Gael. Get him out of here."

"So this witch thought she would use the solstice to create a distraction? Does she not see she cannot win?"

"Whether I beat Enud or not isn't the question, Theron. I only need to empty the village of as many of my people as I can."

"And this witch will bring the power, yes, yes? A good plan, if not flawed."

"How is it flawed? If they can't be bothered to watch over you, then surely the same is happening to Gael. Bodicca is strong enough--"

"The same is surely not happening to Gael."

"What do you mean?"

"Gael is even now performing his service."

"He can't be. The solstice hasn't begun."

"Solstice begins today. Yenic's casting isn't complete, no, no. But the large warrior--well, his fate is sealed already."

"He can't be. He's drugged--"

"Drugged, yes, yes. But not in the way you think. That demon chalk witch uses my own sacred brew against us."

"We have to stop it. Theron, we can't let Gael be

debased that way."

Theron's eye traveled to the two Enyalia battling in the dirt. A collective sigh went up from the crowds when one fell, and a wiry stock woman ran forward, throwing herself onto the prone body.

"The first loser, yes, yes." Theron's face clouded over and he swallowed repeatedly. Alaysha noticed he shivered and pulled his arms together over his chest. "We can smell hair burning, yes we can. Such a terrible smell."

Alaysha reached out to touch him on the arm and he startled. The eyes that he turned on her took a moment to focus. "We will do what we can for the warrior, but know that Uta will not let you win."

"I told you that doesn't--"

"Matter. Yes, yes. The shaman knows that. But what the witch doesn't know is that Uta is not honourable. Even her general doesn't understand that."

"Uta wants me dead."

"Uta will do what she needs to, to keep this witch from draining the village. She will believe it's the right thing, oh, yes, she will. Her komandiri might even come to believe it too in time."

"Because the men will die anyway," Alaysha said, letting what she'd known all along settle into her psyche. They used the casting as a distraction, letting Alaysha believe she was buying time for Yenic, for Gael, when all along they knew that so long as the men lived, Alaysha wasn't a threat. Once they died, things would be different. And they knew Alaysha was capable of killing the entire tribe. She began to wonder if the dead Enyalian raid party had actually encountered the wind witch at all. If those women cast for Edulph somewhere out past the village. Why else would they let such a ceremony occur if they were under threat of attack? Of course there was no threat of attack. She realized that now.

She even started to think that if Enud succeeded in killing Alaysha the problem would be solved--if Alaysha died fast enough that she couldn't bring on the power. That made her wonder if she would be fighting one warrior, or one warrior with an assassin nearby, ready to strike before Alaysha could bring the power to save herself.

Chapter 22

Alaysha did her best to look as though her entire being was focused on the battle she would have to undertake, but her mind was racing behind the mask of composure she wore. She couldn't bear to watch the next battle as it began; this one was between Enud and the victor of the first, and both of them were vicious, not dancing at all. This time, there was a desperate ferocity to the battle. The victor used her feet as well as her sword, kicking at Enud, her entire body twirling full circle, sweeping Enud's feet from beneath her. Enud recovered quickly enough, but she came up bloody from a grazing of her opponent's blade. Three movements later and it actually appeared as though this battle would be over quickly. Alaysha scanned the women watching the battle, searching for evidence of an assassin. Could it be that stock woman there who hung a little too close to where Enud had placed her belongings? It might even be that young girl who was lifting pikes from a pile, testing their weight, thrusting them almost playfully at the air.

In truth, if she examined the area it could be any one of these women. The boys had been set to work collecting wood and tying thatch and dried rushes to a formation that looked like a large sword stuck deep into the ground. It was far back enough into the woods that she hadn't noticed it before, but as it became thicker with tinder, it grew more noticeable.

Outwardly, she knew her posture was straight, but she couldn't stop the fidgeting her toes had started doing. She kept stealing glances at Yenic, his face kept turning into Gael's, and she found herself cursing her stupidity over and over. She glanced at Yenic again now. He stood between two large women, swaying just a bit as though he too had been drugged. No wonder he did nothing to save himself. She wondered just what kind of brew Theron knew how to make that could lay a man as large as Gael out cold on the bed and yet leave Yenic, much more wiry, much slimmer, standing swaying on his feet. His eyes held a far-off look, and he kept straining to stare into the fire pit, shaking his head when nothing rose from it but smoke from a dampened fire.

If only she'd tried to get to Gael earlier. If only she hadn't trusted them to see he was healed. She should have thought it was too easy. But she'd been so worried about him. It was a mistake to think that women of this sort, who cared nothing for men, could be interested in his welfare. She only hoped that Bodicca and Theron could manage to get him out of the bone witch's lodge. She hadn't had contact with Aedus at all since that first day, but she hoped against hope that the girl was somewhere safe.

But Yenic. Even if Theron and Bodicca managed to get Gael away, how would Alaysha rescue Yenic?

It seemed there was nothing to do but wait and watch. And even that time died as quickly as she realized it. Enud stood over her opponent's form already, her foot planted on the woman's back. Her arm raised, sword in the air. She turned her vengeful eyes to Alaysha and then kicked the woman away as if she were a roll of moss.

Alaysha searched for signs of exhaustion in the warrior's face and saw none. Even as her mouth went dry, three Enyalian soldiers came forward to collect the dead woman and they hoisted her onto a pyre laden with fragrant rushes and pine. Enud squatted in the pool of blood that had collected where the woman fell, and without taking her eyes from Alaysha's, she ran her hand through the fluid.

"Come, little witch. The ground is thirsty for your blood." She streaked her hand across her chin, leaving a trail of blood in a ribbon that mocked Alaysha's markings.

Strangely enough, Alaysha thought of Corrin. She'd been trained for battle from the time she was small, and the brutal man had done his job well. She knew how to shut out the fear, ignore the sounds of shouting, of weeping, of cheers. She'd learned under that brutal hand how to focus everything she felt and feared into the energies of her hand and her legs and each muscle and every fibre beneath that muscle.

She stepped forward, pulling her sword from her back, offering her enemy a confident smile.

She only hoped the woman believed it.

There was no fear. There was only a keen awareness. Alaysha knew every hair on her body was straining to feel the currents of movement, the subconscious knowledge that her opponent had shifted, that she had begun to attack. The din of shouting disappeared and in its place rose the sound of her own heart slowing at precise moments, pulsing, then flooding her legs with fuel. She stepped left; Enud's blade swung down straight to the empty space she'd been in an instant before. A small victory to have avoided the first blow, but there was no time to savour it. She was already swinging around, her sword in both hands, aiming it level, catching Enud's blade and biting into the metal. A jolt slammed into her elbow, telling every muscle and nerve in her hand to let go.

Deities, the woman was strong.

She danced to the right, kicking at the ground for purchase and leapt just in time to avoid the sweeping arc of Enud's sword trying to take her from the legs.

It was obvious the woman was playing with her. Testing her patterns. It could be her only advantage; the Enyalia all had similar training and understood how each of them would fight. Alaysha could use her own foreignness to keep the warrior on edge. It wasn't enough to keep her alive long, it wouldn't be enough to draw the battle out very long, but it might be enough for the others to get to Gael, and it might be enough time for the assassin to step forward. It wasn't that Enud could best Alaysha, it was more that Enud needed to make a quick death, one that wouldn't afford Alaysha the time to bring the power. Alaysha wasn't foolish enough to believe that Enud's blade would be the one to strike that blow. And so she had to fragment her mind, split her body awareness into two consciousnesses. One had to deal with Enud, the other had to lie in wait for the assassin.

Almost instinctively she exhaled as she swung, inhaled as she pulled back. She saw a flicker of movement from Enud's eyes; for one moment the warrior had taken her eyes from Alaysha's. It was one instant, but it spoke volumes. Alaysha knew it was the critical moment. She spread her arms, her sword held out to the right, ready to swing; her left arm waiting to feel the shift in the air. The attack was coming from behind. Enud was swift. Too swift. There would be no way to meet the assassin without exposing herself to vulnerable attack from Enud.

And then she felt it. The fine hairs on the back of her shoulders moved enough to lift her skin in tiny goose bumps. She swung halfway to the left, her right hand toward Enud, her left toward the assassin, spinning as Enud stepped left, stepped right, trying to confuse her, to let the murderer in close enough.

She took the chance. It was a mere fraction of her own heartbeat, but she took it. She brought her sword in a solid swing to the left, gripping the handle with both hands, using the weight of her body to arc powerfully to the left. She swung with everything she had, knowing that whatever her sword contacted, would go down if she swung hard enough, she could keep going back toward Enud. She'd have to find her feet, then. Wait for the attack.

Her sword bit into solid wood and Cai's green gaze flicked over her so quickly Alaysha barely had time to register the surprise in them. Cai? The assassin. Alaysha felt a moment of betrayal then of resignation. So be it, she thought and wrenched her sword away from the wood, readying herself to strike again.

The Enyalian pulled her shield away and slipped close to Alaysha all in one movement, grabbing her by the waist, pulling her hard against her. Alaysha could feel the woman's heart tremoring against her back. She saw the young warrior from the day before who had played at battle in the tiltyard so fiercely lying on the ground. A mace three times the size of any Alaysha had ever seen lay next to her. The chalk witch stood over her, glaring at Cai.

"This is not honourable, Uta," Cai said. "The maga said she would leave. She gave her word she would not harm us."

"You're foolish, Komandiri," Uta said. Her gaze fleeted over Alaysha's shoulder and she remembered the battle was not over. The sound from behind her reminded her that Enud was still fighting. Cai spun at the same moment Alaysha realized it, easing Alaysha behind her. "Back-to-back, little maga," she said.

They moved as one, Alaysha feeling each movement Cai made and mirroring it is best she could. It was no longer a simple casting battle; it ceased to be the moment the Komandiri stepped within it. There was no telling how many Enyalia would make this battle their own.

Enud struck out, forcing Cai backwards. Alaysha

moved forward with the warrior at her back. Cai seemed loathe to engage and Enud took advantage of it. She hefted her sword much more fiercely, and Cai blocked each one, seeming to take great care not to strike to do damage. It was obvious she was the greater fighter, that Enud understood it, but that she also knew Cai was not fighting to the death.

"My sisters will not be gentle with the man, witch. Not his body, nor his mind." Enud laughed. She didn't sound the least winded, rather she sounded invigorated.

"Stand down," Cai told her.

"I won this right," Enud said.

"You won the right to battle this woman, but what you've done is dishonourable."

They shuffled, Cai careful to keep Alaysha's back close enough to feel each movement. Alaysha watched the faces of each woman she was spun to see. The pleasure in the battle had left their faces. Now they looked angry.

"Stand down, Enyalian," Cai said again. "We'll stop this madness and resume later."

"You protect a foreign witch over your own people?"

"I protect honour over all," Cai said. "My oath is to my sword sisters and to their honour. We celebrate women of power, we do not murder them."

Alaysha scanned the faces. She watched Yenic, his mouth working as though he was speaking, his eyes glazed over, staring into the fire pit. He managed to draw small fingers of flame from the smouldering logs. She flicked her gaze toward Uta, whose mouth was drawn in a tight line, Thera, standing next to her, whose hand went at the same moment to her neck with a look of confusion; both collapsed in a heap on the ground.

An arrow bloomed in the neck of another, but this

warrior did not collapse. Instead, she spun to face her attacker, sword drawn, blade on the other hand. And several others, who in the same moment had begun gripping their throats with both hands, the mouth gaping open like fish landed on the side of the river.

In the same instant, Alaysha felt her lungs tighten. Power unfurled itself from beneath her breastbone, searching for the source of the attack, wanting retribution for it.

Because an attack it was. Not just from one enemy: but from three.

Chapter 23

Alaysha had one thought: to psych the fluid from whatever was stealing her breath. It wasn't a matter of fear or bravery; it was one of pure self-preservation. The power tingled beneath her skin even as she saw Cai drop to her knees. They'd been back-to-back when the battle began, but now as Alaysha spun, searching for breath to pull into her lungs, she'd fallen away from Cai. She knew she had mere heartbeats to stop the psyching, that within ten, all of the Enyalia, the boys even the one she'd come to recognize, Yenic Gael and Theron would be nothing but dried flesh.

If she could just focus it, she could at least save someone. But where? How?

Her lungs were starving for air and her legs lost their strength, unable to find the fuel they needed as the air was robbed from her lungs. Blackness was overtaking her vision; she could smell the stink from the sweat of the fighters, taste the water from beneath their pores. If she didn't do something immediately it would be too late. It wouldn't matter who took the lives: lack of air or lack of water had the same result, but if she did nothing they would all be dead.

A flicker of movement, there in the trees, past a collapsed Uta and Thera, several Enyalia on their knees struggling not to pass out. A heartbeat more and it would be over.

The easy water had already gathered to a mist, was gathering still. The quick supply from buckets and gourds and water skins, it was all there ready to be used. It would have to be enough. Like she would strike with her sword at an enemy, Alaysha imagined the water as part of her arm. She swung, gathering it into a wide streak and at its apex, she sent it jabbing forward, toward the movement she saw in the trees. It gathered as it hurtled forward, picking up condensation from the psyched breath of each woman and child, and it turned to a sheet of water with enough force that it slammed into a tree, cracking it in two as it crashed into the woods.

Alaysha fell forward onto her chest, her hands splayed in front of her, trying to hold herself up. She couldn't breathe; she had spent everything she had in the attack. She lay there, trying to focus. The Enyalia who had reclaimed enough air to stand were doing their best to sprint into the woods, swords drawn. Alive then. Most of them. But staggering as though drunk.

She felt herself being lifted into warm arms. Strange. She hadn't realized she was cold until just then.

"We have to get out of here." Yenic's voice. "You have to get out of here if you want to live." Shouting at someone, everyone, it seemed. Fires had started somewhere near, she could hear the lightening striking wood and splitting trees. She could smell the stink of char and burning skin. A blur of flame from the edge of the woods where the tinder sword blazed.

Alaysha's vision blurred, but she could see waves of red flashes then of green. Moving. The feeling of awkward loping. "Come, man," she heard her Saviour say. "I know a place."

"It best be far away." Yenic said. He was breathless too, as though he was running and labouring at breath at the same time. But it didn't feel like they were running. It was too awkward, too slow.

A grumble of thought, then darkness. Alaysha couldn't stop shivering. She thought the shadows wanted her to sleep. They crept in from her side vision, threatening to steal even the unfocused power that she kept tightened and in check. But there was something she had to tell these saviours of hers. Something important.

"Gael," she croaked out and her throat burned at the effort. She tried to lift her head because that wasn't what she wanted to say. It had something to do with the movement she'd seen as she felt her power let go, and she needed to concentrate, to get it back.

"Gael," was what came again.

"Her man," came Cai's voice.

"I'll see to it." Yenic again. Sullen but agreeable.

"Use Bodicca and the beast to get him. Meet me at nightfall. She'll know where I'm going."

"Bodicca," Alaysha mumbled, and even that wasn't what she wanted to say, but it was closer. Gael. Bodicca. Theron. Aedus.

Edulph.

Yes. She could picture it now. Remember. Three attacks. A bloom of arrow. A swat to the neck. The loss of air. A complete triangle of attack and at its third point a small child--a girl no more than two seasons old.

The wind witch, surely. And with her two people Alaysha knew on sight. Aedus, her hair and body slicked in mud, holding a blower to her lips. Edulph with a bow. The only people standing, unaffected, by the child's power.

And that could only mean one thing.

They had her blood.

Chapter 24

Alaysha woke to warmth, but when she opened her eyes she saw nothing. So the shadows had taken her after all and she was dreaming. She listened to the fire crackling nearby. Behind her perhaps? She tried to move only to discover she was trussed up into some sort of torturous blanket too heavy to lift. She heard Yuri's voice commanding her to be calm, to stay resolute, stupid girl, and she worked to quell the instinctive panic.

She inhaled slowly as he would have bid her, and forced herself to imagine the air moving to her toes and fingers. There. Much better.

The darkness was merely night, not the gloom of Corrin's dungeon. The trussing material, a warm fur tucked tightly around her, covered her head. It let her face peek through and now that she understood what was happening, she knew that the fire was indeed crackling behind her. She'd rolled over in her sleep, evidently, and now faced the forest. She shook her head free of the fur and worked to unwind her arms from wherever they'd come to rest--crossing her chest, hands jammed into her armpits. Now that she was free, she could make out conversation, hear distinct words.

"She wakes," Cai's voice from somewhere near. Alaysha tried to roll over.

"Careful, little maga. Here. Let me help you."

Meaty hands burrowed beneath Alaysha and twisted, freeing her enough that she could manoeuvre into a semi-sitting position. Cai grew impatient with the floundering to get set right and pick her up, fur and all, then plopped her back down facing the fire.

"What happened?"

They were all there, sitting around the flame: Yenic, Theron, Gael, Bodicca. They all looked sullen. Full recall struck Alaysha like cold water.

"The girl," she said. "What happened to her?" She had a quick image of a toddler knocked backwards, her body broken against a tree, her hair hanging down, wet, against her tiny body. "She's dead," she heard herself say.

Yenic poked at the flames, the light dancing on his brow. "We can't say that for sure."

"She will be dead," Cai said and Yenic looked at her.

"I know the Enyalia are fierce, but you saw what happened. You can't say for sure the girl is dead."

"My sisters would have killed her if the little maga didn't."

He chuckled humourlessly. "Your sisters could barely move."

It took a moment, but Cai did agree. "True," she said. "We were much--drained--but a child? Well, she wouldn't have taken much energy to kill in her broken state."

Alaysha thought of the girl again with dread and imagined the limp body. In her mind's eye she saw someone reaching for the girl and lifting her, even before the Enyalia managed to gain her feet.

"Edulph," she said and Theron's beady black eyes rested on her. "It was Edulph. He took her."

"That madman, he's dead. Surely the Enyalia killed him in the burnt lands." The shaman said, and Alaysha gave him quiet study as she listened to his words. There were too measured. Too careful. Too altogether clear.

"Both he and Aedus saved her. I saw them."

"Alaysha," Yenic said. "You couldn't have. If they were there, they would have been in the same condition as the rest of us. As it was, even the Enyalia struggled to gain their strength. The loss of air, and fluid." He shrugged. "None of us could manage more than an hour's walk even with the beasts. Cai could barely carry you."

"I tell you, they were unaffected."

His brow furrowed and Alaysha turned to Gael. He would understand. The warrior was mostly quiet.

"She shot Uta with a quill. You know how she does it. Uta collapsed. That was it. Edulph left an arrow in Saxon's bed when he stole the boy for Aislin. An Enyalian was shot in the neck with the same." She waited for Gael to support her but it was Cai who replied with a disgusted snort.

"A traitor's weapon, that. No honour in it."

No response from Gael and he wouldn't even meet her eye.

"Gael?"

It was Theron who spoke, and he seemed to be taking great care in putting his words together. "A madman such as that one would use the witch for ill."

"A madman such as that one had no reason to fear the witch, Theron. Why would that be?"

"The blood. Like your nohma. Like Yuri."

"Yes. The blood. He's related, and so must be Aedus."

"Closely too," said Yenic thoughtfully.

"Very close. Yuri and my nohma where the only ones safe from me. My father and my aunt."

Yenic kicked at the fire. "Doesn't make sense. He used you to free his people from Sarum because there were no others left. He wanted them back. He hated the servitude. That's why he forced us there. Remember?"

Cai rose to dig at the fire, and Alaysha realized there was a spit over it, some sort of rodent roasted there. "The highlanders have never been warlike. Only subservient. In my time. In Alkaia's. I would expect it from those in the frozen lands, but they are long gone. Enyalian justice before I was born."

Alaysha tried to pull her gaze from the long tail hanging down from the spit. "Scattered, you'd said. Slowly rebuilding themselves."

"Perhaps to relocate in the highlands as we suspected." Cai said thoughtfully.

Yenic shifted as he sat. "Gathering strength."

"To make war on Enyalia."

"Not Sarum," Alaysha said. "Edulph wanted his people so he could build an army. Even Aedus said so when I first met her."

"To drive Enyalia to oblivion," Cai said. She sighed. "So at least that war is over. We needn't worry about that."

"Why not?"

Cai shrugged. "My sisters would not have let them live."

Gael sniffed haughtily and tried to stand. It took a few long staggering moments for him to catch his balance, but when he did he wrapped his cloak tighter around his chin, staring into the fire, and then he strode off into the trees. Alaysha watched him go with a curious foreboding sitting in her chest. It seemed the drugs had worn off and he was able to move about, but he certainly was not steady on his feet, nor swift. Each of his movement seemed full of effort. She got up to go after him, only to discover her legs wouldn't hold her.

Cai caught her before she fell.

"None of us have much in the way of strength, but you even less, little maga."

"What you did was amazing," Yenic said. Alaysha

never heard that tone in his voice before and it made her feel warm and tingling. "Such control, Alaysha."

"I seem to be paying for it, however."

He nodded, mutely. "It's still a victory. You should enjoy it."

She looked around, as much to change the subject as anything else. "What is this place?"

"This is the pine woods. It's the last piece of land before the journey to the highlander territory." Cai stretched her legs forward and Alaysha noticed her circlets were gone. There was no corresponding rattle.

"That fire," Cai nodded at the flame. "Is burning in the same place my sword sisters say Alkaia lit one her first night in exile."

Bodicca made a sound on the other side and Cai nodded at her "I knew when you found us here that it was true. You met her here, didn't you?"

"We did, yes. She was weak. We had no idea how badly she was bleeding." Her voice seemed far off and Alaysha thought she must be remembering, maybe even watching it again. "She'd already killed four wolves by the time we found her. And the babe."

"Ellison," Theron murmured. "How did you keep him alive until you reached us?"

"Easy," Bodicca said with a grin in her voice. "We let him drink his fill from her after--after she died. Then we stole back into the village."

"So you were the ones," Cai said.

"Yes." Bodicca said. "Corrin and Yuri hid away a host of pre-men too young at the time of the quarter solstice to go to slaughter. Dozens of them." She chuckled. "Together with the stock women and wet nurses, it seemed like a thousand.

The boy had plenty to drink then. Many of us lived on mother's milk for the first sun cycle."

"Fierce leader of a thousand," Alaysha mumbled, thinking of Yuri's title.

"It's easy to re-enslave those already enslaved if you offer things seeming like freedom," Bodicca said. "That was Yuri's enticement. Freedom to live and fight at their will in a city of their own. They slipped away as they did their chores and we lit on our way through the burnt lands before four sun rises."

It was a history of her father she'd never heard, and it held Alaysha rapt. "Why didn't the boys just leave before if it was so easy?"

Cai cleared her throat. "Until then, Enyalia would have noticed. They would hunt and kill anyone who left the village. But then--"

"Then the village was under strain," Bodicca said.

"Strain. A good description," Cai said. "Uta only ever called it difficult. A young warrior choosing to save a pre-man. Our leader gone into self imposed exile, taking an infant male with her and leaving the daughter."

"Self imposed? I thought she'd been banished." Alaysha was surprised to hear this.

"I suppose she knew she'd upset the balance. That to choose an outsider, she was no better than Bodicca. She would expect the same treatment."

"Uta expected us to track Alkaia and kill the boy."

Alaysha sensed something in the warrior's tone. "And you, Cai? Now that you've saved outsiders instead of your sisters?" Alaysha reached out to touch where the woman previously sported her circlets, and the thigh muscle trembled beneath her fingers.

"I can never return," she said.

"It's a hard choice," Bodicca whispered and got up, finally, staggering as Gael had done before she managed a good balance. She looked incredibly old in the firelight and Alaysha realized for the first time that she was old. She'd been such a solid, brusque constant in her life that Alaysha had always assumed she didn't age. But she was as old as her father had been.

Her father. So much she didn't know. He'd saved his half brother from certain death, rescued dozens of comrades from Enyalia, survived the burnt lands.

And had done everything in that power to ensure all but the one witch he could control was dead.

She watched Theron in the light, wondering what he knew, and found herself feeling betrayed by him. He'd known all along that she'd killed his witch--his wife she knew now--and he'd not told her the connection. How much more was he keeping quiet? She was even beginning to wonder if he was half mad at all, but used his speech patterns as a means to stay below the vision line. He'd made her take Yuri's eyes, saying they were part of Etlantium, and she'd carried them with her in her pack.

All that was left of her father after Aislin scorched him to ashes. All she had of a sister she didn't know was a memory. She thought of the warrior Alkaia and how she'd saved her son, the part Yuri played in that and felt strangely proud.

"Do you have children, Cai?"

"I have celebrated two quarter solstices; I did not relish the task, and did not think to repeat it. I am grateful I never quickened."

Alaysha shifted uncomfortably as drums sounded in

the distance, the beat growing more incessant, and she realized Cai was watching her. "Makes me nervous," she said.

"It's meant to. They get into your chest, do they not?"

Theron grumbled from his spot next to the fire and Alaysha peered at him, trying to make out his expression. "Do they bother you too, Shaman?"

He had taken to rocking. "The hair. Stinks of burning."

"Not yet, old man. Not yet," Cai said and his eyes snapped to her, suddenly aware, as though the turn itself had struck a chord.

"And yet this old man smells it. Spectres of men once known, they follow us. They do. And they are not kind. Such is the price of escape."

"What does he mean?" Alaysha asked.

Cai sighed. "My sword has bathed in solstice blood but twice, but even I remember the stink of hair and fat."

She looked to want to avoid the topic, but Alaysha pressed her. "The drums will peak and die even though no men will be sacrificed. The pre-men will have no need to tether the men to the burning sword. Many of them will be forced to walk into the flame. Some, those who are lucky enough, will be killed before, to shed their blood for us. All will die."

Alaysha thought of Yuri, of his knowing what lay ahead of him if he stayed in the village of the Enyalia and realized at once that he'd saved dozens from their fate. She stole a look at Bodicca, who stared into the flame as though reliving her own casting ceremony so many years ago. Her mouth was twisted into a line of revulsion that echoed how Alaysha felt.

"That's savage. You don't kill for a god, or to prevent

disease. You kill because they are men."

Cai pursed her lips, considering. "You speak as though there was something wrong with that."

"There is something wrong with that. You use them to procreate--"

"Not just any male, little maga. Only the halest of them."

"So you use the best specimens, force them to lie with you--"

"Not all are forced." Cai held up her hand. "Quite a few enjoy the activity."

"Only because they have no idea what their end will be. So the ones who don't enjoy it? What do you do to them? You torture them to submit?"

"Little maga, a man is simple, and his manhood even more so. There is no need for torture--unless he wants it."

"And then you murder them."

"They are men. They have no further use."

"I thought the Enyalia felt no fear for any man."

"And what do you think affords us such courage?"

"Surely you can't believe all men are vermin. These here," Alaysha pointed to Yenic and then to Gael who sat by himself hunched fire away from the fire. "These men were useful enough that you brought them here."

"I let them live because you wished it, little maga. Not because they have value besides their seed."

Alaysha groaned, frustrated, and Bodicca spoke finally. Her voice was a gritty whisper. "Had I let Yuri die in our land, this little maga you seem fond of would not be sitting in front of you."

Cai shrugged. "The value of seed, warrior, no more."

"This man was valuable enough to the Enyalia that

Komandiri Alkaia gave her life for his service." She pointed at Theron who squirmed anxiously.

"Again, all has more to do with the power of Enyalia, Bodicca, not the value of men. We birth men, they serve us, and in their time they die. If men were more resourceful, more valuable--even more fearsome a thing, they would not die so easily at the quarter solstice. My blade would not have sent a red grin across two men's throats, the pre-men would not have hoisted dozens of their comrades to the burning sword over and over and over again as long as Enyalia has thrived."

A terrible guttural sound came from the bushes and Gael, his face a fearsome mask of pain and rage, threw himself over the fire and leapt at Cai.

The two struggled, Cai finding her footing first, but Gael meeting her cheek with a resounding blow as she did so. He seemed to know each place she would be and followed her with dogged punches, to the stomach, the ribs by the time Yenic and Bodicca lunged in to separate them. Cai gave in readily to Bodicca, but Gael fought on, thrashing in Yenic's hold until Alaysha shouted that the foolishness should stop. It did stop, but Gael stomped out into the trees snarling to himself. Alaysha looked about the surprised group, all heaving, the tension obvious in their shoulders. She turned and picked her way behind Gael.

She reached to touch him but he shifted away, his shoulder jerking forward. "Leave me be, Alaysha," he said.

"I won't. You're hurt."

"Then send the shaman to tend to me." He stomped a few paces farther, forcing her to step over a fallen tree to get to him.

"Gael?"

The full moon had tucked itself into black clouds, but

it was light enough for her to see his face when he spun back to her. He was closer than she thought and his voice sailed over her head. "I told you to go away."

"No." She didn't understand the coldness in his tone. "You need to rest, to eat. You're still not fully healed."

"I'm as healed is I need to be."

This time when she touched what she thought was his chest, she heard his sharp intake of breath. He gave an audible swallow, then his voice, like grit in his throat. "Leave me alone, Alaysha. Go back to your pup."

The hulking shadow settled down next to the tree. There was a dark movement as though he was pulling his cloak over his head and then all was quiet but for the sounds of bats clicking in search of a meal.

Alaysha picked her way through the darkness back to the fire, feeling confused and concerned. She could make out Bodicca's form hunched next to Theron, mumbling over Cai's upturned face as the komandiri sat against a tree.

"Broken," Bodicca said. "Can you see out of the eye, Komandiri?"

Cai cursed loudly as Theron prodded about, but Alaysha was certain it wasn't because of the pain he might be inflicting on her cheekbone.

"He's quick, isn't he?" Alaysha asked.

"And brutishly strong," Yenic added. He rubbed at his shoulders as though yanking Gael off Cai had torn tissues beneath.

"Imagine the warrior when his strength is returned," Theron said, and Cai swatted the two of them away.

"He is freakish," she said, but Alaysha thought she detected a smile in her tone. A niggle of sadism streaked through Alaysha that she wanted to set free.

"So," she said. "Can you see out of the eye?" It had been a wallop of a punch, aimed at a fellow fighter, not a woman, and Gael had held nothing back.

Cai stood next to the fire and stretched, making a great show of disdain over her own discomfort. "No doubt our Alkaia lends him her strength through her mark." She said it almost as though she was impressed, but Alaysha knew better by now.

"Might your Alkaia have been a bit mad?" she asked a little too sweetly.

Cai didn't take the bait, rather treated the question with all seriousness. "Uta thought her mad, certainly, for choosing exile over her sword sisters. All for a man. But no. I don't think her mad."

Bodicca squatted again next to the fire and poked at it. "She was a komandiri to the last," she said, and Theron made a small sound in his throat that stole Alaysha's attention.

"What was she like, Theron?"

He shook his head, refusing to engage in the conversation.

"My father's mother," Alaysha said, testing the statement to her ears.

"Madre," Bodicca said. "Our word for mother."

"Men don't have a madre," Cai said.

"No," Bodicca agreed and passed Alaysha the poker. "Your father knew he had no such claim to her, but the infant--"

"Ellison," Theron interjected.

Bodicca looked at him thoughtfully. "Ellison might have, had she lived to watch him grow." Bodicca said. "As it was she died true Enyalia even in exile."

Cai shifted as she sat, letting one long leg snake over

top one crossed. "Sword in hand?" She asked.

Bodicca nodded. "Even when the red grin stretched across her neck. We had to pry it from her afterwards."

Alaysha understood their sense of pride; a warrior caste such as these women wouldn't want to die of old, doddering age. But she didn't understand how loving a male of any age could make her less a woman, less fierce. "One would think," she said. "That a true warrior wouldn't be afraid of a small infant in the first place."

Cai's foot moved across the leaf litter, but she said nothing. Instead, she sighed audibly. Alaysha hadn't forgotten the warrior sitting alone in the woods, his cloak over his head, not for an instant. "I would think a warrior such as an Enyalian wouldn't have to drug a man--"

Cai sent a glance Yenic's way. "You gave my sisters quite a fight when you came, but did we resort to drugs to keep you docile?"

Yenic looked at his feet. "I had other things to take my mind."

Cai shifted closer to Alaysha, so close her booted foot nearly crushed Alaysha's bare toe. "It's your large one you ask for, I know. But I tell you the only drugs Thera used were to keep his body quiet during his repair. The rest--I'm afraid would have all depended on my sisters."

Alaysha didn't want to hear anymore. She didn't want to have to think about any woman equally as large as the Enyalian leader settling into bed with Gael, touching him. Rousing him from a wounded sleep.

"I'm tired," she said. "Someone needs to take watch."

"I'll do it," Bodicca said. "I find pain a remarkable antidote for weariness."

Alaysha moved back into her furs and stretched out.

Someone tapped her shoulder and she turned to see Yenic slipping in behind her. He curled around her without a word, pulling her close. His warmth felt right next to hers, the comfort it gave to have another body next to hers helped her eyelids ease closed.

Dawn hadn't yet courted the tree line when Alaysha heard it. Her eyes flew open but she kept her body still, not moving, not shifting or breathing. She could tell by Yenic's arms around her midsection that he heard it too, and like her, he pretended he was asleep. The forest clung to a wet mist, even in the quiet gloom of predawn, a figure would have thickened into a great hulking shape if it tried to move through the wide swath of mist, but still Alaysha knew something was out there.

Bodicca and Cai thought so, too. Neither's eyes were open, but each had tightened grip on their blades. Cai was sitting frozen next to a tree, the obvious lookout for the early morning, a woman who, for all intents and purposes, appeared to have fallen asleep.

It would fool many invaders, but not Alaysha. The warrior looked entirely too comfortable and the woman never looked comfortable.

They came even as Alaysha was contemplating whether Theron understood they would soon be under attack.

One moment there was nothing but mist, the next a savage looking man appeared directly in front of her, his muscled legs springing from a squat as he landed to a full-on run in her direction. There were dozens of them: all-male, all slick with mud, twigs, and branches and leaves in their hair, streaks of soot across their faces. Perfectly camouflaged for dropping out of trees and it was evident that's what they done. Half a dozen still were dropping.

Alaysha had time to bolt to her feet and dart sideways to avoid her attacker. He caught Yenic as he tried to gain speed and together they rolled across the forest floor, Yenic doing his best to avoid the blade in his attacker's hand.

The sound of metal striking metal met Alaysha's ears and she knew she had to get her sword. The man in front of her pulled an arrow from his quiver; Alaysha wasn't fool enough to believe he could use it at such close proximity. She made a lunge for him, thinking to put him off balance and sprint passed him. He held onto the arrow as though it was a blade, jabbing it into her forearm. She felt the bite between the bones and gasped. The arrow head must've been made of god's teeth it was so sharp. She caught the fury in his face as he pulled it out and made to stab again, this time aiming for her throat. His gaze touched for an instant on her chin and she took that moment to swipe with her good hand for the arrow. She grasped it above his grip and broke off the feather fletching, leaving the shaft with the arrowhead still in his hand. No good. She needed to get the black arrow tip away from him.

She would have ducked and swept his legs with her feet except a blow landed on her back stealing her air and dropping her knees from beneath her. Little gnat bites burned into her shoulders two it a time, and the sting went deep into her tissues. It reminded her of the oddly numb feeling in her side when Drahl had tried to kill her--not truly painful, not at least until she saw the blood running down her arms. She peered up to face her attacker, this time with the arrow ready to swipe across her throat.

All sound returned, and she heard her group fighting on despite being outnumbered. Her chest burned to release the power, even as she felt too weak to keep it at bay. She couldn't let loose. Not yet. They were still very much alive. She had to block out the emotion, use the flat heartlessness her father taught her.

She made to come up with fist aimed to block her attacker's swing, but even as she uncoiled the springs in her thigh muscles, the man's head disappeared from his shoulders and his torso fell sideways in a heap.

"Move, Alaysha," Gael ordered and turned to engage yet another attacker. Beyond him, two handfuls of invaders in similar states were all around her. He finished with one and stormed toward where Bodicca was cutting an equally fierce swath around Theron. They all appeared ferocious and vigorous in their battle, but the subtleties were different; Alaysha could detect the slight hesitations in the movements, the heaving chests from effort, the slight sway to their stance. They still battled the invisible enemy of fatigue and recovery from the earlier attack and to her, it showed.

Alaysha searched for Yenic who was grinning madly as he set fires around the feet of his attackers. She found herself wondering how he could wield such power at all, knowing to do so would take an amount of blood. Then she saw him holding onto his side, and his fingers oozed with red. She looked at her own hands, covered in her own blood, swept a glance at Bodicca and Theron and Cai. Blood was to be found in abundance.

But they were winning. At least it appeared so. Cai was chuckling with each man she felled. She barely moved as they came at her from all sides, and each time she did move, it was with such economy Alaysha knew was calculated by the perfect harmony of her senses.

It was time to dart for her pack and pull her sword. Alaysha lost all sense as she spun to meet one, two, three attackers. She sent her whole body into the swings, slicing into their stomachs, then she flung herself past them to where Gael had engaged two of the burliest.

There was something familiar about the way these men moved, the way they herded themselves into battle: without thought, as though fighting was one more chore they had to complete for the day before they settled in to their beds. They seemed almost slave like. Even so, they owned a strange sort of fierceness. Savage. Her father would've used such a crew wisely, she thought and realized the truth of it as it entered her mind.

Her father had used them--or some of them. She thought of the word Cai used to describe them.

"Highlanders," she said. The tribe of people who were fierce at heart, but who did everything they worked at stolidly, like oxen. Edulph's clan.

She stepped forward, hefting her sword and taking aim at the closest of Gael's attackers. He too fell into a heap, his head lolling to one side, cut, but not severed. She didn't have the strength for that.

She knew the battle was dying around her. There were far less noises. Gael sent his last attacker to his knees, but spared him the final blow. Instead, he pressed the man's face down in the blood-soaked moss.

Alaysha couldn't help smiling at him and pointed at the man she'd slain. "I returned the favor."

His face when it turned on her was cold. "One man is equal to a dozen, witch? You're cheap with your favor, it seems." He glared down at the recumbent man. "You'll wish for your death when I hand you over to the Enyalian." Gael didn't look up, but Alaysha knew his next words were for her nonetheless.

"Have the shaman tend to you. You look like you're ready to faint, and I'd rather not shrivel into a husk because you have no control over your power."

It hurt. He had to know it did, and she didn't understand how he could save her life one moment and cause her pain the next. She turned to see where Theron was and noticed him tending to Bodicca's back. It appeared to have split again in spots. Alaysha staggered forward, feeling her strength waning. Yenic came up beside her and she reached for him, thankful to have the support. She'd expected Cai's people to come for them; this attack was a complete surprise.

"Are you hurt?" She managed to get out.

He twisted her around so he could look at her face, and in another moment, she felt his palm press against her belly. "It's not as bad as all the blood seems," he said, lifting her into his arms.

"Are you hurt, Yenic?" she asked him again, fighting the desire to lay her head against his chest. A full night of sleep and she was still exhausted. Now what had this battle done for her stamina, she'd not know. "Tell me, Yenic," she pressed, thinking he had to be hurt because he wouldn't look her in the eye.

"Yenic."

"No," he said, striding to where Theron was busy digging roots from the dirt and stuffing them into a strip of leather. He patched up Bodicca's back again with strips of linen he must have stored away from Sarum.

Not hurt. Good. Alaysha curled an arm around Yenic's neck, holding on as he squatted to ease her onto the Moss. Theron swiped his hands on his cassock and edged closer, poking at the wound in her forearm.

"It's clean," he murmured. "Straight between the

bones." He inspected her shoulders, where the gnat bites stung. "The witch's back is the same. Already knitting back together. Such clean wounds, no tearing. The young witch was never good at healing, but today she has been given a gift."

"Is it bad?" Yenic asked and Theron shook his head. "The blood would still be flowing freely if it was. Oh, yes. But we should clean it." His eyes flicked over Yenic. "And yours too."

"Her first." Yenic ran his hand over Alaysha's hair and offered her a short, encouraging smile. "She nearly passed out."

Theron hummed and thought. "We see. Oh, yes. We have seen it before." He peered down at her. "How long has the power been draining you?"

She eased her eyes closed because it was easier to speak the truth without looking at anyone.

"Always," she admitted. "But never like this."

"Yes, oh yes," he said. "Not something a witch wants anyone to know. We understand. The stronger the power, the more it uses of you. And it is very strong in this witch. Your father knew it, planned for it, but he wouldn't know its cost, would he?"

Alaysha shook her head. That Yuri had engineered her strength by killing her mother and grandmother simultaneously when she was born was not news to her now, but she'd never truly understood why. The discovery of how she'd come into so much power had sent her searching for his blood when she discovered it, but when Aislin had killed him instead, Alaysha suffered too much emotional conflict to give it more consideration. It was one more thing that she slammed down into the dungeon of her memory, hoping to never have to think about it again.

"The power grows, Theron," she said cautiously, opening her eyes to study his reaction.

"As it should. It needs to mature." He poured water over a piece of his cassock he had ripped free and wiped his hands clean it. "The young witch must find a way to ground it, to stretch it past her own breath or when its fullness comes, as indeed will, it will use her up. Yes. Oh yes, yes."

"She needs an Arm," Yenic said. "But how, here with nothing."

Theron's face split into a happy grin. "Warriors think little of shamans, yes they do. So little they go unnoticed right in their own eyesight." He chuckled and Yenic glared at him.

"This isn't the time for foolishness, Theron. We need her mother's ashes and then we need a good candidate. We're lacking both."

"We lack nothing. We have something better. Yes. Oh, yes, we do."

Alaysha was about to ask when her peripheral vision caught Cai stooping over one of the felled attackers. She watched as the woman rammed the butt of her blade against the man's open mouth and extracted several bloody teeth, weighed them thoughtfully in her palm and then dropped them into an already large pile. Alaysha couldn't help the revulsion she felt, and both Theron and Yenic followed her gaze.

Yenic let out a sound of disgust and hearing it, Cai turned. A fiery brow quirked and she shrugged. "I feel naked; a bit of filmy gauze is better than nothing."

Alaysha felt a shudder pass through her, but she wasn't entirely sure with the chill of early morning. Theron ran his palm over her shoulders, much the same as he had to Bodicca in the burnt lands. "She is fierce, that one." His voice held a note of question.

"No," Alaysha said.

"Then who?" Yenic asked and she heard the dread in his voice. She thought it might be because he knew what it meant to be an Arm, the weight of it, but she suspected the real truth.

"Not Gael either," she said, hoping to ease his worry.

"Either warrior would die for a witch," Theron said. "And you can't find a better Arm than that. It must be one of them."

She thought of being tied to Cai for the rest of her days, then imagined it with Gael, knowing how conflicting it would be for him when she was also bound to Yenic and how much the two men hated each other. The price would be too high for all of them.

"Gael has already suffered too much," she said and heard Yenic's relieved exhale.

Theron sighed. "The witch is a foolish one. There isn't a better choice, oh no. And there isn't time either."

Alaysha tried to sit up, fighting the wall of black that weakened her vision. She waited, letting it pass, and watched as both Cai and Bodicca picked a specific dead man one after the other and cracked into their mouths to extract trophies. She noticed Gael, on his side of the clearing trussing the last living attacker and hefting him against a tree. He was breathing hard, she could tell even from the distance, and she knew it was because he still wasn't fully recovered. He never so much as sweat when he fought, and here he was fighting to stay on his feet.

They needed to eat to regain strength, and they needed rest. At least, they could manage one of those things.

They settled quietly, each with a meagre amount of

meat and nuts, chewing reflectively. Alaysha knew they were all surly, thinking the repast a foolish waste of time, but the bare truth of it was she didn't have the energy she needed even to climb atop Barruch and ride. She knew the others were equally spent. The Enyalia would come regardless and overtake them eventually. They would die if they weren't fit enough to face them. The few moments wouldn't matter unless they were used to refuel.

She could already feel the energy creeping into her extremities as she chewed a piece of apple. When she looked around at the group and saw the strained looks fading, she knew she'd made the right decision. Her eyes were drawn to the captive repeatedly, and she caught him staring at her.

"Why did you attack us?" she asked and Gael harrumphed around a mouthful of salted pheasant that Cai had in her tackle.

"I already tried to beat that out of him."

"Foolish man," Cai said, rolling her eyes. Bodicca murmured her agreement.

"What would a fearless Enyalian have done," he demanded.

She shrugged, "Killed him. Why would I care why he attacked, only that he attacked."

"It doesn't matter," Alaysha said. "He's alive. We might as well ask." She turned to him again. "You heard the Enyalian. She would have you dead."

The man blinked but said nothing. Alaysha pressed on, "You see those two stringing your comrade's teeth, would you like to rattle about their thighs with them?"

He spit a gob of blood on the ground in front of his feet.

Alaysha sighed, "I suppose why he attacked doesn't

matter. We'll head on and leave him for your sisters."

She got up and stretched. She did feel better now she'd eaten. Her shoulders still hurt, but like Theron said, the wounds would heal. The others too.

"It's time to go, I think," she said and collected her sword and bedroll. She heard the others doing the same. Both Cai and Bodicca dropped the teeth they'd collected into pouches tied to their waists. No doubt by nightfall the women would have full circlets around their forearms and would feel a little less naked. Alaysha scanned the area, smelling now the stink of the dead that littered the forest floor. The wolves and crows and other beasts would come soon to feast and would no doubt pick the bound man to death. He must know it, and still he said nothing.

She and Theron sat Barruch while Bodicca tried to get Gael to sit Cai's beast with her. The massive man refused and Bodicca leapt up to sit with Cai saying it was just as well--a man had no place on a beast unless it was as a body from a solstice raid.

It sounded like an intentional dig to Alaysha but she noticed that although the warrior clenched his jaw, he said nothing in counter.

"Where to?" Alaysha asked.

Cai spoke with an offhand shrug and nodded toward the dead. "The vermin come from the highlands. Best we not go there."

"Foolish woman," growled out Gael, "That's exactly where we should head."

"Foolish man. My sisters, those who are sent to kill us, will most assuredly be on their way to the highlands. They won't let this go unavenged." She smiled almost nostalgically, "We've not seen a decent war in many seasons."

The man stirred in his bindings.

"Having second thoughts?" Alaysha asked him. Cai had seen no reason to gag him, saying casually that his cries would only bring Enyalia or wolves to his aid.

"We were only one group of many," he said and Alaysha stepped closer.

"Tell me, and I'll loose you."

Cai and Bodicca both protested, but Alaysha silenced them with a glare. She prodded the man with her toe.

"A dozen ambushes, set a day away from the Enyalian village in every direction."

"What for?"

"To wait in case the young one didn't succeed."

Alaysha could feel the hairs rise on her arm. "The young one?"

"Yes. She and her father. Gone to kill as many as they could."

There was no sound to give Alaysha warning, but Cai was next to her in a heartbeat, her face leaning in to the captive, her blade pressed against his throat. "You highlanders forget yourselves."

No fear sat in the man's eye as he responded, and Alaysha's back tingled. "No. We are only just remembering, Enyalian."

"Cai." Alaysha put her hand on the woman's wrist and noted that the blade had pressed far enough into his skin that the folds neatly met over it. "Cai, it doesn't matter."

Green eyes met hers. "It's the only thing that matters."

"Not anymore. Why isn't important." She turned back to the man. "Where are they now, this young one and her father."

He glared at her. "If you're here, filthy Enyalian witch,

then they are dead."

Alaysha pulled back and studied his face, keeping her palm on Cai's forearm. She chewed her lip and noticed Cai tapping her own arm as she too gave the man study. It was obvious he knew little except to guard the escape routes and nothing more. It was also obvious he'd never visited Enyalia, but had heard about Thera and her tattaus. He thought he had the two powerful leaders just within his grasp. That must have been the reason for the attack.

"What if I told you we spared their lives only to be betrayed as they escaped?"

"I'd know you are lying. No Enyalian has such pity."

Alaysha could feel the tension in the woman beside her as she spoke. "What do you know about Enyalia, man?" Cai said. "The little your foolish mother weaned you upon wasn't even enough to fill a frog's tiny mind."

Alaysha squatted down to reach for the man's lashings. "You're wrong," she told him. "Enyalia respects a woman's power. The young one was spared because of it."

The man's eyes never left Alaysha's face, but they were suspicious and wary. "And the father?"

The twigs crackled from somewhere behind her and Alaysha knew it couldn't be from any of her mounted people. She and Cai spun at the same instant to see a horde of men thickening the trees, bows drawn, swords drawn, blades drawn. At the head of the throng stood Aedus, a look of surprised pleasure on her face, and next to her, holding a limp and tender looking toddler's blonde curls draped over his arm, stood Edulph.

Chapter 25

"It was you," Alaysha breathed and he nodded. His face was haggard looking, his eyes swollen and red-rimmed. Aedus would've darted forward, but Cai had pulled her sword from her back and with a blade on her other, was already poised to advance. Aedus was smart enough to speak before making a move.

"We came for you," she said. "I told you I could help."

"You nearly killed us, little one," Gael's voice, closer. He'd snuck over unnoticed and stood on Alaysha's right.

Aedus fleeted a gaze to her brother. "We didn't mean to," she said, and Edulph hung his head. It was obvious he'd tricked his sister yet again.

"She won't wake," he mumbled and the sob in his voice revealed more than Alaysha expected.

"You're her father?" She said.

Aedus answered. "We didn't think she had that much magic. We thought she'd steal enough air that we could get in and rescue you." She looked at everyone but Cai. "All of you."

Aedus might believe such a gallant thing of her brother, but Alaysha didn't. "You knew how powerful she was," she said to him. "You would have had to know. Did you kill her mother, Edulph? Did you take her life as she birthed this weapon for you?" His disappearance all those weeks ago from Sarum before Aislin and Yenic captured him, not enough to count for a gestation period, but enough to return to kill the mother, knowing Alaysha had rid the world of the grandmother.

"Look at him," Yenic said, coming up behind her. "He grieves, Alaysha." He sounded amazed that the man could be sad.

Thankfully, Cai remained unmoved. "Answer her, man."

Edulph bent to lay his burden on the moss. "She breathes," he said. "But she will not wake."

"Did you kill her mother?" Alaysha refused to look at the child, afraid she'd soften. "All along, you've known where this girl was. We knew you wanted her. We knew you wanted to use her. You couldn't use the mother, so you murdered her. Now you have but a small thing to control."

She could see his chest moving, watch the bloodshot gaze harden then send a fury of wrinkles into his brow line. Still, she couldn't expect his sudden primal shriek, or the speed he turned and grabbed the sword from a fellow. He lunged forward, shouting, his face a mask of pain and rage. He swung at the same time as he halted, just in front of Alaysha, his blade neck height.

She dropped to her knees, catching her breath. Metal ground against metal. Both Cai's and Gael's swords met Edulph's, holding it captive between them.

But it was Cai who kicked Edulph's feet from beneath him and sent her blade lunging for his throat. He lay on his back, eyes gawking, chest rising and falling. Gael neatly swept his blade against Cai's, diverting it at the last moment.

"The girl," Gael said and nodded at Aedus who was biting her fingers.

His death averted, Edulph sobbed and rolled onto his side, curling his knees into his abdomen.

No one knew how to react until Theron made his way over to the child and began probing through her hair with deft fingers.

"Swollen, yes. Yes." He laid an ear on her chest. "Losing her air, faltering heart."

Edulph sobbed harder and Cai kicked at him with her booted toe. "She'll live, man." She said.

"Perhaps not," Theron said.

Cai sent a scathing look toward Gael as a way of responding to the shaman's declaration. "This one lived." She looked as though she wished it wasn't true.

Theron scrabbled about like a crab, testing for other injuries. "That one is impossible to kill; oh yes. This one is like air, she's so weak."

Aedus knelt next to Theron. "You have to help her," she said and he smiled at her.

"This shaman knows a few tricks still. Indeed, yes we do."

"I can help," she said and Alaysha's heart ached to see the maturity in the girl's face. It was almost too much until she recalled a time when she was similarly hurt and unconscious. When she'd come too, she'd been afraid, but in control enough to put a short, tenuous leash on her power. Would this small child be aware enough to do the same? Alaysha watched Aedus and Theron together and realized they could all be in danger if the child lacked even the small amount of control that Alaysha had.

She knelt next to Aedus and put an arm around her. "She's lucky to have a blood witch like you."

Aedus swiped at her cheeks and worked to keep her lip from trembling. Alaysha smiled at her. "My own blood witch was my nohma. It's a sacred thing. Your niece couldn't have asked for better."

Theron took Aedus's hand and placed it beneath the child's head. "Feel the lump? She swells there."

Alaysha watched Aedus nod and caught Theron's eye from beside the bent head. He would do what he could for the girl for now and hope Aedus's blood would be enough to keep the girl calm, and him safe if she lived. Alaysha wished she had the right words to say, but all that ran through her mind was that she'd harmed the girl's niece. Aedus was too grief stricken at the moment to remember or realize it, but soon she would.

She turned and faced the horde Edulph had brought. "Collect yourselves and run. If the girl lives, she may well steal all your air before she knows what she's doing. None but her father and this girl are safe."

Several of them sheathed the swords they still held aloft, but many more refused to move. Alaysha motioned to Yenic to hoist Edulph onto Barruch and as he strode over, Edulph rolled onto his back, staring up at the canopy.

"Edulph," she said. "Theron will do what he can, but your men are in danger."

"You're all in danger," he said glumly.

"You and Aedus are safe as you well know," she said. "You can stay, but if your men--"

"Go," he said, waving a limp hand at the group. "Let them take you to the village. If she lives, you live."

Cai snorted. "That's a hollow threat, man. You see the might we wield, the witch we own."

Edulph's head rolled to its side. "Your witch is useless," he said, taking in Alaysha as she stroked Aedus's mud-slicked hair. "As long as you are all with her, she's as good as--"

Bitter fury roared through Alaysha for all she knew of this horrible man and she wanted to strike him. "You're no better than Yuri, using your own daughter for your own gain, forcing her to kill so you can feel some sort of weak power. Have you thought of how much she'll hate you when she's grown? Have you thought what it will do to her, all this killing?"

He curled tighter into his ball, facing the sky again, his arms pulled into his chest. "You know nothing, you stupid witch."

Yenic motioned to Cai for help lifting the man, but Alaysha stopped him. "Leave him," she said. "We'll follow him to their village until Theron can meet us. It will get us out of these woods and away from the stink of trees.

She heard Cai chuckle. "You've never been to the Highlands, then, have you, little maga?"

Alaysha brushed leaf litter from her knees and scanned the troops. "No."

The men had swollen in number, their ranks coming from all of the ambush sites, no doubt. They looked restless and uncertain.

"How far is it?" she asked.

"About a handful of sunsets north." Cai collected her packs and threw them onto her beast. "Then the trees get taller and thicker. Seven more from there until we reach the border." She threw a glance over her shoulder to where Theron had begun sharpening his blade. "He may need some of Meroshi's beetle, eh, little one?" She said this to Aedus and swiped at her neck almost absently, but with a purpose that made Aedus's eyes light up. The girl colored tellingly and then nodded. So Cai had seen the purple stain when Aedus had shot her in the glade and had known exactly what it meant.

"Keep her under," Cai told Theron. "If she seems afraid when she wakes, have the little one use one of her quills."

Alaysha turned again to where Edulph was lying, staring blankly at the sky. It was entirely too contrived. Even if she left with Cai and Gael, would Edulph find a reason to harm Theron or Aedus?

She recalled Yenic's plea that she had to trust someone sometime, thought of her father's teachings to feel for no one, trust no one. She stole a glance at the child with the honey hair, her fat legs lying still, knowing that small thing could take each one of their lives as easily as she breathed.

The decision was easy after that.

"Today is not the time for trust," she said to herself and strode over to where Edulph lay. His eyes followed her keenly.

"Get up," she told him, kicking at his shin. "Your daughter needs you."

"Leave him," Cai said and Alaysha kicked Edulph again, ignoring her.

"Get up, I said," this time she reached down and slapped him hard across the face. His eyes held steel, cold and sharp when he looked at her. "You have things to do while Aedus gathers her beetles."

"Alaysha," Yenic said.

She held up her hand. "You all go. Get to a safe distance. I'll stay here." She watched Aedus ease to her feet. "Find enough to keep her quiet, Aedus," Alaysha told her with a sick feeling she knew exactly why Theron was sharpening his blade so intently. She stole a peek at Gael, and she thought of the bandaged hole Thera had put in the back of his skull. Now, standing in the middle of the woods, hearing the metallic scrape of steel against rock, Alaysha realized why she had drugged him to unconsciousness and in the moment was incredibly grateful to the bone witch.

She felt Yenic's hand on the small of her back. "If you stay, I stay," he said.

"You can't," she told him. "Theron is taking a huge

risk and if she comes to and is frightened, he'll need me to fight back for him."

"If you can," he said and she read the anxiety in his voice. She knew where it came from.

"I managed it before."

"At great cost," he said. "I'm staying."

Theron thumbed the edge of the blade and mumbled in disappointment. Alaysha took it from him and tested its sharpness for herself. "Seems pretty sharp," she said but he only shook his head.

"We need much speed on the edge," he told her and spit on the whetstone in disgust. He reached again for the girl, smoothing her hair and leaning in to test her breathing. "We could lose this little temptress," he said.

Edulph made a sound that surprised Alaysha. It could have been fear, but she couldn't be sure. When she turned to look at him, both Cai and Gael had stepped into place, blocking a now standing Edulph from going near Alaysha. His face was streaked with mud but had a determined look. He pulled a blade from his side that was more black than steel, translucent, with an edge that seemed so thin it couldn't possibly act as anything remotely dangerous.

Cai had him by the wrist in less time than it took Alaysha to draw breath. She heard a crack and Edulph groaned in evident pain. "You should be dead by now, man," Cai told him.

"It's for the shaman," Edulph gasped out. "The edge is sharper than anything you've seen. Take it."

Cai's narrowed gaze didn't drop from Edulph as she took the blade. "I wouldn't have needed your leave to do so, man," she said and in a flash, she'd drawn the edge against his cheek, leaving a streak of blood that welled blood. He gasped, but he didn't pull away. She leaned in and inspected the wounds. "Barely split the skin." She passed the blade to Gael who took it carefully. "Don't worry, man," she told Gael, "if you hurt yourself with it, we'll see Thera finds you to patch you up again."

He glowered at her but passed it to Theron who seemed very pleased indeed. He poured water over the edge, washing Edulph's blood away. He would need to be quick. They were running out of time.

Alaysha faced Edulph. "Tell them to go," she said. "My friends will leave too. It'll just be us: you, me, Theron, and Aedus with the girl. And if you're somehow tricking me," Alaysha crossed her arms. "I will kill you."

"And I you, stupid witch," he said making both Cai and Gael shuffle threateningly. Edulph held his hands up in surrender. "You expect me to trust her? With the shaman, alone with my daughter? You think I'm a fool?"

"We know all too well what you are," Yenic said. "We're not leaving Alaysha or Aedus or Theron alone with you."

Alaysha groaned. "There's no more time for this. You have to gain some distance. Go. Please."

None but the last of Edulph's men scrambled past them, disappearing into the trees. She sighed heavily and sent Aedus into the woods; Gael followed her, mumbling something about wanting to see the nasty sleepers with his own eyes.

Theron hefted the girl into his arms. The poor thing's legs hung feebly over his elbow. "We need to sturdy this small one." He cast about for volunteers, but no one seemed up to the task of holding the frail thing while the shaman cut into her skull.

Alaysha noticed that Edulph's face had gone the shade of new bone.

"I'll do it," she told the shaman and could swear she heard audible exhales from everyone present.

She knelt in front of him, working her knees into a bunch of Moss all the better to cradle her bones when the going got tough as it undoubtedly would.

"This shaman would have used the ghost pipe," Theron told her, nodding toward a small patch of translucent plants that hung over at the top in a U. "Very potent mixture for stealing one's awareness. Too good."

Alaysha knew he'd stuffed some into his pouch, roots and all, but she kept herself from looking at it. "Sometimes they don't wake again?" She guessed.

In answer he took the care to lay the child over Alaysha's lap facedown so that her head hung over just a bit. "We haven't the time to measure correctly or prepare. This young one might well sleep the long sleep from haste if he used too much of the ghost pipe. Yes, yes, oh yes."

"Best we leave it to Aedus, then." Whatever the consequences would be should the child live, would be nothing compared to those if she died. It made Alaysha keenly aware of her own mortality and its effects if she died without a daughter to pass the power to. She couldn't stop herself from running her palm across the child's back, comforting her, wanting desperately to hold her tightly.

"We need to start, oh yes."

Alaysha's heart pounded as she watched Theron part the girl's hair. "Now?" She said and he met her gaze with black determination.

"Can this witch not sense the girl's departure? We have to start now."

Edulph groaned from behind her. "Do something."

Theron remained calm. "We are not as skilled at this as we should like."

"Theron?" Alaysha said. "Are you sure this is right?" She eyed the black edge with anxiety. It had scored Edulph so neatly that the folds of flesh knit back together perfectly within seconds. That meant it was terrifyingly sharp.

"Listen, little witch," he said and put her palm on the girl's back. "Listen with your hands."

Alaysha felt that, the rise, the halt, and the long pause of the girl's lungs. Beneath just the spine, there was a chill waiting, one that made Alaysha's mouth go dry. She dug deeper into the Moss with her knees.

"Do it, Theron," she said. "We haven't much time."

To his credit, the shaman kept his hand steady, his movements were deliberate, not rushed or hasty. First he shaved a square away in the blonde locks. They fell to the Moss like petals from a bloom. "We shall cut here," he said, pointing to the top of her head. "No doubt the bones still knit together and so it will be softer, yes yes. Easier on the poor thing--less of an insult."

The blade brought blood against the white scalp, and Alaysha knew from experience it would be lots of blood, enough to make Edulph sob and stumble to a nearby tree, his fist in his mouth, the other hand cradled against his shoulder. When the skin lifted away, the blade dug into the bone, and the sound of the scraping black edge against brittle bone, sent Yenic to join him. Alaysha could hear his retching and her stomach tried to rebel until she heard Cai complaining about the weakness of men.

Theron had two lines drawn into the skull and Alaysha was beginning to believe they could manage it. She kept reminding herself to breathe. Then she felt the girl's limbs twitch against her thighs. Theron must have noticed it too--his blade paused, his one hand filled with his cassock to sop up the blood, the other pressed into the corner, ready to etch another line. He said nothing but his black eyes were all pupil, making them seem an endless pit of terror.

A movement came from Alaysha's lap, muffled by pain and confusion but most definitely a child's sound.

Even Yenic stopped retching at the noise. Cai stepped closer, her arm raised above Alaysha and it was only when the child twitched again, her whole body bucking upward, that Alaysha realized Cai's arm was filled with the handle of her blade. The Enyalian planned to strike the girl as she woke.

And she was most definitely waking.

Chapter 26

The next few moments passed in a blur. Alaysha heard a sound like a shout, but it wasn't the noise that made her cringe, expecting pain or breathlessness. It was the feeling of having a massive weight fall against her back and the feeling that if she gave in to the heaviness of it, she crushed the frail body that was even now coming to and squirming in confusion. Moments more and the child would know the pain she felt. Would know it and strike out against it in the only way she knew. Another shout came, even as she had the fleeting thought that she'd have to unleash her power and that this release would surely kill them all. This shout sounded like Gael. If only she could wrest herself from beneath the heavy form, she could hear better. And it was a form, she realized now. Cai's body atop Alaysha's shoulders, her sword dropped on the ground. Were they under attack? What was all the shouting? She tried to find Theron who should have been right there in front of her. She worked to make sense of it when the girl's moaning grew louder, turning to a stifled sob. Oh, dear deities. It would be soon. If it hadn't started already--maybe that was why Cai had fallen onto her, maybe--

Then she felt the weight ease and the shouting clarify. Aedus and Gael both yelling at her to move. Theron at her side, pulling the Enyalian by her feet to the ground. Aedus slipped in and blew a Quill into the child's neck.

The squirming halted.

"My hero," she said to Aedus, smiling, and the girl wiped muddy locks away from a harried face. Gael stood next to her, holding a handful of blackish beetles. His palm was stained purple.

"Save me a few quills," he told the girl. "I think I

found a way out of listening to that brute's infuriating pomposity."

"Such words," Alaysha said, relieved to see them both. She lifted the girl back onto her lap. "How close, Theron?"

The shaman's eyes were glassy with exhaustion. "Soon," he said and then bent again to his task.

"We'll need to cover the hole once he's done," Alaysha said, thinking about the hunk of bone that they cut and that they could never thread back into place. It was a small square but still, it would need protection.

Aedus peered over Alaysha's shoulder. "We could wrap a gourd over it, or a nut casing."

"The young one would make a good shaman," Theron mumbled. "Find one of these--not too round." He was on his last cut, the black edge was indeed terrifyingly sharp but it was more brittle than steel.

"We'll need Aedus near when you're done, so she wakes to a familiar face."

"She won't be waking," Theron said and Alaysha heard Edulph curse. The shaman ignored the nasty things Edulph called him. "This little witch needs to stay asleep while she heals," he said.

"Stay asleep," Alaysha repeated. "So we'll need more of Aedus's beetles then."

"Just until this shaman can measure his ghost pipe roots." He put a critical finger on the girl's neck where the flesh rose and fell irregularly. "Far more predictable, when measured, than these beetles."

Alaysha felt the prickle of someone leaning over her shoulder, someone who smelled of onions and sweat.

"You're a lucky father," she told Edulph, not trying to disguise the coldness in her voice.

"She'll live?"

"She has a better chance now than before."

"No thanks to you."

"You shouldn't have attacked us."

"We were saving you."

She snorted. "Your rescue nearly killed us, but then you would have known that." She would never be convinced he wasn't using the child for his own means. "At any rate, she'll need to recover. And you'll need Theron. We're coming to your village." She had no intention of letting this small witch out of her sight now she'd found her.

Edulph said more, but Alaysha wasn't interested. Instead, she told him to sit down and when Theron had the girl safely wrapped, she eased out from beneath the small body and let Edulph take his turn holding her.

She caught sight of Gael edging his way toward the farthest tree. He looked weary and the bandage Thera had wound around his head showed red. When he leaned against the trunk, she could see his legs trembling and noticed that the tree he'd selected was a good distance off. While it was in good view of the group, it was well out of personal distance.

It was time she spoke to him. She brushed the leaf litter from her leggings and took a bracing breath.

"We'll need to set off soon," she told him when she got close enough. "Theron wants to get the girl back to her village while Aedus still has beetles enough to keep her asleep."

He eyed the spot where Cai was just coming to with a curse. He smiled, but said nothing. Alaysha reached out to touch his arm and he recoiled, electing to drop to his haunches and stare morosely ahead.

"Gael, please," she said, falling to a crouch beside him. It was the best way she could to look them in the eye. "I don't understand. Is it because of Yenic?"

Keeping his thighs from quaking proved to be too much, and he ended up sitting on the Moss, his legs outstretched.

"Is the she-beast coming with us?" he asked.

Alaysha followed his gaze to Cai's now standing form, glowering down at Edulph, her arms crossed, fingers tapping on her biceps. Alaysha didn't want to admit that they might need her. Especially not to Gael.

"For now," she said carefully. "Is she what's bothering you?"

"Alaysha," he said, and her heart sank. He never called her by her name, but always with the endearment that she'd come to enjoy from his lips. His hand covered hers where she'd placed it on his leg, and she thought for a moment that he would squeeze it. Then he plucked it off him and placed it delicately in her own lap

"I need you to leave me be," he said.

He might as well have slapped her. She was about to get up, to rush off in embarrassment but she heard the pain in his voice, disguised, yes, but there was pain in it if she listened.

"No," she told him.

He sighed in frustration and before he could speak again, she pressed on. "Where is the Gael of the burnt lands, the one who would swear to help me? Did I offend him somehow? Is it because we found Yenic, because you don't have to be a victim, Gael. I won't ask anything of you, if you need to leave because you hate him or hate him and me or hate me, I understand. Only, please don't keep me in the dark. Tell me what I've done so I can take my leave of you properly. You've been so good to me, Gael--so good for me. I couldn't bear it if I--"

"You did nothing, witch," he said and in his voice was a growl of anguish. He tried to get up, but seeing him struggle to do so, Alaysha leaned against him, hoping to put him off balance.

"Don't, Gael."

"I failed you, can't you see that?"

"Before? With the Highlanders? No. You're still ill--"

"No. With the Enyalia. In the village."

She thought of the fight with Enud and couldn't imagine why he thought she had been failed. "You were unconscious. I couldn't expect you to save me from Enud."

"No." He nearly bellowed, then lowered his voice when Cai turned around. "No," he said. He met her gaze with panic-stricken gray eyes. "I used you, witch. When they came. When I--" he swallowed convulsively, the cords of his throat working to plunge the Adam's apple down. "When they made me rise, I couldn't help myself, and so I used your image, the thought of you, your voice, your touch. I needed you with me in order to bear it, so I wouldn't feel like a weak woman under pillage." He squeezed his eyes closed. "Only now, I feel like a traitor because I used you so."

"But you're a man, surely you can't be forced."

His fingers raked through his hair and he laughed harshly. "You heard Cai before. A man is a man and our bodies are bodies. Can I stop my flesh from pimpling when it's cold?"

"Oh, I see," she said and for the first time realized why he felt so tortured. "But Gael, it doesn't matter to me."

He glowered at her. "It matters to me." He stabbed at his chest. "A warrior doesn't fear assault; that's a woman's fear." He ground his heel into his eye. "How could I stand it if I knew I was being taken so without my leave? And so I used you and it sickens me, both of those truths. I ache with disgust for using our one memory, for my weakness."

She knew better than to reach for him. He'd pulled his blade from its sheath and played at the edge. "Now any thought of you is tied to those beasts with tits and my own shame."

"I would have told you to use me, Gael," she whispered. "If I had known. If I couldn't save you and you needed me. I would have told you to use me."

She didn't know what else to say. There was entirely too much truth hanging in the air to pluck and process. She couldn't help him or heal him, but she could tell him her own truth.

"My memory of our night is sweet, and I carry it here." She grabbed his hand and pressed it against her chest so he could feel her heart beat. When he tried to pull it away, she held it there with both hands.

"You need to know that I cherish it," she said and he met her eye finally. The skin around his were red rimmed, his expression drawn. The fatigue showed in every muscle, the pain of his healing revealed its every twitch. But he, at least, looked at her. She thought she might have broken through, brought him back to the proud warrior he was, that she knew he was.

Then Cai's foot appeared in her peripheral vision and she knew also it appeared in Gael's. His face hardened and he yanked his hand away. The moment died and she doubted it could be re-exhumed. She gave the Enyalian her reluctant attention.

"Does the man need coddling," Cai asked. "Because the shaman of yours has finished with the child."

Even Alaysha detected the mockery in the woman's tone, but to Gael's credit, he didn't respond. He merely worked his way heavily to his feet, and swaying once, picked his way toward Aedus who was holding her niece's hand.

Alaysha saw Cai was again tapping her fingers against her arm.

"You shouldn't goad him, Cai," she said. "And these men are not mine. If you plan to stay with us, you'd do well to remember to be kind."

Cai's mouth twitched. "Why a woman puts such stock in men is beyond me. They're feeble-minded, cock-driven things with no real conscience." She gave her arm with its new circlet a shake and the teeth chattered. "You'd do well to put your trust in women."

"Women like you," Alaysha guessed and Cai squared her shoulders defensively.

"There are no other women like me."

Alaysha couldn't help but chuckle and patted the Enyalian's forearm, being careful to avoid the teeth and the bits of bloody gum that were still attached. "For once, we agree."

"Truly, though," the Enyalian said. "How do you think to proceed? Your large one is--"

"Not mine. Gael."

"*The* large one is unfit because he's not yet healed. This battle could have killed him. Your handsome one--"

"Yenic," Alaysha said patiently.

"*The* handsome one is too preoccupied with the way the large one steals looks at you, and the shaman is as cunning as a squirrel who forgot where he placed his seeds."

Alaysha sighed. Put like that, these men did sound like a bother. But she knew better.

"And Edulph--"

"You're crafty one--"

"That one is most definitely not mine," Alaysha argued and Cai's russet brow lifted in surprise.

"Well, he isn't. He isn't even ours."

"Even so, that one is as true as a lightning strike."

"What do you propose?" She asked, thinking as she did so that Cai already had a plan and that this preamble was nothing but formality. The Enyalian's heavy arm went around her shoulders and steered her farther into the brush. "Let me trail you, unseen, undetected. I can watch from a distance. If your crafty one--"

"Edulph."

"The others are nothing but sick puppies watching for the bitch, but that crafty one lies in wait. Perhaps, if he believes himself free of me, it won't take so long to discover what he's waiting for."

"And you won't have to be nice to the others if you're out of sight."

"I won't argue that I tire of being in such close company."

"I didn't think you'd ever tire of mocking them."

"You are intuitive, little maga." Cai smiled. "Must I admit to you that I tire of being kind for your sake?"

"You were being kind?"

She shrugged. "They live, do they not?"

Alaysha gave it thought and realized that for now she did want the woman with them. "I would like it very much if you stayed," she said. "But in the end, I have no hold over you. You are free to travel as you please."

The Enyalian stared at Alaysha, her fingers tapping against her thigh, the teeth encircling her forearm rattling softly. Before Alaysha realized what the woman was planning, she'd leaned down and covered her mouth with her own, a soft sigh brushing against her lips. Cai's hands gripped Alaysha's shoulders tenderly and squeezed gently, then she pulled back with shuddering breath, her eyes still closed, her expression melted into something Alaysha had never seen on the Enyalian's face.

"You have more power over me then a mere bit of magic, little maga," Cai whispered, and she turned, striding back toward the camp.

It was long moments before Alaysha recovered herself enough to return. She had no doubt that they would have all preferred to see the Enyalian depart--Gael especially. But it meant Alaysha had to be on her guard without her. With both Gael and Bodicca still recovering from their wounds, the only other true help she had would come from Yenic. Edulph would have to be under constant scrutiny. Theron and Aedus would be focused on the child. Seven more sunrises and several more till they reached the Highlands and then what? Better to have the Enyalian a present and visual danger to any who thought to come upon them.

They made camp again, several hours later, at a spot Edulph's men had occupied earlier. It was obvious from the still smouldering fire and the gourd of drawn water that someone had thought to leave nearby. Several flat rocks sat beside the fire, black with the charred remains of the last meal. Gael was already huffing from exertion and the girl had roused twice as she lay on Barruch's back. Barruch nicked Alaysha as she went by.

"I know, old man," she said, patting his nose. "I promised you a peach."

He whinnied softly and batted at her with his nose.

"Okay. I know," she said. "I promised many peaches." She let him graze the short clumps of weeds at the base of a tree.

They all needed a break and sat chewing a meagre fare of mashed nuts and dried apples steeped in water. Bodicca grumbled to herself and eventually went off into the woods, leaving them to stare each other in the hopes that she had gone off to forage. When she returned, it was with a pheasant, several varieties of mushrooms, and stalks of what smelled like wild onion. She breathed heavily and walked slowly, but it was apparent she was on the mend. By the time she had it stuffed and spitted over the fire, Alaysha's mouth was watering.

Without comment, Bodicca pulled the strips of fowl and passed them around to each. She gave Gael double what she gave Yenic, and Alaysha assumed she understood how much energy it took to heal. Gael bent his head to the fare silently and ate it without thanks.

Dusk crept on them and Alaysha looked around at her companions, assessing each's state of ability. With a sigh, she made a decision.

"I'll take watch," she said, half expecting Gael or Bodicca to argue, but it was Edulph spoke up.

"Why you? You could kill us in our sleep."

"I could have killed you long ago if that was my intent," she told him. "So could we all." She didn't lose sight of the fact that Cai was watching Edulph with a narrowed gaze.

Saying nothing more, Edulph put his hand out to the child and touched her lightly on the hair. Thankfully, she didn't rouse. So far, Aedus's beetles were doing their job well. Alaysha wondered how long it would be before the girl became used to them. She hoped it would work long enough for Theron to figure out how many of his more predictable ghost pipe roots it would take to keep the child sleeping. Edulph leaned over and kissed the child on the hair, eying Alaysha.

"That bit of benevolence was all because you needed to know what I know. Now you have it. I'm in danger unless I have more you need."

Yenic stood and stretched, more Alaysha thought to show Edulph the muscled litheness in his body, the strength beneath the evident fatigue. "We know nothing, Edulph, save that you sired this girl. You volunteer no more."

"Nor do you," Edulph returned slyly and Alaysha stole a glance at Aedus. So, the girl had told her brother of the mistrust Alaysha had for the man she was bound to. Cunning of him, to slip in the mistrust now. She had to remind herself of Edulph's method of operation. His own admission to her that what he lacked in fighting skills, he more than made up for in craftiness and that his craftiness would win every time.

"How did you come to escape the Enyalia, Edulph?" Alaysha asked.

He kissed the girl's hair.

"How did you come to find the girl?"

"I told you, any more information and you'll be done with me."

Cai's voice cut across the fire but with bland unemotional words. "I am done with you two sunrises ago." She smiled and Edulph squirmed.

"Even so," he said, nodding at Alaysha. "That one may have need of certain secrets."

"It's true that we all have our secrets," she said to him, but kept Aedus's eye across the firelight until the girl hung her head. "What we keep, we keep for self-preservation."

She turned to Theron. "But a time is coming when we will need to be honest with each other and let go the hidden pieces."

Theron shifted his weight and mumbled to himself. Alaysha chose to ignore it.

"Sleep," she said to everyone. "At first light we press on."

She got up and pulled the fur cloak from Barruch's pack and crept away from the fire so she could hear the noises of the forest over the crackling of wood. She found a place in good view and settled down with the cloak wrapped about her shoulders. She suspected Cai would pretend to sleep. Neither Gael nor Bodicca bothered to as much as lean against a tree trunk. Edulph, however, curled next to his daughter, snicking in close. Theron leaned against a tree. Aedus laid her head on her knees.

Some would sleep. Some would not. It was their decision. Yenic rose from his spot next to the fire and made his way to where she sat; Gael's eyes on his back the entire time.

"I wish Gael would sleep," she told Yenic when he settled next to her.

"He's stubborn. And it just might cost him."

"And what about you?"

"I can't let the fire catch me unaware. Best I'm away from it."

"Meaning you're afraid to stare into it."

"And I'd rather catch my rest next to you." He gave her a heart-stopping smile that made her open her cloak to let him in. The darkness, the chill, the scent of him, the fire, all reminded her of the time when they'd first met and none of this business had yet happened. But then, she'd still had been a killer. Her father's weapon, and she did as she was bid like any good warrior.

"What did the Enyalian want?" He asked and Alaysha

had to force herself not to look in the woman's direction.

"She was tired of being kind to men," she said truthfully.

"Have you given any thought to marking her?"

"Not really, no."

He put his arm around her and pulled her close. "You need an Arm, Alaysha."

"And you don't want it to be Gael."

"I don't want it to be any man."

"But Cai is as good as the man, just not without the worry," she guessed and he chuckled very low.

"I'm selfish. She's better than most men, so you'd be protected and well advised."

"And you needn't fear me succumbing to her charms."

"What charms," he laughed, then in further response he kissed her earlobe. "It's possible," he whispered. "You could succumb, but I don't think it likely, so I'm willing to risk it."

"Is it really that strong, then?"

"The connection is magnified, yes."

"But then, you and your mother..."

"That connection is paternal. She wants me even safer than she would have before."

"And you in reverse."

He paused a moment, thinking. "For me, it's complicated."

"How so?"

"She's the first woman I knew. Loved. She's very beautiful." Each sentence he spoke seemed to drag out, to take time to think over. She guessed there truly was more to it than he could explain.

"Indeed she's all of those things, and just as corrupt," she said in answer.

"I have no argument there."

"So this bond--"

"It draws us together in ways that are more powerful than the intimacy of coupling. What you feel, that desire to be closer, that primal need to be inside of each other, the ecstasy of coming close enough that you cry out in agony of never quite making it--that's the sense of it. Maybe not the desire, not for a parent and child, not always. But the drive is there."

"Have you and she--"

He answered quickly, almost shocked and ashamed. "No. Never. But I feel it, Alaysha. And you will too. So will Gael if you mark him."

She pulled his face closer so that she could lay her cheek on his. "I feel that way about you, despite all the mistrust and uncertainty."

His lips touched hers briefly. "Now you know why I'm so tortured. If you mark Gael, you'll understand it even more fully."

"Won't I feel it for Cai?"

"I can compete against a woman like you can compete against a mother."

It wasn't a real answer, but she thought she understood it all the same. "Assuming she agrees," she said of Cai.

"Oh. She'll agree. I can see it in her eyes, in her posture when she looks at you."

"Maybe I don't need an Arm."

"A witch was made to have an Arm and you're too powerful. Not having one might kill you."

"And then your mother will win."

"You don't understand what she wants. She wants you dead as much as Theron wants her dead."

"But Theron doesn't want her dead. He said--"

"He said we need to pull the god from her. I want that too."

The way he said it, the strangeness of his tone made her realize something. "You're afraid for her."

"Because she would pull the goddess from you."

"I'm not sure that's true. I don't feel like a goddess."

"My mother told me she remembered her birth and life before it. She told me that what she had wasn't a life. It was--different."

"I remember nothing. And what I do recall is too painful." She didn't want to admit that she forced everything she didn't like to think about into some dark recess of her memory never to be seen again.

"How do you know what Theron says isn't true, that you're Liliah in the flesh? My mother believes it. Her mother believed it." His voice choked.

"Your family," she said, realizing. "I took their lives. Your sister, your grandmother."

He gave her a squeeze. "You didn't. They sacrificed themselves. There's a difference."

"The question is what does Edulph know. That's why I held him under my mother's pretence. She tortured him for the information. He never gave it."

"Because the girl is his daughter and he loves her."

"Or, he still hopes to prevail against us. We'll see when we get to the Highlands, I suppose."

All this talk of secrets and honesty and here she was keeping something from Yenic that could make a difference in how he felt about her. It needed to see the light, finally.

"Yenic. I need to tell you something. I already have a connection to Gael."

His hand left her thigh and he tensed. "How close?"

"Close enough that I understand the drive you speak of."

She held her breath, waiting for his response, hoping she could weather it when it came. She couldn't justify it or try to explain it. A warrior made no such excuses.

"All the more reason to mark the Enyalian," he said softly and stood, taking great care to wrap her carefully back into her cloak.

"Go back to the fire, Alaysha, and rest. I'll never be able to sleep tonight. I might as well take watch."

Morning brought grumpy but better rested comrades. Alaysha hadn't slept as well as she'd hoped, Yenic's words crept through her thoughts most of the night. As they packed up camp, Gael fashioned a comfortable seat for the child that he could hoist over Cai's beast and eased her up behind Bodicca and in front of Theron. Alaysha discovered the best way to get Gael to sit Barruch was to offer him to Yenic. With a curse, the large warrior lifted Aedus onto the horse and sat behind her just so Yenic couldn't. She could tell from his expression that he realized his mistake even as he settled in.

That left Cai, Yenic, and Edulph to walk with Alaysha: the hardiest of the group, but all spent, even so. One night wasn't near enough rest to restore the energy they'd lost. She noticed that while Cai walked on the other side of Edulph, she adjusted the blade on her belt to rest just beneath her dominant hand. It seemed she trusted Edulph about as much as Alaysha did.

"Tell me, Edulph," Alaysha said. "How did you escape the raiding party?"

He gained some of his before-Sarum flair for commanding tone. "I waited till they thought me too exhausted to care, then I chopped off the hand of one when she came near me with food."

"That doesn't explain the others," Cai said and Alaysha heard the fury in the woman's voice.

He nodded to the child lying on the beast ahead. "They found me."

"Quite a coincidence," Alaysha said.

"She's remarkable." Edulph's steps lengthened as he worked to outpace them. Alaysha let him go.

"Do you believe it, Cai?"

"I believe only that men think they are too smart for any woman. We've proved them wrong too often."

"You think he's lying."

"Of course he's lying. But for what purpose?"

"Indeed," Alaysha said.

An entire fortnight: that was the length of time it took to gain the Highlands. By seven Sun cycles, the trees had thickened and not just in quantity, but in girth. At times, Alaysha played a game with Aedus to see how many sets of arms it took to encircle the biggest tree. By day ten, it took all of them to do so; by day twelve, there weren't enough of them to wrap around it.

Aedus and Gael did well keeping the toddler asleep, searching for beetles and mashing them down into the liquid it took to fill the quills. Theron tended her with a peculiar compassion that had Edulph hovering over him in a strange measure of respect. Both of them were silent as much as they were anything else. All of them were. The tension was a heartbeat Alaysha used to gauge the passage of time.

Gael wouldn't speak to her. Cai was merely tolerated by the men, and Aedus took to sleeping between Alaysha and Yenic because Edulph wouldn't let anyone near the child at night except for Theron.

The one bright spot in each day was mealtime. Bodicca always managed to hunt or scavenge something delectable, seeming to prefer the solitude of foraging to the company of the group. Secretly, Alaysha believed she was still in mourning and left her be. It was one sore spot she didn't think either of them wanted to open.

To keep the child nourished, Bodicca and Theron came up with a way to boil down bits of meat and bone into a watery broth that Aedus and the shaman dribbled into her mouth by turns. While the child didn't fatten, at least she didn't waste away.

Fourteen Sun cycles would very nearly send Alaysha to the edge of her tolerance and at times, she understood how madness might have crept upon Edulph if he had journeyed this way at all.

By day thirteen, they came upon a body of water that Edulph said would be impossible to cross.

Alaysha stepped next to him at the water's edge. "You crossed it, did you not?"

He stared at the water in the line of horizon that went past site. "I had a boat."

"How often, Edulph?"

"How often what?"

"How many times have you crossed?" She was already tired of the verbal game.

A sly line of a smile slithered across his face. "Enough."

"How many?" She heard the annoyance in her voice.

"Once running from Drahl."

Yuri's lead scout who had tried to kill Alaysha and who, according to Aedus, did terrible things to a young

Edulph. "And?"

"Once returning for my people."

"And?"

"And that's it. I've seen the Highlands." He sounded nostalgic. "I was happy there."

She snorted and he glowered at her. "Think what you like, witch." He walked the edge, thinking aloud. "They should have left a boat." He scanned the waterline in both directions. "I don't understand why they wouldn't leave a boat."

"Maybe they don't want you back in the village," Cai said, coming alongside Alaysha and crossing her arms. "I wouldn't."

He spit into the water. "You know nothing."

"Then explain," Alaysha said. "Tell us."

"Tell the witch who enslaved my people?"

"That was my father."

"But for you, he'd have lost that battle."

Bodicca stepped closer, her hands on her hips. "Don't be so certain, man," she said.

"Oh, yes," Edulph ground out. "He had you, didn't he, and all those others. I remember. I might've been young, but I remember."

"Then you'll remember Alaysha was but a pre-woman, then."

He ignored her in favor of throwing a pebble into the water. Alaysha waded in behind it, testing the depths.

"I suppose it doesn't matter now, Edulph. It only matters that we get across this so we can help your daughter."

He nodded, still sullen. "I didn't kill her mother," he said.

She looked at him. "Someone did," she answered.

"Yes," he agreed, and the way he said it, the way his

tone held a note of accusation, Alaysha knew what he'd been holding back from her. Why he hated her so.

"It was me," she guessed. "But how?"

He shrugged. "How do you always kill?"

"No. How would you know this when I didn't?" Alaysha recalled the mud village, the three crones hunched over a dead fire. Fire, earth, air. All of them dead, but with their power safe in their daughters' spirits. Safe, presumably, elsewhere, far away from Alaysha's power. Sacrificing themselves, so Theron said, to save the line or to thwart the brother god of his legends. She wasn't sure which.

Edulph seemed to tire of the burden of his secrecy and stepped close enough that when he spoke in a whisper, she could still hear.

"Aislin. She knew." His mouth worked in thought. "She told me you dried her out like an apple in the sun for your father."

"I might have," Alaysha admitted. "I can't deny it's possible. But it couldn't have been in the mud village." She looked at the child pointedly. "Because she would be with her mother. Somewhere safe."

He laughed but without humour. "You witches, playing at your own war while people die around you as though we were nothing but beasts."

"That's not true."

"Isn't it?" He nodded at his daughter. "Even she knows it. I couldn't keep her from you when she knew, and now look at her. Payment for her compassion." He turned away.

"What you mean, *when she knew*?" She grabbed his shoulder and twisted him back around. "Tell me what you mean."

"How did you know about *her*?"

Alaysha thought it over. "Yuri," she said. "And Yenic."

He quirked both brows knowingly and Alaysha caught her breath as she realized. "You *were* trying to rescue us," she said.

"I told you so."

"But she can't control her power either."

He shrugged. "She wanted to try. She thought she could."

Alaysha wanted to reach out to him, but found she couldn't. Too much had happened; she knew neither one of them would ever trust the other. But she did know one thing. They needed to cross the water if the girl was to have a chance of surviving.

"We'll get her home," she told him. "I swear it."

She scoped the breadth of the water, scanning sideways, running her fingers across the surface. She considered the amount of power it would take to psych it dry and wondered if she could unleash as much as that, and if she could, would she be able to pull it back before it worked on the latent water resting inside the bodies and breath of her companions.

The girl was sleeping less and less each time Aedus quilled her; how much longer and how many more times they could continue to do so was unclear. Theron wasn't even sure a fortnight was enough restorative sleep for the child to heal sufficiently. It was very possible she'd not recover at all unless he could get access to more than he had in his pack: to a good shelter, to food and support.

They could go around the broad river, or they could go through it.

"Theron, take Aedus and the child. Get on the road

and travel east on the waterline. Go about a lcagua." She hoped a leagua was enough. It seemed her power extended about that far when she'd taken the mud village.

"The witch plans to drain the sea?" Theron sounded anxious.

"We can't lose the girl, and I won't risk Aedus. The rest of you have your choice."

All of them, even Edulph stood silent in acquiescence as Alaysha watched Barruch plod away. She pulled in a bracing breath, held it, and then very purposefully sent her power sniffing.

The ready water, plenty of it, the seemingly endless supply, delighted the power. She felt the latent excitement dancing in her chest. Oh, what it could do with all the fluid. Her chest tightened like the bottom of a riverbed dried out by the sun; she could feel it pull away from her flesh, gathering into one small spot somewhere behind her spine. Her flesh tingled, her mouth went dry. She could sense that certain coiling of it as it began to reach out. It pulled the water like a dying man thirsted for his last breath.

So potent was the thirst that she thought she'd inhaled enough fluid to send her floating on the sea somewhere above her. She couldn't feel her feet or hands. She only felt the filling of her entire being with the bloat of water, as though some part of her was made of it just past her physical body. She swore she could see a second version of herself outlining her skin and marvelled at how big it grew.

She heard excited laughter coming from beside her but didn't dare turn to face it. She needed to keep the focus, stare at the sea, will it to release its water until the bottom showed through. Fish of all sorts flapped on the sea bed, gasping for water. Trout, pickerel, salmon. The men ran forward, collecting them, throwing them into the front of their leathers. The women drug their bedrolls out to the seabed and collected weeds and frogs. Laughing. All laughing. Barruch plodded onto the seabed even as it crackled dry, the Enyalian beast following him.

She'd done it. She drained the sea and they could cross. She should have been ecstatic.

All she felt was the bloat of water swimming across her vision, filling her lungs, driving out her air.

She gasped, flailing about in mockery of those poor fish. She couldn't breathe. There wasn't room for one more breath or one more inhale.

Chapter 27

She awoke to a cacophony of birdsong and discovered she lay on a soft bed, the scent of roasted meat filling the air.

She called out for Yenic, but it was Theron who hovered over her.

"The witch awakes," he said smiling and she eased herself onto her elbows to look around.

"So much excitement and to have missed it all. Such a shame. Yes?"

She didn't need an explanation to understand what was going on. To be inside a lodge, the smell of food cooking, to feel the heat of a fire: they'd made it to the Highlands. So she'd been unconscious for at least two days, maybe more.

"How is the child?"

"The little one rests more suitably, now she's here. Yes, oh yes."

"Yenic?"

"Brooding."

"Gael?"

"Also brooding."

Alaysha chewed her lip thoughtfully. "And Cai?"

A small grin tugged at the corner of his mouth. "Brooding."

"Is there anyone happy that we made it?"

He shook his head soberly, then brightened. "Edulph."

"So they're all mad at me."

"Worried."

"It had to be done."

"Indeed, little witch. Indeed. Oh, yes. But this shaman isn't sure she'll make it through another."

She sighed, feeling the weariness in every muscle. It

even hurt to breathe. "Don't even suggest it," she told him, touching her stomach as it growled hungrily. He fetched a copper bowl and set it close by while he gathered up a spoon and a trencher of bread.

"Broth first," he told her.

She opened her mouth obligingly to the offered broth and swallowed. The taste was pungent of meat and spices.

"Bodicca," she guessed.

"She fills her time re-teaching the women to cook."

Alaysha waited for another spoonful that didn't come.

"The witch needs to mark another," Theron said.

"You don't waste much time."

"There's no time to waste, oh, no."

She sighed heavily. "Cai," she said and his brow lifted like a bird taking flight.

"Cai," she repeated. "Tomorrow." She rolled over and away from him, suddenly even more weary than before.

She slept the day and by early evening felt sure-footed enough to step outside. If anyone visited, she didn't know, but all now sat outside the lodge around a huge communal fire where children roasted bread over tree limbs and a boar, gutted and split, roasted on a spit sending the delicious aroma through the air. Alaysha's stomach gurgled. She thought of the time she'd made Saxa feed her meat too soon when she was recovering from a wound, and how she'd vomited it all up on Gael.

He'd thought her a burden then, and seemed to feel so again. Best she spare him the mark that would connect them for the rest of their lives.

She saw him now, sitting alone, staring broodily into the flames and drinking from a copper goblet. He must have felt her eyes on him because he looked up directly at her and met her gaze. His face changed; it grew stormy and dark. He leapt to his feet and charged for her; Cai, seeing him, was by her side before he could reach her.

"I won't let her," he barked at Alaysha.

"Won't what, Gael?"

"Won't let her take your mark."

"It's too late. I've decided."

"Undecide it."

She shook her head as Cai stepped in front of her. "She nearly died; have you forgotten that, man? Leave her to her decision."

He pushed at Cai but the woman didn't move. "I won't let you leave your life to this woman," he told Alaysha. "I won't let you leave it to someone you can't trust."

"I trust her." She touched his arm and he met her gaze without a change of expression, but his eyes fell to her mouth.

"Mark me," he said, but it wasn't a plea.

"You don't know what it means," she told him.

"I do," he said. "The shaman told us."

Of course he would, the busy bee. "Gael, I don't even know if Cai agrees." She felt weary over it. She didn't want to argue.

"I do," the woman pressed closer, pushing Gael aside. "The shaman explained it, and I do."

Alaysha took her in. She'd given Theron a name just so he would leave her alone. She shook her head, thinking to decline is all when the Enyalian touched her chin at the centre where her mark was.

"You will die, little maga, if your power takes you again. I would rather share you with this man than see that happen." She looked at Gael who gave a grudging nod. "See?" She said happily. "We both would."

From the corner of her eye, Alaysha saw Yenic watching, both anxious and intrigued. She looked past him to the backdrop of tree trunks so broad they sported stairs and sets of stairs that wound around each other and connected to lodges set in the very trees themselves, up dizzying heights that made Alaysha feel faint.

Highlands. It made sense now. They lived high in the trees, all the better to see danger coming.

"Alaysha?"

Yenic's voice. His hand grasping for hers. He'd got up in the time she was thinking, and she wondered how long she'd been lost in her thoughts.

"You need an Arm, Alaysha. Please."

She chewed her lip. It was folly, what they planned to do, out and out folly. The best candidates and yet all hated each other. All connected only because she loved them.

She nodded, finally, mutely.

They were safe for now, all of them. The wind witch. Yenic. Aedus. What better time to marshal all the strength they could.

"Have Theron verse us all," she said numbly, realizing the decision had sapped what energy she had left. "Tomorrow. It'll be done tomorrow."

She stumbled back to the lodge at the edge of the village, out past the trees into a small clearing that smelled of redwood and ferns.

She collapsed on the bedroll and closed her eyes, feeling as though she'd sentenced the two warriors to death. She thought of Thera and her lodge, of the sight of Gael lying naked in the heat, unconscious. How she ached for him to be well, watching the slow rise and fall of his chest, the thigh muscles quivering in drugged sleep. She smelled again the myrrh, the brimstone, imagined Thera piling the furs onto her cot as the smoke rose.

Brimstone. Something about brimstone niggled at her thoughts, but she couldn't grasp at it with the image of Gael lying helpless in her memory or the sight of those furs piled onto that cot moving in a similar way to Gael's chest, almost imperceptible.

Almost as though someone was beneath the pile.Theron had drawn the first of the symbols in for her with wet soot. Both Gael and Cai held their left arms aloft, careful not to smudge them and letting Alaysha inspect the finest of the lines. She wondered how she'd be able to produce anything nearly as shapely with the bone tip he passed her. She ran her thumb along the point and found it sharp indeed. Still, the idea that she could tap such detail onto skin seemed improbable.

"I don't think it will look as good as he's drawn it," she said, letting her finger run absently along the symbol in the middle of her own chin, the one her nohma had put there for her, the one she knew meant water in an ancient language.

Gael dipped his finger into the sooty ash, testing its texture. "I know some sword smiths add bone to their steel, but this seems a little bit disturbing. I mean, your sister's ash." His words had begun to slur, the effects Alaysha knew, of the brew Theron had fed both him and Cai. Alaysha still didn't understand why they needed to be drugged so. Theron insisted it was not a drug but a sacred drink.

"You'll tell me if it hurts?"

Cai made a sound that could have been disdain, but the way the words came out after, all thick and muddy, Alaysha wasn't sure it was something she intended. "Try being branded, little maga, if you want to understand pain."

Gael murmured his agreement but lifted his arm

above his head, all the better for Alaysha to work on a broader landscape. Both he and Cai lay on a thatch mat, stretched onto their sides. Two large copper goblets sat between them and if Alaysha remembered correctly, they were each to save a drink for her, but all the brew should be gone in the end. By the way they grimaced after gulping some of it down, she was sure there'd be plenty left for her. She just worried she'd not be able to stomach it; her belly already gurgled from nerves.

She inhaled. "At least if I make a mess of it, you can cover yours up," she teased and wasn't certain she said it just for their benefit. She tried a trembling laugh, but neither warrior returned it. In fact, both looked unable to muster so much as a smile.

"So, then," she said, trying again to find courage. "So."

"So, get on with it, little maga." Cai sounded irritated. She didn't expect any response from Gael; except for his agreement to do this, he hadn't so much as spoken but a few sentences to her since she'd cornered him in the forest.

Cai was the closest. Alaysha puffed out the air that had collected in her throat. She could do this. She *would* do this. Theron had warned her that the brew, the marking, and the ritual might take more out of all of them than normal because of the exertion they'd all expelled at the broad sea and because of the amount of recovery they were all undergoing to heal. Still, it had to be done.

She leaned over the bowl, working her mouth to build saliva and spit into the pot. Then she held her finger over the same and with an inhale, pierced the tip with a needle. Squeezed. One, two, three drops for each of them. She intoned the words she'd practiced, did her best to recall the face of her nohma as she did so, the only ancestor she knew who could bring her spirit to the magic.

She used the same finger to mash the soot, ashes, and fluid together. Then she began.

It was precise, finicky work and Alaysha was sweating by the time Cai's mark was done. As instructed, she bid Cai swill nearly all her own brew, leaving enough for Alaysha who by now was licking her lips with thirst. She had to believe Theron when he told her she would be begging for the drink by the time she was done. The fragrance of myrrh charring on the open flame was coating her throat in ways that made swallowing difficult and her nose dry. Still, no matter how much she needed a drink, she couldn't until the last of the work was done.

She wished Gael would at least look at her while she did this to him. Cai had stared stonily at Alaysha the whole time and when Alaysha paused every now and then to take a break, Cai had grinned at her.

She expected no such encouragement from Gael. She began on his symbol with reluctance. What good could come from binding herself to a man who couldn't bear to look at her, who tortured himself with things that simply didn't matter. The Enyalian might be pragmatic about her agreement, and her motives had certainly become all too clear, but there was at least some comfort in knowing the large woman would be there always ready to give her self in service. That she'd agreed without hesitation, even after understanding what it meant told Alaysha the woman could indeed be trusted and could be counted on.

Just knowing it lent a flush to Alaysha's skin that had nothing to do with the fire.

Strangely enough, not long ago, she would have said the same of Gael. He'd voiced it with his own lips, assured her of it even. All she had needed or desired of him at the time, the reality of him now taking the steps to demonstrate it was still almost hollow. How could she ask it of him when he felt so tortured over her; it was why she'd asked Cai in the first place.

But here they were, joining together in a ritual Alaysha doubted would even work. Never done before, is what Theron had said. Could her power, as strong as it was, still move through two Arms instead of one? No one had ever tried.

Poor Gael. It might be too much for him, really. She studied the complete symbol critically. It was good, actually. The curves rounded nicely. The lines were solid. Bold. Beautiful, even.

Not bad for a woman covered in nervous perspiration. She exhaled, satisfied.

"The drink," she said. Surely if she didn't wet her lips soon, the stink of myrrh would gum them closed.

Both Gael and Cai held their goblets out and Gael met her eye boldly. She took his first and swallowed everything within, then reached for Cai's and drank deeply.

The flush of heat without was nothing to the flush within when she finished. She felt as though her veins were filling with molten Quicksilver that was coursing and flowing, throbbing beneath her skin. Her ears tingled. The skin beneath her hair prickled.

And then she knew, just knew, what would restore Gael, what would bring him back to himself.

She reached to cup her hand beneath his jaw. "Gael," she whispered. "Let me replace those memories for you. Help me feed you new ones to eat away the ones that torture you."

At first, he tried to wrest his face from her touch, but she grew insistent, more determined. She stood, pulling his head toward her so that she wrapped him with her arms, her fingers roaming his hair, fleeting gently over the healing wound. He was on his knees, cheek against her legs and it was easy to slip her hand beneath his arms and tug, just firmly enough he looked up at her. When he caught her eye, she refused to let it wander. Instead, she leaned forward and captured his mouth, never once closing her eyes for fear of releasing him. Even as her tongue probed his lips open, she watched his pupils dilate and the wrinkles of doubt smooth over. There was an instant when she thought he'd pull away, but then his eyes squeezed shut determinedly and his tongue followed hers, dancing with it in surrender.

At last he stood, letting his hands roam her body as he found his feet. He pulled her against him, letting her hand rest on him so she felt each muscle tense and let go in his chest. His legs moved outside hers, trapping her; she realized how desperately he clung. She thought she felt a tug on her leggings and tunic. Her arms lifted of their own volition and the leather slipped over her skin. The shiver of air danced over her flesh and was gone so quickly she thought she was cocooned within two fires. The flames of one licked her throat, beneath her hair on her nape; the flames of the other captured her breath, fanning the heat as they danced.

Indeed, she was cocooned, she realized. She had to be, and between the two large warriors, both making her flesh feel as if it was on fire. Gael's mouth moved across her chest and throat, Cai's trailed down her spine and rested at the cleft just above her buttocks where it sent a shiver straight up to her neck. The woman's hands, her fingers cupping and probing between her thighs until she felt herself grind against them shamelessly. She pulled her feet from the leggings and lifted her arms to feel all the more deliciously available.

Together, they stretched onto the mat and she let her

own lips travel Gael's throat even as Cai pressed against her, the hard pebbles of her nipples reminding Alaysha that she had two bodies about her, not the one, and that they were both hard, fierce fighters with almost freakish strength. She felt safer than she'd ever felt, more alive. More than that, she felt as though she couldn't possibly be close enough; she wanted more, to feel their hands roaming her skin, entwining together between her legs, making her slick with need.

She became a molded piece of clay, moving with them, letting them press into her, against her, and then finally being lifted and entered. She rode the wave that battered her and let the hands behind travel her skin, gripping her nipples. It was a wild dance, as fierce as the wielding of swords fighting for possession of her, and she couldn't get enough of either body. She wanted them both to win her; she wanted their growling need to each take her.

Finally the rhythm behind became as the one she rode, until the heat, the flush, the desire of it all left her leaning back onto one warrior as she moved like a piece of oiled sinew against the other.

No one spoke. She could only echo the sounds that met her ears, of desire and satisfaction and longing finally met until the only sound she could make at all was a cry of complete surrender.

Alaysha woke to a groggy head. Both Cai and Gael were gone and the only way she knew for certain that she'd marked them at all was that the small copper bowl of soot still lay on the floor next to her, with the blackened tapper resting inside. She eased to sitting, holding on to her head and trying to keep the throbbing she felt contained to the inside of her skull. Even her fingers ached. The fur around her shoulders slipped to her waist. She was nude and the air was chilly. Morning, then. Thank the deities one of them had thought to build a small fire before leaving.

She tried to get up and realized that every movement she made was effort. She did remember having a few small sips of Theron's brew. How must her new Arms feel, having each drunk an entire goblet when she felt this way after so little, she didn't even want to think about.

She stared into the flames, letting the crackle of wood replace the sound of her own heart beating in her ears. She stared at the flames, watching the short peaks lengthen lazily. Letting the heat fill her skin. She felt totally at ease in her own skin; strong anxieties from before seemed to have melted away in the comforting knowledge that she wouldn't need to be alone anymore. That she was now connected to not one, but two others, in a way that would secure her safety and well-being. She had somehow extended--diluted--her power into another spirit, and it felt right.

She could fix her stare if she liked, focus the pain behind her eyes; the trouble was they didn't truly focus at all even when she tried. They seemed to be following a figure within almost as though the flames themselves were twisting into shapes that wanted her to see. She thought of Aislin and of how she'd come to her through the flames back in the mud village. Pyromancy, Yenic called it. The fire witch's affinity with flame, and her ties to Alaysha through Yenic were supposed to give her the same sort of ability.

Alaysha wondered if that connection could work to her benefit. She certainly felt just off enough this morning to do it.

She stared, pinning her gaze on one particular section of the fire, one that reminded her of the fire witch's eyes. She let the flame lick around the edges of her vision and twist within and upon itself.

When it happened, she gasped aloud. Aislin herself, wearing a long linen shift, paced within the flames, the veil of her hair catching a breeze behind her. She stopped short. Looked over her shoulder to the other side. Then Alaysha could see a slow smile spread across the woman's face as she closed her eyes. A tingling shivered down Alaysha's chin and trickled down her throat. She felt hot, as though the flame had entered her. Dryness came after. So dry she could barely swallow.

She scrabbled backwards, even as she heard shrieks of agony and shouts of confusion sound from outside. Despite the pounding behind her eyes, she bolted to her feet, grabbing her tunic and pulling it over her head. She whipped aside the leather flap of the mud hut and ran across broken branches and through thickets that scratched her face and arms to get back to the village. At the edge, in piles of smoking ash, lay copper bowls and smoking water buckets. She leaned to pick up a copper cup and pulled her hand back. There were blisters on her fingers.

It didn't take her but a few moments to realize what was happening. It came to her even as her toe rammed into a copper bowl. She looked down, confused, thinking she shouldn't be kicking at bowls this far from the fires, see ashes in such peculiar grouping so far from the communal fire. Then she saw them: two hard black seeds sitting in the middle of gray ash, and she couldn't swallow back the gasp that left her lungs.

Alaysha cast about blindly, stumbling into Highlanders as they sobbed and ran about, gathering their children. Several of the Highlanders were already sprinting toward her: confused, afraid, shouting at her, flinging rocks. Alaysha cast about, looking for some witness even as she knew she needed none. These people couldn't understand what was happening to them, they would blame her, and she *was* to blame. Aislin had used the connection to force her to kill.

"It wasn't me," she sobbed. "Not me," she spied Aedus, her mouth agape, her arms full of herbs and plants she'd been gathering. She dropped them as Alaysha reached her, and thank the deities, without speaking, the girl knew what was happening.

Alaysha found her hand in the girl's and let herself be pulled along, the satisfied sense of early morning long gone. Now it was replaced by a queer kind of panic.

"The child," she said, gasping for air she ran. "Where is she?" Several hard globes stung her back.

"Theron has her," Aedus got out, and yanked Alaysha toward the tree Edulph had disappeared into with the girl the moment they'd arrived. "He's mixed up his ghost pipe roots and she sleeps far more soundly."

Panting, feeling as though everything in her skull would erupt, Alaysha craned her neck up the tree trunk. The stairs that wound their way up into the brush of the branches and joined several trees together by a wooden lodge looked far too high for her to climb. It was why she chose to stay in the mud hut, instead. Not only did her head pound, but she suddenly grew dizzy.

"I don't think I can," she said.

"It's okay," Aedus always understood. "I'll fetch them. And Edulph too. He might be able to calm them down." She sprinted up the steps as though there was no height to worry about.

Alaysha whirled to face an accusing crowd.

"I did nothing," she said. "It wasn't me."

A woman stepped out from the throng. "Then name the power that could dry standing flesh to leather."

"But they were burned. They –"

"They caught fire with no lightening to hand, no torch near. They simply dried out as they stood until there was nothing left but flame."

"But there *was* flame." Alaysha wasn't afraid; she was ashamed. So ashamed; and she couldn't explain to herself, let alone the simple folk, that the power that could do such a thing wasn't from her even if it came through her. Her tongue felt tied to its palette. She could hear footfalls on the stairs again and realized that Aedus hadn't gone all the way up. Instead, she came back around the tree and stood with her hands on hips, daring the crowd.

"Worry for yourself, then," she commanded. "If you think this woman capable of lighting the flame, imagine your own deaths from such fire and *back off*."

They went quiet but they remained. Alaysha took a bracing breath.

"Your young one can drain air, you know it's true. I can draw water, but there is another. One who sparks fire in a man's own flesh. It's why we're here. We want to help you."

Out of the corner of her eye she saw Yenic rushing toward her, his face a mask of concern. He drew close, his arms opened in question.

"How, Alaysha?" His eyes, so like roasting honey when he looked at her, were clouded with something she couldn't name.

She shrugged. "I don't know. The fire, I guess. I was staring into it--"

It took him a moment, but realization flashed across his face. "Sweet deities. She channelled you."

"No," Alaysha protested. "Not like that. I saw her. She was pacing, angry, upset, something. I caught her unaware."

He grabbed at the spot beneath his arm as though it stung. "My mark. It still tingles." He looked at her and past her at the same time.

"What does it mean?" she asked.

Yenic shifted his weight side to side. "You touched her, Alaysha. She knows your spirit. She knows it without having to search now."

"The bond," she guessed and he waggled his head up and down, stepping now more lively, his hands swatting his ribs.

"She can sense you through me."

Another shriek went up from somewhere near; the crowd parted, pulling back like the ball of fire would reach out to them each with light, leaping fingers. The stink of animal fat and burning hair raced through the air.

"No," Yenic said, stumbling. Alaysha caught at him, leaned down to keep him from falling. He swept her hand away. "No," he said again. "I have to break it," he mumbled to himself and Alaysha thought his face had shifted into something akin to Edulph's when he'd gone mad.

"Yenic," she reached again, but he took a faltering step away.

"Your Arms," he said, his eyes glazed and wide now. "Is it done, Alaysha? Tell me it's done."

"Yes. Yes, it's done." It was true wasn't it? She saw the ink pot, the black and bone. She'd marked them both. They'd finished the drink, she drank the brew. They'd--

Oh, dear deities. She'd done more than mark them. She felt her face flush and forced herself to stay calm. She could explain it to him later. "Yes," she said avoiding his eyes. "Yes, it's done."

His chest was heaving even as another scream rent the air. "Good, good." He staggered. "She knows we're together," he choked out. "She won't stop. I have to break it, Alaysha." His amber eyes were liquid again for one heartbeat, and he leaned in and kissed her, gripping her face, letting his thumb travel her tattau.

"Get the child away from here while you can. All of you." He looked at Aedus who was still standing on the stairs. "Trust only so far, little girl." He told her.

"What are you doing?"

"Whatever I can." He stepped away. "Go, Alaysha. I can gain them some time." He paused, seeming to want to say something more, but in the end, he turned and darted off toward the tree line where the brood lodge stood.

More shrieks now. Too many. The Highlanders had begun to scatter, each to their trees, some away from them, rushing with children in their arms for the woods.

And it was a good thing they were leaving in a rush, because not only were many of them succumbing to Aislin's flame, but a herd of Enyalia beasts split the tree line at the end of the village with Enud at their head.

Chapter 28

It explained why, with all the yelling going on, neither Gael nor Cai had come searching for the source of the trouble. It also explained the obvious state of injury on a few of the warriors as they'd entered the village.

"Aedus, get up to the lodge, get Theron, get the girl, get Barruch and get out of here."

Thankfully, the girl didn't argue. She scrambled up the tree, her grubby legs agile and adept as if they'd been born to climb. Alaysha swallowed hard. She had only to buy time; that was all. Just enough for Theron, Aedus and the girl to find and gallop away on Barruch. If Gael and Cai lived, they'd surely be protected somewhat by their marks. Yenic was gone, hopefully far enough that he'd be safe. The spontaneous lighting of the Highlanders had slowed down, so she thought he must have found a way to stop his mother.

So, all she needed was time.

Enud climbed down from her beast and strode toward Alaysha. She limped painfully, and Alaysha could see a large gash in her side. Even as she came forward, she was pulling her sword from her back. The Enyalia behind her look ragged and weary. Scouting the escapees had taken its toll; Alaysha counted half a dozen beasts. Not so many then.

A scrabbling noise came from behind the tree, and Alaysha knew Aedus had made it back down. She moved away from the Redwood, closer to Enud, whose circlets rattled louder with each step. The tree was thick enough that the inhabitants could slip off into the woods and not be seen.

"I shall wear your teeth first," the Enyalian said. "And then my sword sisters will clear this village as it should have been done seasons ago."

"You'll string no new teeth today, Enud," Alaysha told her and the woman laughed.

The time, if it was ever going to be right, was now. Alaysha wouldn't see one more of these people murdered today. She thought of her father, imagined his icy eyes as he told her to bury the emotion, to see her foes as targets of shield and bone. To think of them as water. Water she needed, wanted, and could use if only she could sniff it, touch it, draw from each pore the way a bucket emptied from a well.

But not from everywhere. From one target. That one right there who was even now swinging her blade, thinking to stop the beating of her heart and take her teeth, to decorate her thighs with a string of white bone.

The power awoke. It unfurled like a leaf to the spring sun. Alaysha imagined the pathways that she knew from past experience were there. She saw them all in her mind's eye, and her tongue tasted the fluid that kept the Enyalian's eyes clear, her lungs moist, her breath in sweat. She heard Enud's short sigh and the hollow thud of steel against ground, and she knew she'd done it.

She'd sent the power in one finger to touch the one target she needed and she nearly wept in relief because it worked.

She stood, heaving with exertion, staring down at the leathered bit of skin at her feet and she heard her own choked laughter ripple across the air because there were no seeds for her to collect. She looked up, searching for someone to tell this to, and she remembered they were all gone and she was left with six furious Enyalia. And she realized she was fatigued but not beaten by the power. And then she realized the power was still unfurling.

And then the rain came.

Chapter 29

The warriors in front of her seemed ignorant of her power or unconcerned at their imminent deaths. Alaysha almost pitied them. Two came forward, circlets chattering in the onslaught of water like beads beneath a stream, rubbing against each other and growing smooth. Both women toed the dried skeleton of flesh that once was there demi-leader, and even so, seeing the state Enud was in, that Alaysha had caused her to be in, they took lazy steps forward. Unafraid, as always.

Alaysha's fingers tingled as though charged with lightning. She could barely inhale for the smothering weight of power that still moved within her. It was building. Far more than she'd ever felt. More than the power that sent a village to ruin, more than the power to drain the ground beneath her feet dry, for the birds to fall from the air above her. She'd coalesced the magic somehow and funnelled it to aim it at one woman, but it was a greedy thing, this power. It wanted unleashed in total and any attempt to hold back made the ready, standing water gather. In moments, heartbeats, even, it would turn all the rest into one great cloud that desired nothing more than to bloat itself on living water.

But they didn't know that.

The two paused a mere leg span from her, seeming to decide which would take the teeth of the woman who had dared oppose them, who had freed one of their brood men, who'd escaped with a band of the hated Highlanders into the woods. No one left Enyalia and lived.

Alaysha knew she had no choice, she didn't want to hurt anyone unnecessarily, but she knew she had no choice. The power was coming.

"Run," she croaked out and then she lost her mind to

the power that was already blackening her vision, letting go a shriek as it took her.

A sort of soft sigh moved across her earlobe. Voices, perhaps. Maybe even birdsong. Neither of these could be true. Either she was dead or everything else was.

Indeed the blackness alone indicated a certain state of unlife. She couldn't open her eyes, move her arms, or even gasp for breath. It was settled then. The power had won.

She was ready to resign herself to being dead except for the incessant hum that bothered her ears. Yes. Low, but most definitely the sound of a bee's wing or the whir of a heat beetle. And now she thought it, she felt air moving across her skin. Or maybe she felt as though she was moving.

Understanding jolted through her. Not dead after all, but whirling about on her own power, traveling through her own veins, watching the lightning rise from inside her mind and fire into another chain, collapsing into liquid and beating again through her heart, her lungs, throat, her breath.

She gasped herself awake to find she had collapsed onto the forest floor. The rain pelted down still, making a deep puddle that was already leaking into her ears.

She made her way on her knees to the fallen warriors in front of her. Leathered husks, yes, but like Enud: no seeds. She swept the hair from her eyes that let rivers run down her face as they collected the rain. She scanned for the other four, their beasts. It seemed they'd tried to do as she'd ordered and all but one were facing the other direction.

This last one, though, she clung to the railing of a step all the way across the compound. With a shock, Alaysha realized the Enyalian looked scared.

In truth, that wasn't the only shock. Alaysha noticed the foliage was still lush and wet, drooping from the strength of the rain but not dried to dust. The trees hadn't crackled to petrified wood. The moss beneath her feet was still spongy.

She heard her own sob of relief and the sound gave voice to the rest of the weeping; it rose like a wave within her and she could no more stop it than she could stop the rain.

Where the water had come from, she didn't know nor did she care. She regretted the lives she'd been forced to take, but for once the torture of it didn't overwhelm her into hardening her heart. She let herself feel the regret; she let herself feel forgiveness in knowing the choice of it had been left in their hands.

She touched her chin absently and in doing so remembered.

"Where are the warriors who met you?" She shouted at the Enyalian.

The woman had regained her composure and her feet. She was picking her way across the bridge she was on and down the ladder.

"You mean Komandiri Cai and her man?"

Alaysha chuckled at she thought of Cai's reaction to that statement. "Yes," she said. "Do they live?"

The woman shrugged. "They were living when last we saw them."

"Where?"

"We left them fighting back to back together against my sword sisters."

"How many?"

The woman paused, seeming to be considering something. "Too many," she finally said.

Alaysha broke into a gasping, forced run. The Enyalian saw how difficult it was for her and caught her as she was sprinting by. Meaty hands picked her up and threw her onto a nearby beast and they begin loping into the woods.

They made about a hundred horse strides when they saw them. Both warriors were bruised and bloody, and both were smiling broadly even as they sprinted forward. Gael saw them first and his face clouded over. In a heartbeat he broke into a sprint, aiming his whole body at Isolde as she dropped from the beast, sword drawn, stance squared.

Their broadswords struck each other and the sound rang out with Gael's bellow of fury. He parried, shifted, swung again. Isolde met him and danced away.

"Careful, man," she taunted. "I may be with child."

'To the god of death go your child." He swung again, catching the woman's leathers with the briefest of the sword's edge. He grinned and made to swing again when Cai shouted at him. He swung on her.

"Would you take us both, man? And after such a wondrous night." The Enyalian's lip curled in a half-smile. She tuned to Isolde as well. "Isolde." There was the undisputed sound of command in Cai's tone, in the stance of defence in her posture. "If you think to take this witch back to Enyalia, you will die."

"I have no such intention, Komandiri."

Alaysha found her feet as Isolde walked hers together in submission. With relief, Alaysha faced the three of them. "Gael," she breathed. "You're alive."

"As am I," Cai said, almost as though hurt Alaysha hadn't noticed it. "Although I had to take two of my sword sisters to his one." She gave Gael a disapproving look.

Alaysha could see no bodies littering the forest floor. "What happened?"

Cai shrugged and clasped Isolde's shoulder. "What of the battle?" It was apparent by the way Isolde's eyes watered that Cai was squeezing the woman into further submission.

"The battle is won, Komandiri."

Cai's expression went carefully blank but Alaysha could see her thinking.

"Enud is dead," Alaysha told her.

Gael glowered at Isolde, still not willing to give in, but he spoke to Alaysha. "How did she die?"

She met his gaze and quirked the corner of her mouth into a knowing line. "You see the rain."

"I do," he said. "And we felt the draining. Those we'd not killed already merely--"

"Dried out," she finished.

"The others who didn't, scattered." Gael looked thoughtful. "I wouldn't have expected it of Enyalia."

Cai looked at Isolde. "Our other sword sisters?"

Isolde's face held no emotion. "All gone but for me."

"Why take to Enud's raid at all?"

The woman shrugged. "Battle is battle, Komandiri."

Cai studied her comrade's face. "You'd forswear your sword sisters, Isolde?"

"I forswear Enud, Komandiri. The death of Yoliri drained the Enyalian from her."

Cai looked at her thoughtfully. "Uta will see you wear the boar grease if you speak of our meeting."

"There is nothing to speak of to Uta."

The two women said nothing more, but a look passed between them that Alaysha didn't understand. Moments later,

Isolde strode to her beast and climbed atop. She loped into the woods and disappeared. Gael watched her, saying nothing but scowling a good deal.

"You're right, man, if I understand your scowl," Cai told him. "Isolde will see the old witch decides it is her time finally to die."

"It matters nothing to me," he answered turning his back on her and striding toward the Highland Village. "What of the rest, Alaysha. Aedus? The girl?"

"I sent them away." She walked with him, thinking out loud. "I had no choice, Gael. Aislin found a way to channel her magic through me. People were dying everywhere." She choked on the memory but continued. "And then *they* came."

"How many?" Cai asked.

She gave the Enyalian a shrug. "You say how many; you saw the most of them. At least they didn't all get into the village."

"Agreed," Cai said. "How many deaths in the village?"

Alaysha sighed. "Too many." She thought of Uta's coming fate and didn't feel sorry for her. "What of Thera, Cai?"

"She will emerge finally from behind Uta's shadow."

"It was a dark one, I admit."

Cai kicked at a pebble. "Even more so of late. Dark enough to change Thera."

"How so?"

The woman shrugged. "Secretive. Always in her garden, always in her lodge, that infernal fire breathing its heat into her lungs. It made her fidgety." She jerked her chin toward the highland village. "Like yon shaman. Peculiar and quiet."

"The brimstone." Gael shuddered. "It woke me each time she fed it to the flames. I don't know how the woman could stand all those furs."

Cai halted and peered at him sideways. "Thera never slept with furs... always naked like the rest of us, ready to spring to combat."

"Not Thera," he said. "The other one."

Alaysha's spine tingled. "The other one?"

"Yes," he said. "The one in the other bed."

"The one in the other bed," she said, recalling the mound on the cot, the stink of brimstone on the flame, the quaking of the earth for days as they travelled. "Brimstone binds magic," she murmured. "Dear deities."

"What?" Gael asked.

"Thera," Alaysha said, realizing it all at once. "The clay witch *is* in the Enyalia village. She has been all along."

"Not Thera," Gael said doubtfully.

"No," Alaysha answered. "Not Thera. The woman beneath the furs. She's hurt, I bet. Thera is healing her and she's binding her magic to keep the quakes down. That's why she was interested in my tattaus--not because of her own marks, but because of the witch's."

"The clay witch," Gael said and Alaysha smiled at him.

"Yes. Finally," she said. "Thera is harbouring the clay witch."

The village was quiet when they returned, and Alaysha sighed in relief. They made their way through the piles of ash, Alaysha bending every now and then to retrieve the seeds she knew were there. Cai said nothing when they passed the drawn and leathered bodies of her comrades, but Gael took the time to kick at each one until Cai gave him a dirty look.

"I want to make sure the she-demons will not rise," he said in explanation.

"Don't worry, man. The only danger they are to you now is in your night visions." She put her hand out to Alaysha as she started past. "Wait, little maga."

Alaysha halted midstep, scanning the trees for danger. "What is it?"

Gael, too, halted, but he nodded just ahead of them where a thicket of brush moved. "Aedus." He chuckled. "Quite a danger."

Cai didn't seem as amused. "Not just the girl." She pushed Alaysha behind Gael and strode forward on her own to meet whatever would come out. "Watch her, man," she said, pulling her sword from her back and widening her stance in readiness. Alaysha couldn't see much past Gael's back and shoulders. She eased her way around him and felt his hand grip her waist. He inclined his head toward the Enyalian and let go a low, throaty chuckle. "High alert, that one, for nothing but Aedus and a few stragglers."

Alaysha smiled with him as Aedus emerged from the thicket, Theron at her back. About a dozen Highlanders emerged as well, seeming to think the worst over. Cai relaxed visibly and sheathed her sword.

"Nothing but weak men and children," she said. She waved them in and Alaysha scanned the crowds as they came, searching for the rest of her crew. Edulph carried his daughter, Theron and Aedus ahead of him, and beyond them, far back past several Highlanders checking for their own loved ones, came Bodicca. Her head and shoulders rose over those of the returning men and women, and it was only as the crowds parted that Alaysha realized she was carrying Yenic.

Chapter 30

She didn't remember pulling from Gael's hold or how she managed to get past the throngs of people without her legs failing her. Alaysha only knew she knelt on the ground where Bodicca laid Yenic.

He was still. Pale and white, so white. White everywhere except for the bloody place where his fire mark was. In its place grinned a nasty red line.

Bodicca passed her a black blade like the one Edulph had given Theron to cut into his daughter's skull in the wilderness. Alaysha held it, not even feeling its weight.

"Who did this?" she asked, aware that she had spoken, but not quite certain the voice was even hers. It sounded off, as though she was speaking from somewhere outside of herself. She reached to touch Yenic's face and the flesh felt strange. It was hard and cold beneath the first give of skin.

"He's dead," she heard herself say. "Isn't he?" She looked up at Theron. "Is he, Theron? Is he dead?"

She wanted the shaman to shake his head. She didn't want to see him nod, and step closer to her, to hear Bodicca say it looked like he'd pierced his own lung with the blade. She didn't want any of that and surely it would all change if she explained it away for them. Surely his chest would move if she touched it.

"He said he had to break the connection." She lay her cheek on Yenic's face, imagining that if he could feel her grief, he'd somehow breathe again. He'd find a reason to live like she had so many seasons ago when he'd first accepted her tears.

"Yenic," she murmured and swatted the hand away that tried to pull her free of him. "Leave me," she said. "Just leave me."

She barely made out the voices around her. They could talk, each of them, if they wanted. They could laugh or walk away or settle down next to her. She didn't care what they did. She stretched alongside Yenic, wrapping her arms around him, trying to warm his skin. She thought of the first night they'd lain together, feeding each other heat. If her tears didn't work, surely her body warmth would.

Still they talked, those around her. She heard her name a few times, made out Theron's voice saying something about death being the only way for an Arm to break the magic. None of that mattered. Not anymore.

She fought them when they tried to pull her free. She might have even shouted, cursed. Eventually, they let her alone but they didn't leave. She felt them around her, forming a protective circle for her grief, keeping the Highlanders out, letting her mourn in some sort of private.

She didn't mark the time. It could have been a day or moment she stayed there; it was a small sound that finally took her attention. She lifted her cheek from Yenic's face to answer the noise--the question, now she realized what it was.

"Why you cry?" It was a delicate bird of a thing who had made the sound. Blonde with curls. Frail looking, standing alone, forgotten.

Edulph rushed to the child and gathered her close, cooing over her hair, her arms where they were bare. Aedus shifted side to side, obviously not sure whether she should go to Alaysha or to her niece.

"Why you cry?" the girl demanded. She broke out of Edulph's embrace and stepped closer to Alaysha. Her eyes swirled with color: green, yellow, blue, brown. Alaysha recalled Aislin's words--that a witch knew another by the eyes, but these were like no eyes she'd ever seen.

"He's dead," she told the child.

"Dead?"

"He's not--he doesn't breathe anymore."

"Oh." The girl cocked her head thoughtfully and the colors melted into one another. "Me fix that."

Alaysha crept to her knees and reached out to touch the child's shoulders. Indeed she was a frail thing. Maybe a season and a half old, but her face: her eyes, were older. As Edulph had said, she was remarkable.

"How can you fix it?" Alaysha asked her and the girl looked confused, as though the answer was obvious.

"Because I Liliah."

The End

Find out what happens to Alaysha and the world of Sarum in the breathtaking conclusion, Breath Witch

Made in the USA
San Bernardino, CA
17 June 2018